CHAPTER 1

Hanging Judge Parker looked down from high up on the bench where he sat presiding. Gat Rutherford returned his gaze stubbornly. To Gat, the Fort Smith court's famous judge looked like an ineffably tired and flabbily overweight old man.

The judge said, "You know who you'll be regulating out there. Indians."

"Yes, suh."

The grinding crush and turn of a beer wagon's heavy wheels, pulling down off Garrison Street, came through the wide open windows at the rear of the courtroom. From the courthouse side yard came a more ominous crash. Hangman George Maledon was testing his gallows. It was a busy Fort Smith summer morning.

"Yes, suh," Gat repeated. "I like Indians."

"And they won't dislike you," promised the judge. "At least not as much as they do my white marshals."

"Yes, suh. White man has lied to them Indians. Cheated them too often. They hate him."

"You'll be regulating white men, too."

Gat hesitated. "That ain't gonna be easy. I'll do my best."

"And Negroes of your own race." Isaac Parker stared down at Gat, his face mottled red and patchy with sick white splotches like dead flesh. He looked almost apoplectic.

Like maybe he wanted to lecture the black man standing before him on being sure that he knew his own place, but needed him too bad right now. The lecture could come later.

The judge said, "Raise your right hand."

Gat stared at his own twin reflections in the round lamp

globes on either side of the judge's high desk. In them he could see himself, with right hand raised, twice. *Two black men; but which one is really me, and which one is what other folks think I am?*

Gar glanced at his son, eyeing him from a few feet away, a rashly handsome young man with his mother's fine features and part Creek Indian complexion.

"Do you solemnly swear . . ."

When Gar had allowed that he did and the oath was completed, the judge handed him a sheaf of papers. Carrying them, Gar and his son left the courtroom. Gar remembered how elated he had been, seeing his son for the first time. Surprised that the boy even existed, it had seemed like the greatest of his blessings. A fifteen-year-old son with a beautiful and personable mother. The boy was going to mission school then and getting book learning. Bound to amount to something!

That was five years ago. The boy was twenty now, and Gar wondered. He knew his son was ashamed of the ignorant way his father talked, and was ashamed of the fact that his burly ol' dad could not read or write any better than an ignorant field hand.

They stood outside the courthouse. The hangman, Maledon, was still exercising his gallows. Built to hang six men at once, Gar could see the hangman's gaunt body standing beneath the gallows, his death's head intent on the traps he sprung and the six sandbags that came falling down through the gallows floor. They were brought up short at the ends of their ropes with a solid thud and hung inert, not even swinging. The air was still. No wind blew on this sultry, warm morning.

"Let's walk a ways from here," newly sworn-in Marshal Gar Rutherford suggested.

The beer wagon's broad, crunching wheels were turning in to the sutler's store at the brow of the hill behind the courthouse. The new marshal led off and his son followed, a little sullenly, Gar thought. They drew up on the greensward where the hill fell away toward the Arkansas River. A little breeze now stirred

Also by Bill Burchardt

SHOTGUN BOTTOM
YANKEE LONGSTRAW
THE BIRTH OF LOGAN STATION
THE MEXICAN
BUCK
MEDICINE MAN
THE LIGHTHORSEMEN

BLACK MARSHAL

BLACK
MARSHAL

BILL BURCHARDT

DOUBLEDAY & COMPANY, INC.

GARDEN CITY, NEW YORK

1981

All of the characters in this book
are fictitious, and any resemblance
to actual persons, living or dead,
is purely coincidental.

Library of Congress Cataloging in Publication Data

Burchardt, Bill.
Black marshal.

I. Title.
PS3552.U65B59   813'.54
AACR2
ISBN: 0-385-17553-1
Library of Congress Catalog Card Number 80–2951

First Edition

PREFACE

To the renegade Indians he was the big "buffalo lawman." To white outlaw scum he was "that nigger marshal." To black outlaws he was "that damn *po*lice."

To reasonable people, of all races, he was Gar Rutherford, black marshal from Hanging Judge Parker's Fort Smith court.

Big (he could palm a .45), black, broad, powerful, phlegmatic, he rode a tall copper dun horse, nineteen hands high, that he esteemed next to his duty.

The few black marshals who served the U. S. Court for the Western District of Arkansas and the Indian Territory worked in a strange aura, a unique atmosphere of prejudice and acceptance. Accepted by Indians, who intensely hated white people; held in contempt by racially prejudiced whites; confronting fetid resentment from members of their own race who were lawbreakers.

It was a time of witchcraft. Indian medicine men had not yet lost their power. Hoodoo conjurers had been brought by the slave ships from Africa. Prejudice was abysmal and almost universal, directed against any person whose skin was a shade darker or, for that matter, a shade lighter.

Bill Burchardt.

BLACK MARSHAL

the broad current below them, helping to alleviate the humid warmth of the day.

A steamboat was pulling in at the foot of the Garrison Street landing, roiling the muddy river water as it backed its giant stern wheel, taking off way. As it came alongside, Gar saw the heavy mooring lines being heaved out fore and aft.

The gangway swung out smartly, hovered over the landing, and dropped into place. Passengers began to disembark. Among them, surprisingly, was a black passenger. He was not a deck-hand or a dockworker, Gar knew, because the black man was well dressed, carrying a satchel in one hand and a heavy portmanteau in the other.

Gar handed his son the sheaf the judge had given him. "Whut do the papers say?" he asked.

The boy scanned them, reading hurriedly, before replying, "This top one is an order on the Fort Smith Hardware store. Says to facilitate your arming yourself. Here, the judge has written you a note: *I suggest you purchase either a .44 or .45 calibre revolver, a heavy rifle, and a shotgun,* it says. *These will be charged against the federal court account, which will reimburse itself by drawing on your fees and commissions.*"

"An' whut's the others?"

"What are the others," his son corrected him. "Why they are warrants, Papa. Here is one for an Indian named Vkéeē."

"Read 'em to me while we walk," Gar said. "I got to memorize them."

As they turned toward Garrison Street white woodsmoke came chuffing from the steamboat's stacks as its cargo boom swung to begin unloading cargo from the afterdeck. The jet of steam that burst from the whistle had become a hovering cloud by the time its hoarse toot reached the top of the hill, informing Fort Smith merchants that steamboat freight had arrived to be claimed at the wharf.

The cargo hook began sorting among the afterdeck stores of barrels, bales, rough wooden crates. The black passenger who had disembarked from the steamboat, doing a little huffing and puffing himself with his heavy luggage, came climbing the hill to hail them.

"Pardon me, gentlemen," the dark pilgrim said, lowering his satchel and portmanteau to the ground. "My name is Ross Stephens. I'm looking for work."

Gar knew he did not look like an employer. He also knew that if this jet black traveler asked any of the white gentry hereabouts they would send him hustling off to Spoon's Shoeshine Parlor, figuring maybe Spoon could use another shoeshine boy.

"Whut work you know how to do?" Gar could see his son's eyes roll with pain, listening to such crude talk.

"I've been on the Saint Louis police force," Stephens offered.

"Patrolling niggertown," Gar guessed.

Stephens nodded. "Got to where it looked like that was all I was likely to do. So I took the man's advice. I'm going west."

Gar stood thoughtfully. In contrast to his own hulking size, Stephens was a small man. A sort of dandified dresser but compact of frame and muscular. "So you know how to roust out a felon?"

"I've caught some."

"Then whyn't you go in there," Gar nodded toward the courthouse, "an' talk to the judge. He just hired me."

The newcomer picked up his duffle. Gar struck out toward town, his son alongside.

"Now them warrants," Gar prompted.

"Yes, Papa. This first one, as I said, is for a fellow named Vkéeē. Says he's a Cherokee full-blood. Charged by a woman for killing her husband. *Said assailant did, on the fourth day of June last, feloniously assault and unlawfully cause the death of—*"

"All right," Gar said. "That's enough. You got some more."

"Yes. Two 'John Doe' warrants. Seems like the court only knows their last name. The description says they are *negro individuals, twenty to twenty-five years of age, living with their mother in the north vicinity of the settlement of Bokoshe.*"

They've been charged by several of their neighbors with *petit larceny*." He looked up at his father. "That means stealing little things," he explained.

"Sho' nuff," Gar mouthed in an exaggerated dialect. "Whut else you got?"

"One for a white man. Name of Frank Eads. The charge is vague. Looks like somebody dragged his sleeve through the ink while it was still wet. Down here at the bottom the court clerk, or the judge, has written, *detain this man and bring him in for questioning*."

"Does that sign over there say Fort Smith Hardware?"

"Yes, Papa. Right there catty-cornered across the street."

Gar swung to cross the dusty intersection, dodging among vehicular traffic. His son fell into a lope to keep up with him. They stepped up on the boardwalk in front of the store's narrow, fly-specked bay window, and entered. The counters were stocked with ancient hardware, thickly covered with Garrison Street dust. Reaching to take the court order from his son's hand, Gar gave it to the ascetic merchant who sat, flint-skinned and scowling, in a wicker chair just inside the entry screen where he could watch the horse-drawn wheel traffic and pedestrians passing along the street outside.

The hardware merchant gave Gar, and his son, a long look, dropped his eyes to the paper, and read. When he had finished his knuckles rapped the paper sharply. His tongue raked a dip of snuff from beneath his lower lip and spat it into the corroded spittoon beside his shoe.

"Arming niggers!" he said angrily. "Has Isaac Parker taken leave of his wits?"

Gar was already beyond him, staring through the dirty glass of a showcase behind the counter. "I think I'll take that second-hand Colt's there," he said. "It looks to be in pretty fair shape. Then the thirty-thirty Winchester in the rifle rack above it. And the new double-barrel ten-gauge that's still in its box here in front of me."

The surly hardware merchant sat, stalling. "I'll have to talk to Judge Parker about this," he said petulantly.

Phlegmatically, Gar unfolded the signed U. S. Marshal's commission from among the papers and, wordlessly, handed it to the hardware man, but his son burst out heatedly,

"You *know* Judge Parker, don't you? You recognize his hand-writing? My father has four warrants the judge gave him to serve *with all due haste!* You've got a government contract here and if you don't want to fill it—"

Gar interrupted, "Be quiet, boy. Wait for me out on the side-walk."

His son stormed out, banging the front screen door. The flinty merchant sat studying the papers in his hands. He made no move to get up, and Gar went about gathering up the three weapons he had indicated, along with boxed ammunition from the shelves above. The hardware man grunted gruffly, "I'll have to keep this court order." He dropped Gar's commission on the floor beside the spittoon.

Stuffing the ammunition boxes in his pockets, except for the shotgun shells, which he carried with his armload of weapons, Gar leaned to retrieve his commission from the spit-dirtied floor.

"You want to make out a bill?" he asked the merchant.

The merchant reached for a pad and wrote on it. Gar studied what he had written, decided to take a chance on it, put his X at the bottom of the paper, and, painfully, drew his initials, G.R., then sidled out the screen door, beside which his son stood pout-ing.

"Let's walk on down to the grove," he told the boy.

There in the grove, beside the river, their horses waited, graz-ing in thick shade under the spread of huge pecan trees. They mounted up and rode out into the sluggishly running waters of the Arkansas River. Gar was recalling the argument when he had first found out what his wife had named their boy.

"Phenunda Sterling!" she had proclaimed, glowing with pride.

"Whut?" Gar had demanded.

She had repeated it.

"Whut I gonna call him?" Gar remembered asking dully.

"Phenunda, or Sterling," she had said aggressively.

"Huh-uh," Gar had shaken his head.

"What you want? You want some common name everybody got? Like Sam? Or maybe Rufus, or Rastus? This boy going to *be* something. He got to have a name that *sounds* like he bees something!"

The Arkansas River water roiled around their horses' fetlocks.

"P.S.," Gar ordered his son, "read me the warrants again."

The rising water slopped up around the horses' knees.

"All right, Papa," P.S. responded, taking the papers his father handed him. "This top one is for a full-blooded Indian up in the Cherokee country around Oktaha," he reminded. "Some Indian lady is accusing him of murdering her husband."

Gar repeated the name and charge aloud, imprinting the information on his brain.

P.S. shuffled Vkéeē's warrant to the bottom. "This one is for Frank Eads, a white fellow who lives at Porum. I can't read the smeared writing, but it looks like these two words might be *grand larceny*."

Gar kept at his memory work.

"These last two are the John Doe warrants I told you about, except I don't think I said the mama's name is Gertrude Cabot."

He folded the warrants and handed them back to Gar, who was still moving his lips in the memorizing chore. Gar found himself once more wishing that his master had taught him to read. It was a good thing he had a stick-to-itive memory, and something tugged at his memory now. Gertrude Cabot. Something about that woman's name. But it wouldn't surface.

The swirling river water had risen to their horses' bellies. Impatiently, P.S. spurred his horse forward, forcing it to stride on out ahead, and Gar thought, *There he goes, heading out into deep water without knowing what he's getting into; but I can't teach him nothing!*

Gar contemplated how little he knew his own son . . . how

little chance he'd had to get to know him. It had been back
when he was about P.S.'s present age that Gar and his young
master had undertaken the long trip from Texarkana Plantation
to Kansas City, Gar's first buying trip for the plantation.

Halfway across the vast expanse of the Indian Nations they
had stopped at the log cabin of a Creek chieftain named
Opothleyahola. A palatial cabin by the standards of that day, for
Opothleyahola was a well-to-do chief, himself a slave owner,
who raised extensive crops for barter and ran wild hogs and cattle in the surrounding mountains. He and young master Bedford's father were old friends.

Chief Opothleyahola had invited them to stay the night, and
that was when Gar had first met his son's mother. Young master
Bruce Alan Bedford had slept up at the big cabin, but Gar,
being a slave, had been banished to the slave quarters.

The young girl that he had met was not a slave. She was part
Creek, a young beauty living in that *demi-monde* limbo which
was then the lot of the half-caste. Her mother Creek, her father
a Negro freedman, she had inherited all the finer traits of both.
She was Missy Bernice Hērusē. Though she lived in the half-
world between Indian and Negro her beauty was legendary.
Her lively wit had lifted her to a peak of popularity and she
lived like a queen in the small settlement that constituted the
headquarters of Opothleyahola's operations.

She was used to being the center of attraction. Among the
shops and outbuildings around Opothleyahola's sprawling and
palatial two-storied log cabin, adjoining the smithy, was a harness repair shop. It was here that Gar had first encountered her.

He had gone there to repair a broken buckle from the harness
of the light buggy in which he and his young master were traveling. Bernice Hērusē had ridden into the harness shop, sidesaddle, on a white-maned *palomilla* mare. The sidesaddle's flank
cinch had come unriveted and broken loose. Casually, Gar had
stopped working on his master's harness and repaired her saddle
cinch. She was flippant toward him.

"You're new here," she challenged.

Young Gar Rutherford, broad of chest and as strong as a young horse, had cinched up her saddle and lifted her easily back up into it. His attention was piqued, but seeing no need to tell her his business he had maintained a closemouthed silence.

"Speak up," she demanded. "You new here?"

Gar eyed her. "I reckon," he said.

She watched him thoughtfully, and pensively commented, "Hmmm." Flipping her skirts bewitchingly then, showing a variety of glimpses of her pretty legs as she rearranged her dress across the *palomilla's* withers, she lifted the reins adroitly, made persuasive noises with her pink little tongue, and rode off.

At suppertime they had met again, and by this time, Gar soon discovered, she had learned a good deal more about him. She did not yet know his name, but knew that he was not a new slave owned by Opothleyahola, but was attached to the young master traveling north from Texas who was just passing through.

Gar was seated on a stump outside the cookhouse, which stood separate from Opothleyahola's main house, and was waiting for the cook to pass a plate of supper out to him when Bernice Hērusē came switching by. Her brown eyes flashed past him as if he were not present as she went into the cookhouse kitchen. Gar could hear her questioning the cook, from whom she then learned his name. After a considerable time and the occasional clatter of impatiently handled utensils, she came marching back outside, carrying a picnic basket.

"Hello, new boy," she said. "I've gotten your supper. Come along."

And he had followed her off.

The journey became an increasing revelation. The spot she chose for their picnic, beside a stream with mossy banks amid lacy overhanging ferns, was idyllic. Isolated and quiet except for bird songs and the rush of trickling water where the stream ran from a clear pool to cascade over low, rocky falls. From the basket, she produced a bottle of Opothleyahola's dandelion wine and challenged him to share it with her, and then go swimming with her. Her flashing eyes had melted to become warm and round and shining as she said, "I never did anything like this before," and then proved herself right.

They had concluded by spending the whole night there, with Gar arriving back at the big house the next morning barely in time to harness the team to the buggy for his and his master's departure. When they came back through on their return trip, three weeks later, Gar tried to persuade Bernice Hērusē to return to Texas with him.

She had refused. And Gar had understood. For if she crossed the Texas border her half-black ancestry at once made her fair game to be taken by any Texas slave owner and made a slave. At best, as Gar's wife, she would be considered no more than another slave by Gar's master. At worst, she might be kidnapped and Gar would never see her again.

Gar, a fully owned chattel, as much the property of his master as a horse or a dog, did not have the choice of remaining in the Indian Territory. So he and Bernice Hērusē, however overcome with sadness, were parted.

Gar watched the boy riding far out ahead of him in the shoulder-deep waters of the Arkansas River. He was a fine-looking young man, riding erect and easily as his horse took swimming water briefly then began the slow ascent out of the river toward the west bank. The boy had Gar's height, but not his breadth, and apparently none of the grim, patient tenacity that had enabled Gar to endure and survive through years of slavery, and years as a runaway renegade during the War Between the States.

His son's horse emerged, dripping, from the river and Gar yelled at him, "P.S.! Hold up there! Wait for me!"

When Gar rode up on the bank his copper dun horse was winded from the strong push through the resistant water trying to catch up. His son's roan mount, now dry and shining, was caracoling and ready to run.

Gar grunted, "We might as well split up here, I expect. You ride on back through Yahola. Yo' mama will be worrying about you. Tell her I'll be home as soon as I serve these warrants and deliver my prisoners to Fort Smith."

"All right, Papa." Without hesitating, Gar's son spurred his horse and rode off northwesterly. Gar watched him go, already feeling a pang of lonesomeness, the strange mix of regret at seeing the boy ride off alone shaded by a touch of relief at being free of his son's disapproving eyes, critical comments, and unpredictable impetuousness.

Gar rode due west. Into the Indian Territory hills and mountains. Through the long afternoon he thought of his years of servitude. Years of daylight to dark hard work, but years of as near freedom, he figured, as any owned slave could know. From the time they were nubbins, he and "Mastah Bruce" had played together almost as equals. They were about of an age and had always been agreeably compatible. Satisfying their always avid curiosity about life, in games of make-believe, in mischief, they had never seemed much like slave boy and master. More like friends growing up together.

As they had grown older, into young manhood, they had grown slowly apart, but in the growing apart, "Mastah Bruce" had gradually given Gar nearly total control of Texarkana Plantation. It was only with the approach of the War Between the States that the barrier between them became uncrossable. Though Gar had lived his life as an almost free boy and a free man, bossing the huge cotton and cattle-raising enterprises of Texarkana Plantation, he knew that he was not a free man, and the thought rankled.

As Bruce Alan Bedford passed into his mid-thirties, growing more and more addicted to alcohol and self-gratification, Gar had fallen to thinking that the day might come when out of gratitude and recognition of Gar's service and ability, his old friend and master might make him a free man. But, soon after the firing on Fort Sumter, "Mastah Bruce" had taken a commission as captain and formed a company to serve in the Confederate Army. Gar was convinced that the whole reason for "the war" was to prolong slavery and prevent its ever ending.

When Bruce Alan became a Confederate officer, Gar knew that if the South won, he would never be granted full freedom. So, in the confusion of those tumultuous times, he simply laid down his tools, and disappeared into the Indian Territory.

There, throughout the war, he had lived "on the scout." An outlawed, escaped slave. He had, in fact, learned the ways of the fugitives he now pursued, for he had lived as one.

As the afternoon latened, Gar rode beyond Vian, into the Cookson Hills. As night began to close in on him he saw a kindled signal fire spring into life in the misty summer dusk atop Blue Mountain. It had burned only moments before a kindred spark flickered on Tenkiller Mountain's round top ahead of him.

Gar had expected no less. He swung off the trail in the deep vastness of a timber-locked valley between the two peaks, lit no fire, but put rawhide hobbles on the copper dun stallion, turned him loose to graze, and spread out his saddle blanket near the grass-cropping horse.

He lay waiting for sleep, letting his thoughts wander back over his search for Bernice Hērusē after his runaway from Texarkana. On fleeing the plantation he had headed directly for the long-ago rest stop, the Creek Opothleyahola's headquarters settlement not far from Tullahassee. Still cherishing warmly stirring recollections of the idyll with the beautiful half-caste Creek girl, he had tried not to let his hopes rise greatly, though even after nearly sixteen years the seductive vision of her was sharp and unfaded in his mind.

Her recollection of Gar Rutherford was equally sharp, for she had special reason to remember. Gar's joy on finding her had turned to pure delight at the discovery that he was the father of an almost-grown son. His comings and goings through the rest of the war had included frequent concealment near the Opothleyahola settlement so he could see his son and be with Bernice, planning for their life together if the war ever ended and Gar could count himself a free man.

Those years had slowly filled with disillusionment as Gar began to comprehend the results of Bernice's raising of the boy. She had sent him to mission schools. He could read and write. He was educated. And with education had come a feeling of superiority. As the object of all his mother's attention the boy had become self-centered, even selfish.

Before the war's end Opothleyahola was forced by Confederate troops to flee to Kansas, leaving the Yahola settlement to become only a whistle stop on the Texas Pacific Railroad. Gar and Bernice married and as the war finally ended moved north to a small black settlement called Pleasant Hill.

There they established a home of their own that was too often a sad place of discord in an ongoing struggle as Gar tried too late to mold the boy Phenunda Sterling, whom he cynically called "P.S.," to some of Gar's own standards of manhood and ideas of conduct.

It was hard, uphill going for Gar. His every effort met stubborn, determined opposition from Bernice, now his legal wife. Gar pursued the futility of this train of thought until he was drowsy, then rolled over on his blanket and tried to go to sleep, but even his drowsiness was haunted by thoughts of his learning that he was wanted in Fort Smith on an old charge resulting from his runaway from the Texarkana Plantation.

Not knowing what he might encounter, Gar had taken P.S. to Fort Smith with him, and in sleepy half-consciousness Gar relived the embarrassment of his son's reading aloud to him every posted notice, every sign, with a kind of supercilious arrogance that bred in Gar a stifled frustration and wrath. Young P.S., now twenty years old, did not seem to notice his father's growing anger.

Instead, tall, angular P.S., haughtily patrician in mien, basked in the importance of frequently explaining to Gar that Judge Parker's summons could not amount to much because it resulted from an old charge grown dusty in the docket.

When Gar had been arraigned, the Hanging Judge had asked, "Would it seem strange to you, being hailed into my court on an old charge made by your former master, to have me seek your services as a deputy marshal?"

"No, suh," Gar had replied steadily. "I know I ain't guilty of nothing, and I'm a good man."

Parker's mottled red face was staring down from the bench. "I have many men brought before me and have learned to judge their qualities. Marshal Dan Wells, who has talked with you, says you are a good man. I also have confidence in Marshal Wells's recommendation."

"I nevah stole nothin'," Gar declared sturdily.

"You ran away from your master, making you guilty of the theft of the very clothes you were wearing. But a war has intervened. You are a free man, and the statute of limitations makes the prosecution of the theft charge marginal."

P.S., standing alongside, looked pained at the accusation, but Gar suspected the boy's ears had been even more pained by the ignorant cadence of his father's thickly slurred protests of denial. The judge was vindicating him, but his own son was finding him guilty of untutored ignorance.

The painful spectacle faded and dulled in Gar's mind as he eventually eased off into sleep.

He was awakened by sounds crashing through the brush. At least his first response to the sounds as they jerked him awake was that they were crashing. But as he lay still and listened they came to seem more like an attempt at stealth. No, he finally decided, not stealthy, just the normal sounds of someone walking along a trail with no caution, or perhaps with no knowledge of how to keep quiet.

Gar glanced around, looking for his copper-tinted horse. It was nowhere in sight, but cropped grass and a heap of horse droppings marked the direction of the stallion's grazing off through the thin timber. Gar slithered over to where he could

deer. Stephens stopped to watch him skin the carcass. "How you going to keep all that meat?" asked the pilgrim.

"Jerk most of it," Gar said. "While it gets started drying out I'm going to cook us up a big stew."

Gar dug a hole, lined it with deerskin, flesh side up, and put in water, salt, chunks of venison haunch, wild onions, tubers, and herbs. He heated round stones in a blazing fire he built beside the smoky one that smoldered beneath the drying jerky, and he eased hot rocks in among the raw meat and vegetables in his earthen stew pot. The mixture was soon boiling.

As he retrieved stones from the cooking stew, replacing them with freshly heated ones, Gar warned, "Don't use no rocks you fetch out of that cold creek. They look mighty clean and nice but they'll blow up when you put them in the fire. A rock exploding is as deadly as a shotgun going off aimed right at you."

Gar stripped the rest of the deer meat from its bones and began cutting it in long, thin strips which he suspended above the smoldering fire. Flies and insects would swarm in toward the drying meat, hit the rising currents of smoke, and sheer off buzzing, leaving the meat to dry cleanly.

Ross watched him intently until curiosity overcame him. "How you learn all this stuff?" he asked.

"You a town boy," Gar said. "I been mostly on the scout for years. Ever since I run away from my mastah down in Texas."

"How come you do that?" Stephens asked. "Ol' mistah Butler said you was your master's prize boy. Like a house nigga. Wasn't that better than livin' on the run, out here in the woods?"

"Well, first off, I reckon I was proud he picked me to run his plantation," Gar speculated. "It was good work, me bein' the boss. But when the war came along and he signed up to be an ficer I seen he wasn't ever going to let me go. He was fightin' keep slavery goin'. He wasn't never goin' to give me no free- n. I expect I could still be bossin' his place, livin' like a house er. I wanted to be my own boss."

he stew cooked. The jerky seasoned, the gently rising hick-

see the trail clearly through a patch of black haw brush, and waited.

The man he saw, after a few minutes, was the same pilgrim who had approached him and P.S. above the steamboat landing back in Fort Smith. What had he called himself? Gar reflected. Ross Stephens. He was still afoot, still carrying the portmanteau and the telescope satchel. Sweating in the humid coolness of the morning, but plodding along the trail doggedly.

With his burdens, he was as wide as the trail he walked and one or the other of his pieces of luggage frequently scraped noisily through outhanging brush along the trail. Gar waited until Stephens came up even with him, not ten yards away.

Then he said softly, "Hey, pilgrim. Over here."

Stephens stopped, and looked. His shoulders were slumped a little, not from lack of determination, but from tiredness.

"Man, you crazy?" Gar asked.

Stephens saw him now. Gar got up and stepped out to the trail.

"No," said Stephens. "I figured I'd come up onto you."

"Afoot?"

"I policed them Saint Louis wharves afoot, walkin' a beat, come to near thirty miles every twelve-hour shift."

"Carryin' two big suitcases?"

"I didn't have no place to leave 'em," Stephens declared.

"I just been easin' along," Gar said. "What if I'd been hurryin'?"

"Figured you'd have to stop some time."

"You been readin' my sign?"

"No, just followin' this footpath."

"Footpath!" Gar snorted. "Hasn't anything but horses' hoofs ever marched up and down this trail."

Ross Stephens shrugged.

Gar asked, "Why for you followin' me?"

Stephens set down his suitcases. "I got a warrant to serve. You the only brother likely to have the kind of advice I need to get."

"The judge hired you?"

Stephens nodded. "I was carryin' a letter of recommendation from the Saint Louis police chief."

"Who Parker send you after?"

"Well, you first. After that some Indian named Crawford Goldsby."

Gar whistled. "Cherokee Bill! He started you out on the head hooligan. That man a murderer!"

"Where'm I likely to find him?"

"Afoot? Carryin' two suitcases? You got a gun?"

"I've still got my service revolver. Here in my suitcase."

"It'll do you a lot of good in there." Gar suppressed his sarcasm. He stood thoughtfully. "Well, give me that telescope. We got talking to do."

He led the pilgrim back to where he had slept. Gar retrieved his saddle and blanket, then followed the copper dun's trail off through the timber. They found the horse grazing in a small clearing a mile off the trail. Gar looked around.

"This place will do as good as any," he said. "Let's make camp."

Gar took a small hatchet and a heavy, handmade chopping knife from his saddlebags. By the time he had selected a place beside the narrow creek below the clearing, and showed the pilgrim how to cut and thatch bundles of bunchgrass, Stephens had removed his coat, tie, shirt, and undershirt. He was sweating heavily.

"How long you going to stay here?" Stephens asked.

"A while," Gar replied.

He showed the pilgrim how to select, cut, and trim willow withes and began setting them in the earth to erect a lean-to wigwam. As the shelter took shape, Stephens asked, "You aiming to winter here?"

Gar shook his head. "Coming in last evening I saw signal fires being lit along the hilltops. By now every owlhoot from here to Tenkiller Ferry knows Isaac Parker has sent a deputy marshal through this way. Onliest thing they don't know is who he sent,

and who he's after. I expect to hole up here in the brush long enough for them to forget about me, or anyways lose track of where I am."

"What about me?"

"You got a lot of learning to do. Along about dark, I'm going to tell you how to find Rentiesville. That's a black folks' town where I got friends. You got money to buy a horse?"

Stephens nodded.

Gar nodded. "Good. You can find old man Butler. Buy one of his horses. He won't skin you. Tell him Gar Rutherford sent you, and I want a gun holster that will carry this Colt's. I need a couple ca'tridge belts and two saddle scabbards. One for this rifle and one for my shotgun. When you get back we'll take up where we leave off this afternoon."

It was long past noon the next day when Stephens return[ed] Gar was still busy with camp work. He showed Ross Steph[ens] how to twist the wiry grasses native to these steep hills and [val-]leys into stout twine, and how to lay the cords into useable [?] From Gar, the nimble-fingered pilgrim quickly learned h[ow to] swing himself a hammock between a pair of shady pin oak[s.]

Gar took time to show him how to knot the grass [?] catch a jutting rock on the far side of a deep ravine [?] running, swimming-deep mountain stream, secure it, [?] the slack line for crossing, and remove it from b[?] "Don't never let your hurry or your courage get the [best of your] judgment," Gar cautioned. "Man working by hisself [?] out of danger. You can break your bones falling dow[n] these coulees an' lay there till you die. This fa[?] sweep you off and carry you under and drowned [?] know what it's about. Now you keep on thatchi[ng] of that wigwam we started yesterday. Cinch '[em so] they won't leak. You'll be surprised how chill[y?] drench these mountains can git this time o[f year. ?] hunting now. Be back pretty soon."

Gar was back before sundown carrying [?]

ory smoke flavoring it as it kept off the insects, and as the darkness intensified Gar made a slush lamp out of a clay-lined pine knot, deer grease, and a cotton rag. By its flickering light the two sat talking, getting acquainted, yarning about the past, until the stew was tender. Each ate a bellyfull, and turned in to their hammocks.

At sunup, Gar swept the camp with a newly tied twig broom. He rigged a vine clothesline and both did their laundry in the creek, using yucca root for soap. Gar showed Ross Stephens how to draw a sun clock on the ground.

"When we going to serve them warrants?" Stephens asked, showing some growth of impatience.

"Ain't no hurry," Gar said. "Let them two-legged hooty owl varmints make up they mind we ain't going to do nothing at all. Now here is how you make a fish hook out of a long greenbrier thorn. Fust off, you harden it in the fire . . ."

By the time a fortnight had passed Ross Stephens knew how to set a killer bow trap for man or animal in any place he was eager to avoid making the noise of shooting. He learned how to construct snares to trap live food. How to make baits and small game lures from wild grain, grubs, blood, and earthworms, and to bait larger game animals by using their own musk over deadfalls and beneath logfalls.

He had seen the piling up of cumulus clouds, ragged gray nimbus and storm scud that prefaced a mountain storm with driving rain, then followed by mare's tail clouds and mackerel sky, signifying fine weather. He had been taught to measure the passing hours by lofting his knuckles, or his outspread hand, against the sun, and how even a hazy sky can be used to correct a faulty sense of direction.

Late on their fifteenth evening together Gar said, "Now let's take a real close look at that horse you bought."

Stephens' horse was a dusty chestnut Morgan with a strain of wild barb in him. The chestnut horse stood restively while Gar Rutherford lifted each hoof, prodded its pasterns, opened its mouth, and poked its chest and belly. He backed off to study the set of the horse's hips and its stance, rechecked each iron shoe, then pronounced his verdict.

"Old man Butler didn't skin you. That horse has been gelded real neat. I anticipate he'll have good bottom and will do to ride the river with. Now if you was to ride off anti-gogling northwest from here for pretty near a hundred miles, pretty soon you'll come to a little Cherokee village called Lenapah. Right near there, in a cabin out on Going Snake Creek, a young girl named Maggie Vail lives. She is part Cherokee and part black sistuh, and she is the light of Cherokee Bill's life. If you can find her maybeso you might be able to persuade her to tell you where her sweetheart is."

"And you—"

"I aim to head off toward Oktaha in the Cherokee country and see if I can take this fellow Vkéeē."

Gar helped Ross gather his gear, saddle up, and watched him ride awkwardly away.

"You going to have a sore butt after while," Gar called after him. "Keep your matches dry."

At some time during the night Gar departed camp and disappeared. Thus their camp was left empty and deserted, with no indication of how, or when, or what direction Gar had gone.

CHAPTER 2

Gar inquired at the gristmill an hour's ride before he reached Oktaha, hoping to learn how to find the young woman who had accused Vkéeē of murdering her husband.

The miller, gaunt and work driven, looked at Gar as if he was dirt, but seemed to perceive that the quickest way to get rid of his stolid inquisitor was to answer his questions as quickly as possible. Outside, the run of the millrace filling the millwheel buckets, splashing their water down into the stream below; inside, the steady abrasive rumbling grind of the heavy millstones made talking difficult, but Gar learned that the girl's name was Yúkpē Afvc'keko and that she was living with her brother on his farm, the other side of Oktaha.

Gar gave the copper dun horse an affectionate slap on the neck as he climbed back astride and rode on through Oktaha, a village still decimated from the Civil War Battle of Honey Springs. The forces of Union General Blunt and Confederate General Cooper had taken turns occupying the town and it was mostly a ruins of burnt-out and blackened foundations with stark standing chimneys. A smithy and the Oktaha store had been rebuilt, and the ringing of the blacksmith's anvil hung suspended in the noonday air.

Rutherford found Afvc'keko's brother's cabin, not far from the Honey Springs themselves. The girl talked volubly. Vkéeē wanted her, she said, and in trying to get her, had killed her husband. Vkéeē had witched him to death. That gave Gar pause. He wondered how well a charge of witching would hold up in Hanging Judge Isaac Parker's court in Fort Smith.

Concluding that was not for him to decide, Gar followed

Yúkpē Afvc'keko's directions on to Vkéeē's hut another three quarters of an hour's ride on the far side of the springs. Reaching it, he sat his saddle in silence on a low rise above the clearing, studying the situation below. Vkéeē's hut was the old-fashioned Cherokee kind, a round mud and wattle dwelling between brush arbor and o-si, the o-si a small oven-shaped sweat lodge where Vkéeē doubtless purified himself before casting up his spells.

The clay-plastered dome of Vkéeē's hut was strewn with medicine objects. There, stretched out, lay the foot-wide skin of a six-foot-long water snake, and the bleached white skulls of several small animals. A wolf's pelt hung beside the door opening, over a rustic stick-and-pole table on which stood a variety of clay pots. Containing God knows what, Gar thought, but for sure pulverized owl's entrails, weasel eyes, ginseng, spikenard root, wormwood, along with the paraphernalia for ceremonially mixing them.

Vkéeē was a well-equipped doctor. From the overhead of his brush arbor hung dried claws, quills, bones, antlers, terrapin shells, and feathered corncob totems spinning slowly in the warm summer breeze. Gar surveyed all this with a slight chill of dread, despite the heat in the air as the season moved toward midsummer.

He did not have to wonder long where Vkéeē was, as the Cherokee warlock came crawling out of his o-si, donned a hairy, horned mask, and squatted by his fire, intoning a monosyllabic medicine song. Gar remembered what Yúkpē Afvc'keko had told him in parting: "Vkéeē is making spells now to kill my brother. He will keep on until he destroys my whole family, to get me."

The dun horse on the knoll was upwind of Vkéeē, its presence well obscured by the timber. *He is thinking about his medicine too strong to know I'm here,* Gar hoped. Gar eased his rifle from the saddle boot that Ross Stephens had brought him from Rentiesville. Aiming quickly, Gar shot.

His bullet clipped the green twig pothook over Vkéeē's fire

and the black iron pot it had suspended fell, throwing hot charcoal sparks over the squatted conjurer's legs. The pot rolled over and the liquid it contained flooded out, hissing, over the fire.

"Lay out there!" Gar yelled. "Flat on your belly!"

The medicine man hesitated. He backed and filled, and Gar shot again. His bullet spanged off the iron pot and went squeeing off into the woods. Vkéeē flopped, stretching himself out, head and hands toward the hissing fire. Gar rode down off the hill.

This medicine man was young for a doctor. Gar guessed him to be no more than maybe thirty years old. A good-looking fellow, brown as a ripe sumac berry, long and muscular, wearing only a ceremonial deer hide breechclout suitable for medicine making. When he stood up, there was a remote mysticism about his face, as though he was seeing Gar Rutherford, but had become totally unperturbed by his presence.

Gar thrust out his warrant and told him in the Muscogee tongue, "I have got a *nakoku* for your arrest. For murder. You want to get some clothes before we start for Fort Smith?"

"You should not do this," Vkéeē said in English.

"Don't make me wait," Rutherford ordered hollowly. "I'll have you stretched out on yo' belly again. This time from a rap up alongside yo' head from this rifle barrel."

Vkéeē delayed, but not too long, entering his lodge while Gar peered squint-eyed into the dimness of the clay-whitened hut, watching him fetch out clothes. The Indian then stood beside Gar's horse as if expecting to be invited to mount up behind the marshal.

Gar declared, "This hoss ain't been sentenced to carry double. You going to walk down to Porum anyhow. Heah, I'll carry yo' stuff."

They struck out with Vkéeē striding on out ahead. Gar, riding, decided that from too much sun, or too much tension in making the capture, he felt a little woozy. Vkéeē still wore only his breechclout and moccasins. Gar had tied the Indian's pants and shirt into the latigos behind his saddle. The marshal, his head light and swimming a little, ordered a halt, dismounted, and watched the Indian with sidelong eyes while they both drank out of the creek they were following down toward the Canadian River.

The drinking didn't help. Gar leaned with his arms across the copper-haired horse and tried to clear his head. He mounted then, and they went on. *I feel like I am trying to run a little fever*, Gar thought. His eyesight was slightly blurry. The terrain ran gradually downhill. Leaf mold crunched and rustled with every hoof fall, but Vkéeē's moccasins threaded among the leaves silently, as quiet as the passage of a serpent that was part of his legerdemain.

Gar let Vkéeē pick the route, warning him, "Don't try to lead me off wrong. I know this country like the shape of my own face."

They cut away from the stream where it curved off in tortuous windings. Gar knew they were easing downgrade, but in his growing misery it seemed like they were climbing uphill and, as the hours wore away, his discomfort increased. Long before sundown he was aching in every bone and joint and knew he was coming down with the flu.

What am I going to do, Gar began asking himself. *By dark I'm going to be too sick to keep track of an Indian killer.* His fever was still rising. The timber ahead took on a yellowed, feverish hue. The aches in his bones and joints were now intense. Gar felt his body sway, groggily, in the saddle and the way before him lurched and buckled.

As the sun tucked itself below the horizon the stomach sickness overcame him. His gorge rose and he leaned aside over his horse's mane and vomited. He thought that might make him feel better, but it did not. His face, his tongue, his whole body was hot and dry and fevered, and as they came again alongside the stream, Gar half fell from his horse, clinging to saddle horn and cantle as he ordered, "Hold up, *hvtetvs*. I got to have some water."

Vkéeē stood and watched him, blandly. Gar pulled his revolver and pointed it waveringly at the Indian while he knelt and dipped up creek water with one hand, splashing it on his face, then lay flat to suck up water. The coldness of the water on his face and in his belly turned his fever into a chill and he lay shaking with ague, trying to fix his attention on his prisoner.

Vkéeē said pleasantly, "Who lies on the ground on his belly now, buffalo lawman?"

He stood watching Gar as though amused, then laid himself down, on his back, staring patiently up at the evening sky. Gar struggled around onto his side, unrelieved, shivering, but watching. The thought began to form that there was no way he could turn this Indian loose or confine him. Before he completely lost consciousness, if he could lift and steady his gun, he should kill him.

Gar suspected that if he fell into a faint with the Cherokee still lying alert beside him, he would never awaken alive. The Indian's supine body was blurred in Gar's vision. Beyond a moccasined foot, near Gar's face, the marshal let his gaze wander up the tawny body, seeking a vital target. His eyes paused dizzily on a leather thong hanging out of Vkéeē's breechclout.

The Indian still stared at the sky, utterly patient. Gar steadied his hand and reached up between Vkéeē's thighs to grab the thong. He knew at once what ailed him, and as he pulled the thing came free. Gar now held in his black hand Vkéeē's medicine bag. As sick as he was, he felt a temptation to open it, to see the medicine objects it contained.

Vkéeē sat up quickly and came launching himself across the ground. Gar, resisting his temptation, threw the medicine bag in the creek. The current caught it. Vkéeē changed directions, squirming past Gar in pursuit of his medicine. Gar managed to grasp one brown leg, grappling with it and restraining the Indian as the medicine bag was swept downstream, floating away in the swirling water, at last disappearing, sucked down in a whirlpooling eddy.

As it went out of sight Vkéeē stopped short and sat up. His face was pallid. Both fearfully and angrily he said, "You have stolen my power, buffalo man."

Gar, too, sat up. If there had been any doubt in his mind

about Vkéeē witching the Afvc'keko girl's husband, it was gone now. He was feeling a little better. As the chill went away and the grogginess cleared he felt weak and tired, but better. Gar felt his body break out in sweat. The fever was leaving. He held his gun more steadily on the Indian.

Vkéeē promised, "If you will let me dive down into the water and find my medicine I will do anything you want me to."

Gar shook his head. "Onliest thing you've done, conjure man, is witch yourself out of supper," he said. "My stomach is too sick to cook anything, or to eat."

He got up and went shakily to fetch his rope from the saddle horn. With it, he trussed the Indian, feet to hands, behind him, and pointed out, "You ain't going to bed down any too comfortable but I expect you'll be here when I wake up."

He threw down his saddle and propped himself against it with conviction. The Fort Smith court could judge this particular Indian however it wanted. Gar Rutherford judged that Vkéeē was a killer conjurer and that he himself would never have reached Fort Smith alive if Vkéeē's power had not floated off with his stolen medicine bag.

At daylight, Gar was feeling fine. They moved on to Porum, proceeding down its frontier village street around midmorning, with a ringing anvil at the far end of the street reminding Gar of a chore he had meant to accomplish back in Oktaha. He marched Vkéeē straight down to the Porum smithy and was relieved to find that the blacksmith here was a brother, one Matt Wiggins, as big and black as Gar himself.

Gar told Wiggins, "I need to hire a helper—a gent with a wagon to transport my prisoners. Be a help if he could cook. Know anybody? Reckon the store here will take an order on the Fort Smith court for some fatback and red beans?"

The sweaty smith stood cooling the iron rim he had just welded, holding it in a tub of water. "They was a traveling white man in here yestidy—no, it was the day afore. Said he was looking for work. He was driving a wagon. Times is hard. I

down to bright metal, and tossed them up to Gar. "That's the las' ones."

They shook hands.

"You tell folks," Gar said, "that you met the new marshal. He'll be doing his best to stand with Judge Parker betwixt them an' the ragtags."

"If you want me to testify, I'll go," Wiggins replied.

Hesse clucked to his mules, backing them out of the shady doorway, and turning them into the sunlit road.

"Marshal," Hesse mumbled, "don't you reckon you ought to ride where you can watch your prisoner close? You ought to keep a careful eye on him."

Gar understood. His wagoner-cook would rather not be seen riding through town with a black man on the seat beside him. Without a word, Gar straddled the back of the spring-wagon seat and walked unsteadily across the moving vehicle's bed to the dropped tailgate. He sat down and rode with his back to Vkéeē, legs hanging out over the tailgate, carrying on a *sotto voce* conversation with his cherished copper dun horse on the way to the pecan grove where they picked up Hesse's scanty camp gear.

South of Briartown, in a thick tangle of timber, Gar left the wagon with Vkéeē chained to a wheel and Hesse guarding him. Gar rode on down to the river, and Frank Eads's farm. It was a layout altogether impressive. Sandy rich bottom land, a big two-story house of sawed lumber painted white, sizable barn with hayloft, and pole-fenced stock pens. A long, metal-roofed machinery shed covered a riding plow, an iron-toothed harrow, a corn planter, a cultivator, a sickle mower, and a hay baler, each implement still paint bright, indicating it was no more than a year or so old.

Farmer Eads, pink of face and freckled, was throwing a set of harness across the high top poles of the horse pen. He had evidently just come in from cultivating his field, for his team of draft horses was still rolling in the dust, getting rid of the sweaty itch of harness straps.

expect the store will credit you. Better take a chance on selling something and taking an order than not to sell nothing."

"Wherebouts might this white man have went?"

"He been campin' down in the pecan grove the last night or so. Expect he's tryin' to get credit at the store, too," the leather-aproned smith grinned.

Gar left the blacksmith making handcuffs and leg-irons for him and went, taking Vkéeē, to hunt the out-of-work drifter. He found him watering his team at the town trough. Gar explained his need.

The seedy white man worked the pump handle thoughtfully. He equivocated. "I was about to head on west. Came up here from Briartown looking for some kind of a part-time contract for my team," he related pompously.

The pair of jack mules slurping water from the green moss-lined trough were as seedy-looking as their owner.

"Can you cook?" Gar asked him.

"Sure I can cook," the man declared. "Anybody travels alone like I do has got to cook. I been down in Chihuahua in the mining game. I'm headed for the Wichita Mountains. Folks around here think there ain't no gold over there, but I got information from the Mexicans that there is." The flabby-skinned drifter leaned on the pump, smirking.

"I got one prisoner here already," Gar said. "The federal court will pay you for your team, and your time."

"Pretty fair-looking buck redskin," the man granted. "And you figure to ketch some more?"

"The Lord willing," Gar nodded. He said nothing about Vkéeē's casting of spells. There were some things white folks had trouble grasping. Gar took out his commission and unfolded it for the slatternly white drifter to view. There was no way to hide the tobacco stains the paper had acquired when thrown on the floor by the Fort Smith hardware man.

"Deputy Marshal Gar Rutherford," the white man read. "I don't doubt your credentials. Even if it does look like you're a little careless where you spit." He grinned at his own wit. "I'm

Jake Hesse. Since the federal government, not you, would be my employer I guess I'll go along. I do need something for a while to pick up enough money to get myself on over to the gold fields."

At the Porum store, Gar signed a government chit for groceries, loaded them, and prepared to ride in the wagon to the blacksmith shop. He tied his copper dun horse to the wagon's tailgate, and gave Vkéeē his choice of riding or walking. The Cherokee preferred to walk.

At the smithy, Gar ordered Vkéeē into the wagon and used a pair of his new handcuffs to lock the Indian's left wrist to a seat brace. Gar asked the blacksmith, "You know a farmer around here named Frank Eads?"

The smith thrust the last link of a length of chain into the forge and worked the bellows. "He got a place down on the river. You got business with Mistuh Eads?"

Gar pulled the warrants from his pocket, all three of them, and proffered them to the blacksmith.

A smile creased the smith's broad, sweat-streaked face. "I can't read neither," he admitted, "but them sure looks like lawin' papers. Come out here to my junk pile an' pick out how thick strap iron you want these leg-irons made of."

In the weedy backlot behind the smithy, they sorted pieces of strap iron with their heads close together.

"Never thought I'd see the law catchin' up with that Eads," the blacksmith murmured. "Hmm-hmm!"

"That paper only say to *bring him in for questioning*." Gar repeated the phrase memorized from P.S.'s reading of the warrant.

"They sho' ought to ask the right questions!"

"Like what?"

"He got a good thang goin', according to what the folks tell me. Steals horses from the cowboys down in Texas—takes 'em up an' sells 'em to farmers in Kansas. Steals farm horses in Kansas, carries 'em down to sell in cotton country. He don't nevah do nothin' wrong around here. Keeps his nose plumb clean."

"Folks around here think he's honest?"

"White folks, sho' nuff! He a deacon in the Methodist Church South. Big givah, I heah. He rob a post office—grocery store way up at Skiatook, steal a load of hogs down south around Honubby. Rape a woman over in Arkansas when he got horny. All kind of devilment a long ways from home. But he nevah do nothin' but smile a big goat grin an' pray around heah."

"You got any proof?"

"He still runnin' them Honubby hogs out in his pasture. Eatin' the groceries from Skiatook. I expect a friend of mine knows the name of that woman over in Arkansas. She a sistuh, an' she'll sho' remember his goaty red face. Ought to be a dozen Kansas farmers an' Texas ranchers remember the business he done to them."

"Would you tell Parker's court? What you know?"

"I'll answer any questions the ol' Hangin' Judge ask me. He the onliest thang stands betwixt us an' the riffraff in this whole territory."

Gar handed Matt Wiggins the strap irons he had collected during their soft-voiced conversation. There were eight straps, about the same length, each an inch wide.

Matt hefted them. "They'll make four pair, heavy enough to hold, light enough not to burden a man."

"Mighty fine," Gar agreed. "I'll step on back there to you outhouse while you finish up."

As he sat in the outhouse, Gar could hear the steady, po pous, nasal drone of Jake Hesse's voice lecturing the blacksm on how to make up the leg-irons properly. It was irritating, Matt Wiggins' ball peen hammer was busy, molding and w ing. Its rapid taps and ringing blows made long stretche Hesse's discourse unintelligible.

Gar returned to the smithy as Wiggins' tongs tossed a ch red pair of the leg-irons, hissing and smoking, into his w tub of cooling water. The marshal climbed up on the seat with Hesse.

Wiggins retrieved the irons, wire brushed the scal

Gar rode directly to him. "Mistuh Eads?"

"Yes."

Gar leveled the shotgun. "You are wanted in Fort Smith."

The stuffy Eads's face flamed crimson. "Wanted? For what reason?"

"For questioning, the warrant says." Gar fingered the documents from his pocket and passed them down. "You can hire a expert lawyer to help you out when we get to Fort Smith. For now, you better come along easy, less'n you want a load of double-aught buckshot where your belly is." He paused. "I am a deputy marshal and determined to serve this warrant."

Eads fumbled with the warrants, sorted out and read his own, plainly trying to make time while he considered what to do. He ventured, "I'm going to have to go in the house and talk with my wife."

"No, you ain't," Gar said. "She standing on the back porch now, watching us. Walk up that way if you want to. Tell her you in the hands of the law. Then come on. If I see any kind of a gun, in her hands or yours, I'll kill you. I expect you can see I'm mighty nervous."

The woman came down off the porch. She was raw-boned, ungainly, and, when she spoke, coarse-voiced and strong-tongued, "I been a-hearing all this, nigger. Let me see that paper." She read it unhurriedly. "You better be what you say you are. No harm better come to my husband. I'll see you lynched!"

"Maybe so," Gar admitted. "But you ride roughshod over me now, you'll sure see your husband dead."

Again she studied the warrant, and asked, "You want me to come with you, Frank?"

"I don't know," he said uncertainly.

"I suppose I had better stay here," she decided. "I'll saddle up your horse for you. You go straight to lawyer Polk when you get there. He'll put this nigger in his place!" She went on to the barn.

On the way back to the camp wagon, Frank Eads rode

stolidly. Not with the bouncing air of a farmer, but with the steady seat of an experienced long rider. At the wagon, Gar made him dismount. He turned Eads's saddle horse back toward the house and slapped it on the rump. "I ain't got eyes," Gar said, "to guard a prisoner on a horse, another one in the wagon, and maybe some more bringing they buggies or riding bicycles." The horse galloped off through the timber with stirrups flapping.

Eads turned sullen, saying in petulant protest, "That horse comes back without me, riderless, my wife is sure going to worry."

Gar said, "The kind of traveling I hear you been doing, she has worried about you before. Ain't no help for it this time."

With Vkéeē and Frank Eads leg-ironed together in the wagon bed, the marshal said to Hesse, "We is ready to hitch up an' head on to Bokoshe."

At a little coal and water stop named Keota on the Texas & Pacific Railroad, Gar halted their procession to ask questions. The station agent allowed that, yes, he'd heard of Gertrude Cabot and her two sons who lived due north of Bokoshe, not far from the railroad right-of-way.

"If you'll wait here till number six comes in from Kanima the conductor might be able to tell you more. I've heard him say he throws a bunch of old newspapers, stuff like that, reading matter, off the train for ol' lady Cabot, every once in a while." The station agent looked at Gar oddly. "Surely you've heard of ol' lady Cabot?"

"I don't rightly reckon I have," Gar said. He did not show the station agent his warrant, nor identify himself. The agent was one curious white man and there was no telling how loyalties might stack up down in this lonesome, far country.

"We have some trouble with those Cabot boys," the station agent said cautiously. "They ride the blinds a lot. Brakemen are always having to chase them off one of our trains. Seems like they feel the T. & P. owes them transportation wherever they want to go. No better than a pair of bums." He was getting warmed up to the topic and tugged his eyeshade down. He peered up through it at Gar and suddenly seemed to realize he might be getting on shaky ground. "No reflection on your race, you know." He kept peering up at Gar through the green isin-glass of the eyeshade.

One thing you know, Gar thought, *ol' Miz Trudy an' her boys are black folks.* As soon as he abbreviated her name something tugged at his memory. Well, it was gone now. "I thank you kindly, Mr. T. and P.," Gar offered. "I'll travel on down to Bokoshe."

"Aren't you going to wait for number six? I'll flag her for you. Even sell you a ticket. The train don't normally stop here, but we do like to accommodate folks."

Even black folks, Gar thought. "I appreciate it," he said, "but I'm ridin' my hoss." He nodded toward the telegraph bay. The copper dun stood outside, ground tied, clearly visible through the windows.

The agent nodded. "Fine animal." His curious eyes again sur-veyed Gar Rutherford from black hat to boots, then the scab-barded Winchester in the dun horse's saddle boot, the clearly visible side arm on Gar's hip, and Gar could almost read the question welling up in the railroad employee's eyes—who is this big buck nigger with his well-oiled firearms and his high-faloo-tin' horse—

Gar provided no answer. He went back outside, swung into his saddle, and rode down the tracks to the water tank, out of sight from the depot, where he had left Jake Hesse, the wagon, and his prisoners.

The wagon was empty and his two prisoners were standing beside it, dripping wet. Frank Eads was fuming. He turned a torrent of profanity on Gar.

Jake Hesse was laughing uproariously. "They was both stink-ing with sweat. I figured they needed a bath, so I lowered the water spout and pulled the rope."

Both Vkéeē and Eads were drenched.

Eads still shouted angrily, "Up to now I ain't complained

about being arrested by a nigger, and being chained to an Indian, but making me take a bath with him—that is too damn much! I aim to let the authorities know about this!"

"Where's our groceries?" Gar asked.

"I shoved 'em up under the seat. They're dry," Hesse said. "Took my duffle out. It's stacked over on the other side of the wagon." He turned mean, grouching irascibly, "Ain't nothing hurt but that fellow's feelings. He ought to appreciate it. Maybe he ain't sensitive to Indian stink, but I am. He ought to simmer down. The sun was rendering grease out of that redskin."

Vkéeē stood with his eyes fixed on the wet boards of the wagon bed. Gar asked him, in Muscogee, if he was all right. Vkéeē made no sign that he had even heard.

"By god," Hesse said, somewhat awed, "you speak that Indian gobbledy-gook?" He grinned meanly, "Maybe the Injun don't, though."

"I can talk Muscogee," Gar said, "but he's Cherokee and it may be that he don't." He screwed up his courage to squarely face this white man wagon driver he had hired. "Mr. Hesse, I mean for you to carry and cook for these prisoners. Nothing else. Now we have got to have an understanding. If you are going to keep on making trouble, we ought to unload these prisoners right here. You can stay here in Keota, and I'll figure out what I'm going to do."

Hesse stood, glaring at him, hotly.

Stubbornly, Gar pressed. "Well, let me know. What's in your mind?"

"I didn't mean no trouble." Hesse turned away surlily.

"I understand that," Gar reasoned. "The Fort Smith court gives me authority to hire a helper. I can see that you get paid according to the distance that we travel, the number of prisoners you guard, and how many meals you cook. I ain't authorized to pay for no trouble making. Not nothing like this," he said, nodding toward the wet prisoners.

Frank Eads offered, "Turn me loose and I'll whip the hell out of him."

Hesse glanced at Eads, and at the silent Vkéeē. It may have

occurred to him that if Gar turned the prisoners loose he would stand alone.

"Why . . ." the wagon drover's bravado declined. In a voice reduced to a near whine he proclaimed, "Why, I ain't even armed. Oh, I got a old squirrel rifle over there among my truck, but I ain't equipped to defend myself against the three of you."

Gar knew that if he turned anybody loose, it would be every man for himself. But he offered the wagon driver no encouragement. Hesse walked grudgingly to the wagon and began loading it.

"You want," he asked, "that we should head on out somewheres from here?"

"I want that we should circle wide out around that depot, then head on down the tracks toward Bokoshe." Gar felt no immediate triumph from the doubtful standoff with Hesse, but he knew that if the station agent saw his cargo of leg-ironed prisoners it would be a dead giveaway. He wanted to keep his business quiet.

Beyond the freight yards they pulled back up on the right-of-way, driving parallel to the tracks for easier traveling. The country sloped gently away from the graded right-of-way on either side of the tracks. For as far as Gar could see it was clear and open country, variegated with low mottes of persimmon and black locust trees, and the worn-down hollows of long forgotten buffalo wallows.

About a dozen miles short of Bokoshe, with nod and pointing finger, Gar indicated the first railroad trestle they approached. "Le's pull in under there," he suggested. "It will make us some shade."

Hesse swung the wagon down off the right-of-way and drove in beneath the trestle. While he unhitched the team and led them down the ravine to graze, Gar dug into his war bag to pull out a dirty, worn shirt. He swapped his high-heeled rider's boots for Frank Eads's plow brogans. Before thrusting his revolver into the waistband of his pants, inside his shirt, he reluctantly removed his hat and shot a hole in it.

He used his bandana then to make a bindle, tying in it, along with a handful of .45 cartridges, the things he figured a hobo's bindle would contain. With the bindle lashed to a stick and shouldered, he struck out, figuring he had considerable walking ahead of him before he reached his destination. He had planned it that way on purpose, for he wanted to look as if he had walked a long way when he arrived there.

The feel of walking, after the last several days in the saddle, was good. Gar felt his spirits rise. He felt good about having taken two prisoners. He began to feel better about having won an encounter with a red-necked cracker of a white man.

The twisting songs of meadowlarks marked his passage along the flat land as the railroad trestle faded into the distance behind him. He walked a good six or eight miles without seeing any sign of human habitation. In his deep, rich bass voice, Gar began making up a little song:

> Oh, I am just a railroad bum
> A-wandering through the prairie.
> A-tum de um de tiddle de um
> I'm ornery and contrary.

He spotted the ramshackle, unpainted little house off to the left, some three-quarters of a mile from the tracks. Gar altered the rhythm of his marching. He had been moving along steadily, Eads's rough, worn shoes hitting every other one of the creosoted railroad ties. At a more leisurely pace now, he turned his course down off the right-of-way, studying the unpainted, poverty-marked little dwelling as he moved across the flat valley toward it.

As he approached through the wavering heat waves rising from the pasture grass, the primitive cabin became more discernible. Constructed of rough, adz-hewn boards put together with wooden pegs, no drop of paint had ever touched its walls. He could tell it was pegged instead of nailed together, for there were no streaks running down from rain-rusted nailheads. The two rooms of the cabin were separated by an open, roofed-over dogtrot, in the familiar way of this cross-timbers country. It

see the trail clearly through a patch of black haw brush, and waited.

The man he saw, after a few minutes, was the same pilgrim who had approached him and P.S. above the steamboat landing back in Fort Smith. What had he called himself? Gar reflected. Ross Stephens. He was still afoot, still carrying the portmanteau and the telescope satchel. Sweating in the humid coolness of the morning, but plodding along the trail doggedly.

With his burdens, he was as wide as the trail he walked and one or the other of his pieces of luggage frequently scraped noisily through outhanging brush along the trail. Gar waited until Stephens came up even with him, not ten yards away.

Then he said softly, "Hey, pilgrim. Over here."

Stephens stopped, and looked. His shoulders were slumped a little, not from lack of determination, but from tiredness.

"Man, you crazy?" Gar asked.

Stephens saw him now. Gar got up and stepped out to the trail.

"No," said Stephens. "I figured I'd come up onto you."

"Afoot?"

"I policed them Saint Louis wharves afoot, walkin' a beat, come to near thirty miles every twelve-hour shift."

"Carryin' two big suitcases?"

"I didn't have no place to leave 'em," Stephens declared.

"I just been easin' along," Gar said. "What if I'd been hurryin'?"

"Figured you'd have to stop some time."

"You been readin' my sign?"

"No, just followin' this footpath."

"Footpath!" Gar snorted. "Hasn't anything but horses' hoofs ever marched up and down this trail."

Ross Stephens shrugged.

Gar asked, "Why for you followin' me?"

Stephens set down his suitcases. "I got a warrant to serve. You the only brother likely to have the kind of advice I need to get."

"The judge hired you?"

Stephens nodded. "I was carryin' a letter of recommendation from the Saint Louis police chief."

"Who Parker send you after?"

"Well, you first. After that some Indian named Crawford Goldsby."

Gar whistled. "Cherokee Bill! He started you out on the head hooligan. That man a murderer!"

"Where'm I likely to find him?"

"Afoot? Carryin' two suitcases? You got a gun?"

"I've still got my service revolver. Here in my suitcase."

"It'll do you a lot of good in there." Gar suppressed his sarcasm. He stood thoughtfully. "Well, give me that telescope. We got talking to do."

He led the pilgrim back to where he had slept. Gar retrieved his saddle and blanket, then followed the copper dun's trail off through the timber. They found the horse grazing in a small clearing a mile off the trail. Gar looked around.

"This place will do as good as any," he said. "Let's make camp."

Gar took a small hatchet and a heavy, handmade chopping knife from his saddlebags. By the time he had selected a place beside the narrow creek below the clearing, and showed the pilgrim how to cut and thatch bundles of bunchgrass, Stephens had removed his coat, tie, shirt, and undershirt. He was sweating heavily.

"How long you going to stay here?" Stephens asked.

"A while," Gar replied.

He showed the pilgrim how to select, cut, and trim willow withes and began setting them in the earth to erect a lean-to wigwam. As the shelter took shape, Stephens asked, "You aiming to winter here?"

Gar shook his head. "Coming in last evening I saw signal fires being lit along the hilltops. By now every owlhoot from here to Tenkiller Ferry knows Isaac Parker has sent a deputy marshal through this way. Onliest thing they don't know is who he sent,

expect the store will credit you. Better take a chance on selling something and taking an order than not to sell nothing."

"Wherebouts might this white man have went?"

"He been campin' down in the pecan grove the last night or so. Expect he's tryin' to get credit at the store, too," the leather-aproned smith grinned.

Gar left the blacksmith making handcuffs and leg-irons for him and went, taking Vkéeē, to hunt the out-of-work drifter. He found him watering his team at the town trough. Gar explained his need.

The seedy white man worked the pump handle thoughtfully. He equivocated. "I was about to head on west. Came up here from Briartown looking for some kind of a part-time contract for my team," he related pompously.

The pair of jack mules slurping water from the green moss-lined trough were as seedy-looking as their owner.

"Can you cook?" Gar asked him.

"Sure I can cook," the man declared. "Anybody travels alone like I do has got to cook. I been down in Chihuahua in the mining game. I'm headed for the Wichita Mountains. Folks around here think there ain't no gold over there, but I got information from the Mexicans that there is." The flabby-skinned drifter leaned on the pump, smirking.

"I got one prisoner here already," Gar said. "The federal court will pay you for your team, and your time."

"Pretty fair-looking buck redskin," the man granted. "And you figure to ketch some more?"

"The Lord willing," Gar nodded. He said nothing about Vkéeē's casting of spells. There were some things white folks had trouble grasping. Gar took out his commission and unfolded it for the slatternly white drifter to view. There was no way to hide the tobacco stains the paper had acquired when thrown on the floor by the Fort Smith hardware man.

"Deputy Marshal Gar Rutherford," the white man read. "I don't doubt your credentials. Even if it does look like you're a little careless where you spit." He grinned at his own wit. "I'm

Jake Hesse. Since the federal government, not you, would be my employer I guess I'll go along. I do need something for a while to pick up enough money to get myself on over to the gold fields."

At the Porum store, Gar signed a government chit for groceries, loaded them, and prepared to ride in the wagon to the blacksmith shop. He tied his copper dun horse to the wagon's tailgate, and gave Vkéeē his choice of riding or walking. The Cherokee preferred to walk.

At the smithy, Gar ordered Vkéeē into the wagon and used a pair of his new handcuffs to lock the Indian's left wrist to a seat brace. Gar asked the blacksmith, "You know a farmer around here named Frank Eads?"

The smith thrust the last link of a length of chain into the forge and worked the bellows. "He got a place down on the river. You got business with Mistuh Eads?"

Gar pulled the warrants from his pocket, all three of them, and proffered them to the blacksmith.

A smile creased the smith's broad, sweat-streaked face. "I can't read neither," he admitted, "but them sure looks like lawin' papers. Come out here to my junk pile an' pick out how thick strap iron you want these leg-irons made of."

In the weedy backlot behind the smithy, they sorted pieces of strap iron with their heads close together.

"Never thought I'd see the law catchin' up with that Eads," the blacksmith murmured. "Hmm-hmm!"

"That paper only say to *bring him in for questioning*." Gar repeated the phrase memorized from P.S.'s reading of the warrant.

"They sho' ought to ask the right questions!"

"Like what?"

"He got a good thang goin', according to what the folks tell me. Steals horses from the cowboys down in Texas—takes 'em up an' sells 'em to farmers in Kansas. Steals farm horses in Kansas, carries 'em down to sell in cotton country. He don't nevah do nothin' wrong around here. Keeps his nose plumb clean."

"Folks around here think he's honest?"

"White folks, sho' nuff! He a deacon in the Methodist Church South. Big givah, I heah. He rob a post office–grocery store way up at Skiatook, steal a load of hogs down south around Honubby. Rape a woman over in Arkansas when he got horny. All kind of devilment a long ways from home. But he nevah do nothin' but smile a big goat grin an' pray around heah."

"You got any proof?"

"He still runnin' them Honubby hogs out in his pasture. Eatin' the groceries from Skiatook. I expect a friend of mine knows the name of that woman over in Arkansas. She a sistuh, an' she'll sho' remember his goaty red face. Ought to be a dozen Kansas farmers an' Texas ranchers remember the business he done to them."

"Would you tell Parker's court? What you know?"

"I'll answer any questions the ol' Hangin' Judge ask me. He the onliest thang stands betwixt us an' the riffraff in this whole territory."

Gar handed Matt Wiggins the strap irons he had collected during their soft-voiced conversation. There were eight straps, about the same length, each an inch wide.

Matt hefted them. "They'll make four pair, heavy enough to hold, light enough not to burden a man."

"Mighty fine," Gar agreed. "I'll step on back there to your outhouse while you finish up."

As he sat in the outhouse, Gar could hear the steady, pompous, nasal drone of Jake Hesse's voice lecturing the blacksmith on how to make up the leg-irons properly. It was irritating, but Matt Wiggins' ball peen hammer was busy, molding and welding. Its rapid taps and ringing blows made long stretches of Hesse's discourse unintelligible.

Gar returned to the smithy as Wiggins' tongs tossed a cherry-red pair of the leg-irons, hissing and smoking, into his wooden tub of cooling water. The marshal climbed up on the wagon seat with Hesse.

Wiggins retrieved the irons, wire brushed the scale away

down to bright metal, and tossed them up to Gar. "That's the las' ones."

They shook hands.

"You tell folks," Gar said, "that you met the new marshal. He'll be doing his best to stand with Judge Parker betwixt them an' the ragtags."

"If you want me to testify, I'll go," Wiggins replied.

Hesse clucked to his mules, backing them out of the shady doorway, and turning them into the sunlit road.

"Marshal," Hesse mumbled, "don't you reckon you ought to ride where you can watch your prisoner close? You ought to keep a careful eye on him."

Gar understood. His wagoner-cook would rather not be seen riding through town with a black man on the seat beside him. Without a word, Gar straddled the back of the spring-wagon seat and walked unsteadily across the moving vehicle's bed to the dropped tailgate. He sat down and rode with his back to Vkéeē, legs hanging out over the tailgate, carrying on a *sotto voce* conversation with his cherished copper dun horse on the way to the pecan grove where they picked up Hesse's scanty camp gear.

South of Briartown, in a thick tangle of timber, Gar left the wagon with Vkéeē chained to a wheel and Hesse guarding him. Gar rode on down to the river, and Frank Eads's farm. It was a layout altogether impressive. Sandy rich bottom land, a big two-story house of sawed lumber painted white, sizable barn with hayloft, and pole-fenced stock pens. A long, metal-roofed machinery shed covered a riding plow, an iron-toothed harrow, a corn planter, a cultivator, a sickle mower, and a hay baler, each implement still paint bright, indicating it was no more than a year or so old.

Farmer Eads, pink of face and freckled, was throwing a set of harness across the high top poles of the horse pen. He had evidently just come in from cultivating his field, for his team of draft horses was still rolling in the dust, getting rid of the sweaty itch of harness straps.

and who he's after. I expect to hole up here in the brush long enough for them to forget about me, or anyways lose track of where I am."

"What about me?"

"You got a lot of learning to do. Along about dark, I'm going to tell you how to find Rentiesville. That's a black folks' town where I got friends. You got money to buy a horse?"

Stephens nodded.

Gar nodded. "Good. You can find old man Butler. Buy one of his horses. He won't skin you. Tell him Gar Rutherford sent you, and I want a gun holster that will carry this Colt's. I need a couple ca'tridge belts and two saddle scabbards. One for this rifle and one for my shotgun. When you get back we'll take up where we leave off this afternoon."

It was long past noon the next day when Stephens returned. Gar was still busy with camp work. He showed Ross Stephens how to twist the wiry grasses native to these steep hills and valleys into stout twine, and how to lay the cords into useable rope. From Gar, the nimble-fingered pilgrim quickly learned how to swing himself a hammock between a pair of shady pin oak trees.

Gar took time to show him how to knot the grass rope to catch a jutting rock on the far side of a deep ravine or fast-running, swimming-deep mountain stream, secure it, then use the slack line for crossing, and remove it from both banks. "Don't never let your hurry or your courage get the best of your judgment," Gar cautioned. "Man working by hisself ain't *never* out of danger. You can break your bones falling down into one of these coulees an' lay there till you die. This fast water can sweep you off and carry you under and drowned you before you know what it's about. Now you keep on thatching up the sides of that wigwam we started yesterday. Cinch 'em up good, so they won't leak. You'll be surprised how chilly the rains that drench these mountains can git this time of year. I'm going hunting now. Be back pretty soon."

Gar was back before sundown carrying a small eviscerated

deer. Stephens stopped to watch him skin the carcass. "How you going to keep all that meat?" asked the pilgrim.

"Jerk most of it," Gar said. "While it gets started drying out I'm going to cook us up a big stew."

Gar dug a hole, lined it with deerskin, flesh side up, and put in water, salt, chunks of venison haunch, wild onions, tubers, and herbs. He heated round stones in a blazing fire he built beside the smoky one that smoldered beneath the drying jerky, and he eased hot rocks in among the raw meat and vegetables in his earthen stew pot. The mixture was soon boiling.

As he retrieved stones from the cooking stew, replacing them with freshly heated ones, Gar warned, "Don't use no rocks you fetch out of that cold creek. They look mighty clean and nice but they'll blow up when you put them in the fire. A rock exploding is as deadly as a shotgun going off aimed right at you."

Gar stripped the rest of the deer meat from its bones and began cutting it in long, thin strips which he suspended above the smoldering fire. Flies and insects would swarm in toward the drying meat, hit the rising currents of smoke, and sheer off buzzing, leaving the meat to dry cleanly.

Ross watched him intently until curiosity overcame him. "How you learn all this stuff?" he asked.

"You a town boy," Gar said. "I been mostly on the scout for years. Ever since I run away from my mastah down in Texas."

"How come you do that?" Stephens asked. "Ol' mistah Butler said you was your master's prize boy. Like a house nigga. Wasn't that better than livin' on the run, out here in the woods?"

"Well, first off, I reckon I was proud he picked me to run his plantation," Gar speculated. "It was good work, me bein' the boss. But when the war came along and he signed up to be an officer I seen he wasn't ever going to let me go. He was fightin' to keep slavery goin'. He wasn't never goin' to give me no freedom. I expect I could still be bossin' his place, livin' like a house nigger. I wanted to be my own boss."

The stew cooked. The jerky seasoned, the gently rising hick-

stood in a planted orchard of apple and pear trees and beyond it, Gar could see a timber line of trees along the creek that supplied it with water, flushed its outhouse, and carried off its trash.

As he entered the orchard Gar paused, sweating profusely, and shouted, "Hello the house."

A wrinkled, humpbacked, tiny, but still brisk old woman stepped down out of one of the rooms into the dogtrot. Her skin was grayish black, like ancient soot.

Gar took a few steps forward.

"Evenin', ma'ma," he called out to the old Negro woman. "Would you give a sandwich to a tired an' hongry man?"

Her answer came back in a tart, cracked voice. "You willing to wuk fo' it?"

Gar let a grudging tone of reluctance color his voice. "Yes'um. I'm mighty thirsty, too." He proceeded on up into the yard.

"My cookstove ashes need emptyin'," she was eyeing him suspiciously. "I'm plumb out of firewood. My boys always take care of these chores, but they been gone a few days."

This must be the place, he thought. Gar followed her into the house, removing his hat as he passed through the door. "Mighty warm travelin'," he declared, "an' I'm a man that ain't as young as he used to be."

"Where you bound?" she asked.

"The brakeman threw me off the blind baggage this morning, from the southbound freight as we was pullin' into Keota. Ain't nothin' much at that town. I figure to wander on down an' have a look at Bokoshe."

"You ain't goin' to find much there, either," she said. "Here the axe. The drinkin' dipper hangin' by the water bucket. He'p yo'se'f."

Gar drank, then went out into the backyard on the creek side of the house. He stood sizing up a pile of dogwood poles stacked there.

"Don't cut them sticks too long for me to get in this firebox," she yelled from inside the house. "I'll use what coals I got left to heat you up a plateful of turnips, an' poke greens with hog chitterlings. Be ready about the time you finish."

Each of Gar's powerful, accurate axe swings lopped off a cookstove length of the cured dogwood. He had a pile more than hip high when the kitchen screen swung open in the dogtrot and he was summoned.

The old woman's voice was gravelly. "Yo' vittles is a-waitin'," she called.

Gar washed up carefully at the pitcher and basin beside the kitchen door, wet his hair and combed it, and surveyed his reflection in the scrap of broken, peeling mirror beside the unbleached muslin towel. He decided that he looked like an honest tramp, went in, and sat down to eat.

"When you finished," the shriveled crone hostess said pointedly, "here is the scuttle. Empty that hopper an' carry the ashes down by the outhouse. Dump 'em in the crick. They's still some fire in them."

Gar ate patiently.

A letter envelope lay on the table, its closure of sealing wax broken. As the shriveled old woman carried iron kettle and skillet from the stove to the dishpan, Gar reached to turn over the envelope while her back was turned. He could not read its crude scrawl, addressed to Gertrude Cabot, Gen. Del., Bokoshe, I.T. The first name was longer than the last. There seemed little doubt about it. This was likely the place. Gar chewed his chitterlings.

"Missus," he said, "these vittles is sure rightly seasoned."

He ate a while longer.

"Maybe," he said, "after I empty yoah ashes I ought to make that firewood pile a little higher. I only laid up enough for a day or so out there."

She was intent on her kettle scrubbing at the dishpan.

"Maybe," he went on, "you might let me spend the night under yo' dogtrot before I drift on down towards Bokoshe. Got to where these dewy nights stiffens the rheumatism in my joints."

CHAPTER 3

She turned from her work at the dishpan. Her gnarled hands suggested that Gar's plea about rheumatism would be as likely as anything to touch her sympathy.

"I reckon you cut enough firewood," she said. "My boys is overdue back."

"Yes'um," Gar temporized, "But they may have other work that's got behind. I ain't in no hurry. To tell the truth, a night out of the weather would be downright welcome. I could enjoy one of yo' breakfast meals before I go movin' on down the road."

She worked at the dishpan without replying. He could hear the gritty sound as she scoured the skillet with sand and lye soap.

"Seems like, too, they might be a law on my back trail," Gar said. "You see there, the marshal shot a hole through my hat." He reached to poke a finger through it. "They more likely to expect a fella on the scout like me to be a-layin' out in the brush than sleepin' peacefully at some civilized householder's house."

She said thoughtfully, "Seems like them laws is always troublin' my boys, too. Maybe you an' them ought to try to get together."

Gar nodded in agreement. He finished eating, shoveled out the ashes, went to dump them, then remained outside chopping wood. Along about dusk, with the pile of chopped wood now grown as high as his shoulders, he stepped back under the dogtrot to sit down and rest. A screech owl's quaver sounded from some distance upstream along the creek. The old woman came hustling out, throwing a shawl over her head. She hurried across the clearing and disappeared in the direction of the spooky quavering of the screech owl.

Little bit early for that critter's talking, Gar thought. *It ain't even dark.* He sat quietly, listening. He could hear the sound of faraway talking, timber-muffled, indistinguishable, but there were male voices, as well as the old woman's higher-pitched cackle. Presently, he could hear them coming up through the timber.

One of the boys went riding around the house. The other emerged from the near side of the clearing, but both halted in the periphery of timber to scrutinize him. Gar could see the dim form of the old woman, standing even farther back, a faint shape among the trees in the gathering darkness.

"You see," Gar heard her declare grimly. "He just an ol' bum."

The boys rode on in, keeping Gar bracketed as they dismounted.

"I'm Albert," said the one facing him.

"An' me, I'm Squint," came the voice from behind.

Gar twisted around carefully, so that he could see both of them. Albert looked to be the leader. He was squarely built, serious in demeanor. Squint was fat, self-indulgent appearing, with a querulous twang in his voice. By the time their horses were unsaddled, hobbled, and turned loose for the night, it was fully dark. They went inside. The old woman lit the kitchen lamp and its yellow light flickered on expectant, waiting faces. The four of them sat facing one another around the kitchen table.

Gar talked, long and garrulously, mumbling out hard-luck stories that he made up while he told them. The boys stared at him, saying nothing. They made no comment whatever about the substantial pile of wood he had chopped for their mother. "Yo' mama says you boys been having trouble with the law," Gar wound up.

Squint complained peevishly, "We didn't do any good a-tall

this time, Mama." He directed his attention at Gar, "Who you?" he asked. "You ain't said."

"What difference do a name make?" said Gar. "Mine is different in different places. Call me whatever you want, as long as you ain't nasty about it."

"He an older man," urged the boys' mother. "He got a good gift of talk. You heard him. Seems to me you might do good together."

"How?" asked Albert.

"Well, say you pick out a store," said the old woman. "He could go in askin' for chores. Like he done from me. Pretty soon he could meet up with you all. Tell you how the place lays out. Then you git yo' guns an' go in together."

"You ever done anything like that, old man?" Albert asked.

"There's his hat, layin' by the stove," said Mrs. Cabot. "See that hole in it? The law was shootin' at him, up at Keota befo' he come down here."

"That right, mistuh?" Albert asked.

Gar reached to pick up his hat by sticking his forefinger through the bullet hole. Squint took it, peering at the hole through narrowed eyes. He sniffed the hole, and whined querulously, "Seems like I can still smell burned powder."

Albert got up. "I'm tired, Mama. We been a long time ridin'." He looked at Gar. "You can sleep in the dogtrot, mistuh. We can talk some more tomorrow."

"You got laws followin' you?" Gar asked, manifestly apprehensive.

"Could be," Squint complained sourly.

"Then we startin' out wrong," Gar said. "We ought to all sleep together in that other room. It's got windows on all four sides. Can yo' mama shoot?"

"Pretty good," Albert admitted.

"Then anybody comes up along our back trail we can shoot out all four windows and drive 'em off."

Mama Cabot thought this over. "I think he right," she decided.

Mama and the boys apparently slept in the single room regularly. There was a cot for Mama, and a tarnished old brass bedstead with a cornshuck ticking mattress for the boys. They threw a quilt on the floor for Gar. Everyone made ready to go to bed, again apparently by custom, fully dressed.

Gar brought in his bindle for a pillow. All four windows were opened. He lay on the quilt pallet, listening to the night sounds, breathing deep and regularly, too taut to sleep, but trying to appear to do so. Gertrude Cabot, visibly worn out by age and the day's tensions, went to sleep almost immediately, with a soft and gentle snoring that lulled Gar's tense nerves.

The boys, overtired from too long in the saddle, turned restlessly, making the dry cornshuck mattress crackle noisily. Gertrude Cabot, the words filtered back through Gar's thoughts and he tried to remember why they seemed familiar to him. The boys were quieting down, though Gar could hear one or the other of them jerk occasionally in the nervous reflexes of exhaustion. They lay with their heads toward Gar in the musky dark, their hands above their heads and thrusting out through the scrollwork of the brass bedstead like shadowy animal paws hanging out through the bars of a cage.

As Gar's eyes accustomed themselves to the darkness, he studied the hanging hands beside him in the dimly reflected starlight to make sure he knew which belonged to who, then felt in the bindle, took out handcuffs, and handcuffed Albert's right wrist to Squint's left. The reaction was immediate.

The racket of opening and closing the wrist irons roused their mother. She breathed a soft snort in awakening, and said, "Whut that noise?"

Both boys seemed momentarily immobilized in the half world between sleeping and awakening. Then both came around fully, startled, and tried to extricate their hands from the brass bedstead. The handcuffs rattled brusquely on the scrollwork as they found they could not pull their hands through. Gar pulled his revolver from beneath his shirt.

"You boys under arrest," he said. "I'm Marshal Gar Rutherford, serving you a warrant from the Federal Court for the Western District of Arkansas in Fort Smith." He fumbled in his shirt pocket to take out the warrants, now oft folded and sweat-soaked.

Albert hissed, "Light the lamp, Mama."

Squint was whimpering.

She lit the lamp, holding the sulfur match until it almost burned her fingers, then threw the match at Gar.

"Judas goat!" she accused.

Gar caught the match, squeezing its glowing end between thumb and forefinger before he dropped it on the dirt floor.

Silhouetted against the kerosene lamp's glowing chimney, the humpbacked old woman glared like a satyr, her eyes catlike, yellow in the lamplight, as she snatched the warrants, sorted and read them, and said, "You think you can do this to Trudy Cabot's boys?" She spat in the dirt.

Trudy Cabot! It was the "Trudy" that this time got through to Gar, unlocking his memory. He struggled to master himself before he spoke.

"You 'Old Winged Trudy'!" he said in amazement.

"She sho' is." Squint's whine turned hopeful.

Gar backed slowly toward the dogtrot door. "We heard of you clear up past Muskogee," he marveled. "Folks say that hump is really yo' wings folded against yo' back. You live by stealing. Folks say you can fly up on the house top an' perch there. Chillun an' grown folks throw rocks at you but nobody can hit you. They say ever'body begs you to go away but you jus' settle up there an' laugh, clucking and cackling like a hen!"

She did it. Old Winged Trudy began to laugh and cluck and cackle. Gar half expected her to unfold her wings and fly over his head, out the door. When she didn't, he took courage and forged on. "Folks say you can only be killed with a silver bullet. That you won't stay dead unless they drives a stake through your heart. Now, Trudy Cabot, you think I'm a fool? Before I come to serve this warrant I sent to a foreign country an' got me a silver bullet. It's the ca'tridge under my hammer right now. You move to give me any trouble I'm going to shoot you with it. I chopped a sharp-pointed stake to drive through your heart this very afternoon. I'll sho' drive it through befo' you can move to git up off the ground."

"Don't pay him no nevah mind, Mama," Squint whined. "Witch him!"

Gar swung the pistol barrel to hit the side of Squint's head. The fat brother cowered, whimpering, and Gertrude Cabot watched the yawning orifice of the pistol barrel as it returned to bear on her heart.

"I won't witch you," she promised warily.

"Let's go outside." Gar unlocked the handcuff on Squint's wrist.

Old Winged Trudy led, carrying the lamp, and Gar prodded the boys out into the dogtrot. He told them, "Now you go saddle your horses. I'll keep your mama here an' anything bothers me I'll shoot her and you two later."

While the boys went to fetch the horses, Old Winged Trudy squatted on the ground before the burning lamp. She reached up under her skirt, brought out her hoodoo bag, and Gar devoutly wished he had the silver bullet he had bragged about.

"I ain't going to witch you, Mista' Law," she promised again. "I'm jus' goin' to conjure up a spell so the Fort Smith judge cain't keep my boys in his jail."

That, Gar decided, was Isaac Parker's responsibility. While her boys unhobbled and saddled the horses, Gar watched her open her red flannel hoodoo bag and spread out its contents. He recognized redshank root, devil's shoestring, and the herb cruel man of the woods. He saw that the bag contained a lodestone, steel filings, red pepper, and gunpowder.

"This heah's graveyard dirt," she muttered, sifting it into a pile. "These is fingernail trimmings from the slavery-days hoodoo doctor who taught me."

The boys came bringing the horses up under the dogtrot.

"Mount up," Gar ordered them, "both of you on one horse. I'll ride the other one."

Watching them do so, he grabbed the saddle horn with his left hand and swung aboard the scrubby horse. Together, they rode off into the night.

"Do what the man tell you," Old Winged Trudy called after her boys. "You ain't going to be gone long."

When they reached the railroad trestle Gar leg-ironed them with his two earlier prisoners, hooked stirrups over saddle horn and released the two horses to return to Trudy's cabin, then turned in himself to get some sleep. Up at daylight, he roused Hesse to make breakfast for himself and the four owl-eyed prisoners.

With the prisoners leg-ironed together in the wagon bed they got underway, following the wagon road northeast to Sallisaw, then turning due east toward Fort Smith, pulling up to camp on the west side of Muldrow. Gar shot and dressed a brace of prairie chickens. As they prepared to eat supper it was apparent that Hesse was beginning to favor Frank Eads, in spite of the white man's offer to whip him if turned loose.

"Mistuh Hesse," Gar complained. "You currying up to one of our prisoners. You figuring to give Mistuh Eads the breast parts. Now that won't do. A man with a brown skin or a black skin gits just as hungry as a white man. If you aim to get fair pay for your work, you going to have to be fair with ever'body." Unholstering his .45, Gar palmed it easily in his huge black hand and spun the cylinder to check its loads, eyeing the white cook with callous, phlegmatic gaze.

Hesse eyed Gar's determined face, and let his shifting eyes wander, his glance including the revolver Gar held in loose and easy grip. Hesse's complexion became suffused with angry red, but he put the chicken back in the fry pan, split the two breasts, then redistributed the portions on the tin plates before he passed them out.

Gar ate with a growing awareness that they were about to have company. He could hear the usual timber sounds falling silent, but not from the approach of evening. He heard the scuffling sounds of horses' hoofs, coming out of the timber, toward them, headed east along the trail bound for Fort Smith. Recognizing the gait of one of the coming pair of horses then, Gar ate, and waited patiently.

Ross Stephens hove into sight coming around the gentle bending of the trail. Riding the horse beside him was an Indian prisoner, his hands rope-tied to the saddle horn.

Gar put down his plate and walked out to meet them. "I see you got him."

Stephens, as immaculately dressed as he had been when he stepped off the steamboat, was more than a little proud. "Marshal Rutherford," he said, trying in vain to conceal his pride, "I want you to meet Mr. Crawford Goldsby, alias 'Cherokee Bill.'"

"I recognize him," Gar said. "How are you, Cherokee?"

The half-blood Indian prisoner stared obtusely, and spat on the ground. Stephens dismounted and led Gar barely out of Cherokee Bill's earshot. Gar, keeping everyone in clear view and in revolver range, listened.

"I done it your way," Stephens admitted, visibly avid to tell his tale. "I hunted up that gal, Maggie Vail, out on Going Snake Creek, then I got lucky. The quarry was already there, visiting her. I asked to spend the night, and knew I'd have to sleep with one eye open. I think she was trying to make her lover jealous. She kept talking about how good-looking I was."

Ross Stephens paused, as if inviting comment. Gar made none.

Stephens went on, "By morning we was all three in a pretty bad humor. I gave the girl money to go to a neighbor's and buy us some breakfast eggs and bacon. Cherokee Bill and me waited for her. He didn't know me and assumed I didn't know him. We just sat on opposite sides of the fireplace watching each other with our Winchesters laying across our laps. When she came back he made the mistake of glancing at the door as she came in. I picked up a stick of firewood and hit him in the head."

"I see his forehead is skinned up," Gar said, nodding.

"Thought I hit him hard enough to kill him," Ross declared. "It barely knocked him down."

"Bring him on into camp," Gar said. "We'll add him to the stringer. I'm anxious to get an early start for Fort Smith. I want to get home to see my wife and boy."

"You've done me a-plenty favors. Why don't you let me take them all in?" Ross suggested. "I'll collect your fees, pay your wagon man, then bring him, your money, and whatever warrants the judge wants you to serve. Where do you want me to bring them to?"

Gar grinned quizzically. "You figure one little Saint Louis policeman can do all that?"

"We're less than fifteen miles from Fort Smith," Stephens shrugged. "If I can't carry five prisoners fifteen miles, you've been helping out the wrong fellow."

"I trust you," Gar said, "an' your offer is mighty welcome." He glanced back at his wagon. "Be careful of that cook I hired. He ain't decided for sure whose side he is on yet."

Ross Stephens looked over the assemblage camped beside the trail ahead of him. "Marshal Rutherford," he said, "I believe I can sleep for one more night with one eye open."

"Then I'll ride all night with both eyes open," Gar said. "Home for me is a settlement right close to Tullahassee. It's called Pleasant Hill, and it seems like it's been a long time since I been there."

"I'll find it," Stephens assured him.

Gar walked back to the wagon to get the copper dun horse. He told none of his entourage where he was going or who Ross Stephens was. Stephens' deputy marshal badge was attached to his neat pinstriped shirt in plain sight of all, and Gar Rutherford figured it was no more than professional courtesy to let Ross Stephens handle the change of command in any way he wanted to. Might as well, Gar thought, let Hesse and the prisoners think he was only going on a short errand and would be back any minute.

Pleasant Hill, a scattered community of board and batten shacks with a few substantial homes and stores, welcomed Gar with silence when he rode in after a night and a day on the trail. The town's residents were freed men and women, *wachinas*, emigrant Negroes who had come in since the Civil War, and half-bloods, Indian-Black descendants of generations of mixed Creek-Negro parentage.

Gar went directly home, to his own yellow, four-room house, an upper-class abode for this community. Tying the copper dun horse in the shade of a front yard cedar tree, he walked up on the low front porch and into the living room. It was furnished with a utilitarian walnut and leather couch and chair, a split cane rocking chair, worn pseudo-Persian rug, and a reed organ.

The house seemed empty. It, too, was silent. "Bernice," Gar called, and walked into the next room, a combined dining-bedroom crowded with circular dining table, chairs, the bed where P.S. slept, a corner cupboard for dishes, and a wardrobe cabinet for P.S.'s clothes.

Still silence. No response from Bernice. Gar went on into the kitchen. It, also, was full of furniture, a big Queen Bee cooking range, kitchen table, pantry shelves, handmade tin sink and drainboard boasting its own stubby water pump. But no Bernice. Gar glanced in the bedroom at double bed, dresser, chiffonier, curtained clothes-hangered shelves. Everything spic and span, neatly in place, but no Bernice.

He saw her then. She was out in the backyard hanging clothes on the line. Gar went out into the yard. It was wide and grassy with a mounded root cellar, garden space, a small barn on the back of the lot and, beside it, an outhouse with crescent moon vent cut in the door. Gar's entry into the backyard brought his hound, a bluetick hunter, charging out of the barn with raised hackles and raucous barking.

The anger changed to body wiggling, tail wagging, whining

welcome as soon as Blue recognized his master. The dog came leaping with upraised paws. Gar caught the dog in his arms, hugged him as if he had been a human, then forced the ecstatic hound down, to sit, then lie, and Blue rolled and wiggled, too joyful to lie still. Bernice came across the yard carrying her empty clothes basket, unhurrying, her face warm with welcome.

She set the basket down on the well curb beneath the shade of a green-leafed grape arbor, and came to embrace her husband.

"Honey," she said, and kissed him.

The soft heat of her lips sent Gar's pulse to stirring. She was in no way less pretty or less enticing than she had been the first time they had met and promptly conceived a son, down at Yahola, less than five miles from where they stood at the moment. In fact, maturity had brought a fullness to her figure that was altogether lush.

"I been a-hurrying with just this in mind," Gar said.

She turned a hip against his belt buckle. "It will have to wait till evening," she told him. "I've got clothes soaking in lye water that have to come out, and more boiling in the soap kettle that are ready for rinsing." She loosed herself from his arms and went to thrust her washing stick down into the huge black kettle on the fire by the back door.

"How come you washing on a Saturday?" Gar demanded.

"'Cause tomorrow is Sunday, and—"

"Monday is Emancipation Day," Gar finished. "I had done forgot!"

"You been gone quite a while," she reminded him.

"That's what I'm a-feeling," he insisted. "I got behind—"

"And you'll get caught up quick," she promised, "but not while I'm finishing this washing."

"They expecting a big crowd in town on Monday?"

"Like always."

"Looks like I got home just in time."

Her eyes flashed with glowing wickedness. "Haven't you got anything else on your mind?" she asked with a touch of impatience.

"I mean to bring some law and order to this Emancipation Day," Gar explained. "Celebrating is fine, but last year it almost got out of hand."

"And you going to fix all that," Bernice teased, "all by your big self."

"Well," he said, lowering his shoulders in a suddenly defensive posture. "Maybe I'll be better than no law at all—" His voice trailed off, as though apologizing for an unnecessary conceit.

Ignoring him now, she fished steaming clothes from the kettle with her bleached and frayed washing stick, piling them high in a dishpan, then lifting a scalding garment gingerly to wring it out over the black kettle.

"Bring me my clothes basket," she ordered peremptorily then. Gar hurried to do so. She kept on wringing out garments and tossing them in the basket.

"Where is P.S.?" he asked.

"Phenunda Sterling," she emphasized the full pronunciation of their son's name, "is helping Etta LaPlace."

"And who," Gar asked, "is Etta LaPlace?"

"She is the Whartons' niece."

Gar knew that Byron Wharton and his dicty wife were mister and missus socialite in Pleasant Hill.

"Their niece is here visiting," Bernice said. "She is running for Emancipation Day Queen, and Phenunda is helping her with her election campaign."

"Then he ain't likely to be home for awhile."

"Your son has spent every waking moment with Miss LaPlace since she arrived here," Bernice said. "He is fully single-minded on that lovely girl. I can't get any help out of him at all. Gar, this fire is dying. Get me some wood—"

"Let it die," Gar commanded. "My fire ain't going out. You're coming in the house with me for awhile." He took the half-filled clothes basket from her, set it back under the grape arbor beside the well, and took her hand.

"Gar! What about the clothes in the kitchen soaking in lye?"

"*He* better take a little time to think. Give me time to make up my own mind. Then listen to me."

"She has been elected Emancipation Day Queen, I hear. If you're going to be law and order man on the grounds, you're going to have to make way for her tomorrow. You'd better be ready to do it!"

Gar had arisen with apprehension. He had dressed antici- pating trouble, and ridden the copper dun to the east edge of town, tying him there so folks would think he was patrolling there. Then he had walked across town to do his scouting around the west side. There was bound to be some drinking.

It was early, but most everybody was up and out, wandering around, visiting in pairs and bunches, getting ready for the pa- rade, claiming picnic areas under the trees to serve as gathering places for family reunions. While white folks in Territory com- munities celebrated July 4th as Independence Day, black folks celebrated August 4th as Emancipation Day.

Past midmorning, Gar heard the cannon near the flagpole go off for the first time. He moved toward the center of town to watch the Yahola clan ride in. They were mostly half-bloods, Creek-Negroes from Bernice's old settlement. She would have many friends and relatives among them and her day would re- ally begin now as she gathered with them to talk and visit.

Gar went on across town to untie his horse, ride through town, tie the copper dun on the west side, then walk slowly back to scout the east side. He thought about Sunday dinner yesterday, its strained atmosphere, and the interminable after- noon that had followed it.

He had tried to be friendly with P.S.'s fancy girl. But she wouldn't have it. Etta LaPlace was beautiful, haughty, un- smiling, expecting others to pay court to her but giving nothing in return. P.S. seemed satisfied with that. Every time she gave her long, dark tresses a toss, P.S.'s eyes rolled like marbles in a game for keeps.

He released her, went back into the kitchen, and returned carrying a washboiler from which he emptied the lye water. Hurriedly, he drew two buckets of fresh water from the well, emptying each bucket into the washboiler of clothes. He hung up the well rope.

"There," he said. "That will soak out the lye. Now—" Again he took her hand and drew her into the house. Her eyes still sparkled wickedly. Her lips were half smiling.

Gar sat, near dozing, beside Bernice, in the Sunday morning service. Lazy summer insect buzzes came in through the open church house windows. Marshal Rutherford gave his full, but drowsy, attention to the Reverend Haworth's sermon. The preacher was in full cry.

"Now de sea parted; split open wide; anybody here gonna say it didn't?

"Anybody gonna say, I was deah, preachuh. I saw dat de sea *didn't* part, *didn't* let de chillun of Israel come a-walking through; *didn't* close down on ol' Pharaoh an' his chariots an' drowned dem Egypt land oppressors daid?

"No, sah! No! Ain't nobody gonna say dat!

"Because de word of de Lawd tell us it's true! An' if dat ain't enough, ain't we in our own time seen de sea of slavery part? Open up an' let us all out? Uh, huh!

"Seen de sea of slavery part in Civil War like de bloody Red Sea an' all us chillun heah today walked right through. An' when de whole phalanx of de Confederate soldiers an' pa- terollers come a-runnin' in to catch us it close down again; some- times they drowned in they own blood. Amen! Ah, hah!

"An' it's gotta be like that, brothern. When you see dat sea of trouble rollin' an' tumblin' out dere befo' you, you gotta pray! 'Cause de Lawd God Almighty can part dat sea of trouble jus' like He part de Red Sea, an' de Slavery Sea, an' you can come on through . . ."

Gar listened, knowing he was no amen shouter, but knowing that he would stand his ground for this small church. Black people's burden was made a little lighter because of the church. Some folks learned to read and write here, they partied here, young folks met their future husbands and wives here, men argued politics here. The church was high society for the ladies. In this plain and simple meeting house human joy and sorrow were shared. Gar's religion was his fellowship with men, and this meeting place with God. It gave him strong force when courage or endurance showed no special promise in the face of dehumanizing pressures. The sermon came to a close and the congregation began singing.

If I can only climb de hill to heaven's pearly gate
It won't matter that I'm weary, it won't matter if I'm late;
I won't care if I am ragged, downhearted, sad, and poor.
It jus' won't make no difference can I walk through heaven's
    door.

Backbreakin' work behind me; here I done the bes' I can,
Ol' Satan an' his devils lef' behind with evil man.
I nevah made no money an' I often was afraid,
Makes no difference can I only climb the heav'nly grade.

With the church service ended they made their way down the aisle toward the bright sunlight outside, shaking hands, exchanging friendly small talk as they went. Nearing the entry-way, Bernice gripped Gar's arm and whispered, "There's Phen-unda Sterling and he has Etta with him. Isn't she pretty?"

Gar saw his son shaking hands with the preacher. Etta, standing beside him, *was* pretty. She nearly reminded Gar of the Bernice he had encountered on his way up through the Indian Territory twenty years ago. If anything, Etta was a more striking beauty than the young Bernice of Opothleyahola's settlement had been. But there was something about this girl's demeanor . . .

They were passing through the church's double doors then, and Bernice was introducing her. Etta LaPlace offered her hand, held high. Gar could not hear what she said through the

chatter of departing churchgoers, and he had to reach far up to touch her tan fingers. He backed down the top step, thinking, *This girl is looking down her nose at me,* but he smiled—reservedly.

She was overdressed for churchgoing, he thought, and her clothes fit too tight. Gar scanned her bracelets, beads, and rings. P.S. was wiggling like an overeager puppy and Gar squeezed against his son to whisper, "Boy, if you had a tail it would b wagging so hard you'd be hitting people."

The boy's face clouded.

Bernice was saying loudly, "You young folks don't forg You're coming to our house for Sunday dinner now."

The heavy press of people thinned in descending the chu house steps and Gar said to Bernice, "It appears to me tha harness may be worth more than the hoss."

She pinched his arm, hard, and hissed, "Shhh!"

When they were completely clear of the crowd, Bernic "Gar Rutherford! Your voice carries like a bullfrog croakir July night. Everybody heard what you said!"

"Ever'body don't know what I mean," he contested.

"Glowering like you do, anybody can guess," she said.

They walked on toward home, disputing.

"She says her father is a fine guitar player, d Orleans way," Bernice informed him. "He grew up or Creole plantation. That's how they come to be named

"Your church-lady friends won't approve of no ma a box."

Bernice ignored this. "Her father is part white, I'm part Creek."

Gar persisted, "A Frenchy nigga who plays on In some New Orleans house of joy?"

He felt the hard edge of her shoe hit as she kicl

"No," she ejaculated. "When we get home that girl! Heah? Phenunda Sterling has got his I think."

Gar had called him into the kitchen to caution him, "Boy, you going to fall out of your chair." P.S.'s response had been a caustic, burning glare at his father.

During the afternoon, P.S. had launched out in a long, philosophical speech to impress the girl.

"Our world," he said, "has never moved forward in a straight line. It moves in circles, like a wheel going. Or better to say like any given point on a wheel. While we think we are moving forward we are really moving up, forward, down, and *backwards*. Like the spot on the wheel. So our future is always the past. Ladies' skirts are long now, but they'll get short like they were in ancient times. Men are wearing stiff collars, but they'll return to soft collars like our great-grandfathers wore. Progress may be into the future, but life's best teacher is experience."

Gar thought about that. It seemed true enough, but he was convinced that the boy was just spouting high talk, showing off for Etta.

Bernice had changed the subject to lecture about her church. "God is at the head of it," she said, "followed by the living spirits of our ancestors, then the people here on earth, and even animals and plants. Everything is necessary for a harmonious universe. Everything reacts to something else. Everybody reacts to somebody else. Life is a sum of reactions between things, spiritual and material. Opposites attract each other." She looked fondly at her son and his pretty companion. "The way we react to each other creates our quality of life."

Gar saw no reason to argue with either. He felt a strong need to make a speech of his own. "The main thing," he said, "is that learning is not in books. Knowledge comes from living. Some of the important things, we already know when we're born. Some others we learns as we go along. Anybody who thinks he is smart just because he knows books, big words, and how to talk polite is a educated fool. He done gone to school an' read all them books, but he don't know nothing!" He glared at P.S. accusingly, but the boy made no reply.

Etta didn't talk. She smirked, and looked high-toned, and

blinked her flirty eyelids. Gar began to wonder if she had any brains at all behind her pretty face.

The flagpole cannon went off again, jarring Gar back to the present. He headed for the middle of town to see who was arriving. This time it was the Choska clan, the men on fine horses, the women riding in brightly decorated wagons and buggies. Their costumes, both men and women, were of buckskin and colorful Indian prints, streaming with multicolored ribbons. Gar kept up his routine, leaving his horse at one end of town, scouting around the other on foot. Word of mouth passage of the fact that there was a marshal in town seemed to be keeping down the drinking. The celebration grew noisy, but mostly joyful.

Etta was parading on as fine a horse as Gar had ever seen. A blood bay mare, her saddle mounted with silver, with silver bangles dangling from its skirts. Etta LaPlace wore a shiny silk crown draped with pearl beads, with every unmarried swain in town in attendance, and plenty of attention from some of the married men. P.S. was prominent in her retinue, but scowling and looking frustrated from all the competition he was getting.

Along late in the morning, the contingent from Tullahassee arrived, completing the coming of visitors. The Tullahassee celebrants were *wachinas,* recent black emigrants to the Indian Territory. They stood apart somewhat from the Indian-blood bands, and, among them, Gar was sure he caught a glimpse of Dick Nash, who already had a reputation for outlawry and troublemaking over most of the eastern half of the Territory. Gar made a note of that in his mind and went off to hunt up Bernice and her clansfolk for the noontime picnic.

The marshal was filling his plate at the food-laden tables when P.S. moped by, without Etta and conspicuously nettled. The courtly activities surrounding the Queen were keeping Etta away from him. With a passive sympathy, Gar stopped him and offered to make conversation.

"Seems like I'm seeing a few brown bottles here and there amongst these Yahola folks," Gar said.

"Pop, you can't have an Emancipation Day picnic without a little brew circulating," his son remonstrated.

"That home-brewed Choc beer is near as strong as white lightnin' sometimes," Gar put in.

"*Choctaw* beer," Phenunda corrected him quietly, "is *nearly* as strong as *illegally distilled whiskey.*"

"Son," Gar asked, "did you understand what I said?"

"Certainly. I was explaining—"

"Let *me* explain," Gar said gently. "If'n I say something so's you can't understand, ask me. Don't be telling me how I ought to have said it."

Bernice came up. "The boy is only trying to help you," she said with asperity. "He's been to Tullahassee school. You should appreciate him trying to teach you how white folks talk."

Gar turned belligerent. "Why ought I to care how white folks talk?"

"If you're going to be a U.S. marshal, you're going to have to work with them."

"Onliest kind of white folks I work with is the kind I have to put in jail," Gar asserted. He turned away. It was like the two images he had seen in the globes of Judge Parker's desk lamps. There were always *two* of him. An officer of the court trying to do his duty, deserving some respect, and an ignorant black-skinned bumbler deserving contempt. Which one was really him? *Seems like I get plenty of contempt,* he thought, *from honkies like the Fort Smith hardware man and Jake Hesse—and my wife and son.*

Bernice was comforting P.S. "Etta is just being Queen, Phenunda, like she's supposed to be. Maybe it has turned her head a little. But it's only for this one day. Remember what you said about the wheel cycles? Tomorrow things will turn around and be just like they used to be."

Gar's appetite gone, he put down the picnic plate and headed for the community auction lot beside Waterman's Mercantile, where the parade would form up. He got there early. Too early. Only a few young men were standing around. They had evidently expected privacy in the vacant lot this early. They were openly passing a bottle around. Gar casually stepped into the circle of young men beside the one who was at that moment taking a nip, and accepted the bottle from him when he passed it along.

The young sport stood transfixed, his eyes watering from the heat of the potion he had drunk, too busy trying to swallow it to try to retrieve the bottle. It was a pint flask of clear glass, as flat as a rattlesnake's head, and three-quarters full of reddish-brown liquor. The young man who had passed it to Gar, now fully aware of what he had done, coughed, backed out of the circle, and faded from sight around the corner of the mercantile store.

Gar sniffed the bottle. It had a unique, strong, and spicy smell. The circle was breaking up rapidly as young men disappeared among the helter-skelter of parked teams and wagons in the vacant lot, sidling then behind the mercantile or the greasy spoon café bordering the vacant lot's other side. Gar put the bottle to his lips.

Cayenne pepper! "Hot!" Gar exclaimed, his own eyes watering.

Only one of the young men still remained. He watched Gar superciliously.

Gar assayed the contents of the bottle out loud. "Jamaica ginger, tobacco juice laced with red pepper, and plenty of grain alcohol!" The bottle seemed small in his huge hand as he reached to offer it to the supercilious, and familiar, young man.

The slender youth, a few tough beard hairs thrusting out from his chin, shook his head. "My momma didn't birth me to be a fool!" he said scornfully.

Gar urged, "Taste it!"

The youth wore a slouch hat over a thick mat of hair. He was brassy, self-assured, boldly handsome. Again the head shake.

"That stuff was made to sell, not to drink," he sneered.

"You Dick Nash, ain't you?" Gar said. "If you not drinking it, maybe you selling it?"

Young Dick Nash's eyes were hot with resentment. "My

momma didn't raise me to have no truck with a nigga law that come down on the brothers."

"Yo' momma raise you to *poison* yo' brothers?"

Dick Nash shifted his weight slightly forward. "Yo' ol' momma sure musta been ugly! That all right. But she done took advantage!"

Gar could see no weapon, but he thought *knife,* and as Nash leaned forward Gar could smell the Jamaica ginger on his breath. If he had been selling it, he had also been drinking it. "Yo' momma raise you up to git drunk? To make a bum outa yo'se'f?"

"Yo' ol' momma musta *been* drunk. Less'n she wouldn't of birthed you *a*-tall!"

"Yo' momma gonna see her boy in jail, or laid out dead in a coffin," Gar suggested.

He heard horses entering the auction lot, coming in among the vehicles and teams parked between the mercantile and the café. Gar kept his eyes on Dick Nash, letting the riders come up beside him. It was Queen Etta LaPlace and her retinue, arriving to lead the Emancipation Day parade. P.S. was riding among them.

CHAPTER 4

Gar assumed that he and the aggressive young outlaw were at an impasse. The marshal knew that he was not going to pull his gun and kill a young buck for smarting off with his mouth. Or for having a few drinks on a holiday. He suspected that young Nash, however aggressive, had better judgment than to go up against a gun with his knife, however sharp the knife and agile his skill in using it.

Queen Etta LaPlace and her retinue seemed to fail to apprehend the tension into which they had ridden. She seemed fully preoccupied with the attention being paid her. Her followers were equally preoccupied with paying attention to her. All of them were insensitive to the face-off between Gar Rutherford and Dick Nash.

Etta's flirting eyes took in the handsome young highwayman. She saw a bold, swashbuckling youth, and promptly evidenced a desire to add him to her cluster of admirers. She rode away from them, close to Nash, giving him the full fragrance of her perfume, for Gar, too, could smell the heady bouquet of her. Here she pretended to lose control of the mettlesome horse she rode.

Pulling up the blood bay's head, she cried out, "Oh, my goodness!"

Before another of her retinue could ride to her side, Dick Nash spun away from Gar. Seizing the blood bay mare's halter, Nash stared up at Etta with the dawn of a new interest. Ignoring Gar as if he had departed from the scene, Nash drawled, "Lovely lady, would you object if I was suddenly to start spinning the wheel of my lively life around the smooth axle of your understanding?"

He released her, went back into the kitchen, and returned carrying a washboiler from which he emptied the lye water. Hurriedly, he drew two buckets of fresh water from the well, emptying each bucket into the washboiler of clothes. He hung up the well rope.

"There," he said. "That will soak out the lye. Now—" Again he took her hand and drew her into the house. Her eyes still sparkled wickedly. Her lips were half smiling.

Gar sat, near dozing, beside Bernice, in the Sunday morning service. Lazy summer insect buzzes came in through the open church house windows. Marshal Rutherford gave his full, but drowsy, attention to the Reverend Haworth's sermon. The preacher was in full cry.

"Now de sea parted; split open wide; anybody here gonna say it didn't?

"Anybody gonna say, I was deah, preachuh. I saw dat de sea *didn't* part, *didn't* let de chillun of Israel come a-walking through; *didn't* close down on ol' Pharaoh an' his chariots an' drowned dem Egypt land oppressors daid?

"No, sah! No! Ain't nobody gonna say dat!

"Because de word of de Lawd tell us it's true! An' if dat ain't enough, ain't we in our own time seen de sea of slavery part? Open up an' let us all out? Uh, huh!

"Seen de sea of slavery part in Civil War like de bloody Red Sea an' all us chillun heah today walked right through. An' when de whole phalanx of de Confederate soldiers an' pa-terollers come a-runnin' in to catch us it close down again; some-times they drowned in they own blood. Amen! Ah, hah!

"An' it's gotta be like that, brothern. When you see dat sea of trouble rollin' an' tumblin' out dere befo' you, you gotta pray! 'Cause de Lawd God Almighty can part dat sea of trouble jus' like He part de Red Sea, an' de Slavery Sea, an' you can come on through . . ."

Gar listened, knowing he was no amen shouter, but knowing that he would stand his ground for this small church. Black peo-

ple's burden was made a little lighter because of the church.
Some folks learned to read and write here, they partied here,
young folks met their future husbands and wives here, men
argued politics here. The church was high society for the ladies.
In this plain and simple meeting house human joy and sorrow
were shared. Gar's religion was his fellowship with men, and
this meeting place with God. It gave him strong force when
courage or endurance showed no special promise in the face of
dehumanizing pressures. The sermon came to a close and the
congregation began singing.

If I can only climb de hill to heaven's pearly gate
It won't matter that I'm weary, it won't matter if I'm late;
I won't care if I am ragged, downhearted, sad, and poor.
It jus' won't make no difference can I walk through heaven's
    door.

Backbreakin' work behind me; here I done the bes' I can,
Ol' Satan an' his devils lef' behind with evil man.
I nevah made no money an' I often was afraid,
Makes no difference can I only climb the heav'nly grade.

With the church service ended they made their way down
the aisle toward the bright sunlight outside, shaking hands, exchanging friendly small talk as they went. Nearing the entry-
way, Bernice gripped Gar's arm and whispered, "There's Phenunda Sterling and he has Etta with him. Isn't she pretty?"

Gar saw his son shaking hands with the preacher. Etta, standing beside him, *was* pretty. She nearly reminded Gar of the Bernice he had encountered on his way up through the Indian Territory twenty years ago. If anything, Etta was a more striking
beauty than the young Bernice of Opothleyahola's settlement
had been. But there was something about this girl's demeanor . . .

They were passing through the church's double doors then,
and Bernice was introducing her. Etta LaPlace offered her
hand, held high. Gar could not hear what she said through the

P.S., sitting on his mount, listened and glared with barely re-
strained jealousy and anger, but other paraders were pulling in
now. There were paper-decorated floats, the leading one replete
with blue and gold foil, fresh flowers, girls in long calico gowns,
the whole labeled EMANCIPATION, and epitomizing an ideal at
last achieved. Another wagon, carrying rustic desks and benches
on which small children were seated was labeled EDUCATION.

A black teacher in cap and gown stood before the children,
pointing to letters and figures drawn on a slate board attached to
the wagon driver's seat. Gar moved over by his son's stirrup.

"P.S.," he said, "take a look at those girls wearing calico up on
the EMANCIPATION wagon. In the long haul, any one of them
will leave that dicty high-yellow French doll a long ways behind
in the dust."

In an outburst of fury, P.S. jerked his horse's reins around.
The startled animal's eyes rolled white as P.S. bristled. "Mind
your talk, Papa!" He jabbed his spurs and charged away in heat,
creating confusion and near collisions among the mounted riders
still arriving on the lot. There were black cowboys in chaps,
checkered shirts, and bandanas, representing the livestock raisers
in the Territory. Part Creek Indians wore leather coats or ribbon
shirts, their pants legs gathered below the knees with ribbons or
thrust into high buckskin leggings.

With time lost in getting organized, a good deal of backing,
filling, and jockeying for position, the parade got lined out and
began moving off down the street led by a black Union soldier
carrying the United States flag of thirteen stripes and thirty-
seven stars, sided by uniformed guardsmen.

Queen Etta followed, trailed by her admiring court, Dick
Nash in the forefront now, riding bareback on a heavy draft
mule he had quickly unhitched from one of the teams standing
in the wagon lot. Gar doubted that the mule belonged to him.

The decorated floats came along, showing up in brave colored
gaiety as they pulled between the drab and sparse buildings
along Main Street. They were aiming to disband at the picnic
grounds for an afternoon of contests and games. Gar thought

then that he knew the man who rode counter to the parade's course, approaching through the scattered crowd of parade watchers.

It was Ross Stephens. He was finally beginning to ride like a seasoned horseman instead of a St. Louis foot policeman who had suffered the misfortune of becoming a mounted lawman on the western frontier. Gar went to meet him.

Stephens' shiny marshal's badge glinted in the nooning sun as he stepped down from the chestnut gelding old man Butler had sold him. Without palaver, Ross handed Gar a warrant. Gar, knowing he could not read it, did not even look at it. He stood holding it in his hand as Stephens said, "The judge wants you to pick up a pair of prisoners at McAlester's store, too." He watched the short parade passing by. "Big celebration?"

"Sho' nuff," Gar quipped.

Ross ignored his facetious dialect. He reported seriously, "Your prisoners that I carried in are repining in the Fort Smith lockup. I've got your fees and mileage money in my pocket. Maybe we could find someplace less prominent for me to turn it over to you. Your wagon and man Hesse are camped out down by the river."

Gar grinned. "Hesse didn't want to come in for the celebration?"

"He didn't fully say so, but I gather he did some asking around and concluded that this is a black man's town and he didn't have no place here."

"Uh-huh." Gar was still grinning. "Well, you're dark enough to join up in the big doings. I'll introduce you around. Expect I can get you entered in the shooting contest this afternoon."

"Reckon I'll have to leave that joy to you." A ghost of a smile flickered across Stephens' firmly serious face. "Soon as I give you your money I'm on my way up to Tulsa town. Seems like there's some hard feeling between black and white folks there, too."

They sat, watching the tail end of the parade, and Ross asked, "Aren't you going to read your warrant?"

Gar cleared his throat, embarrassed. He opened his mouth,

but something seemed to cut off what he had started to say and he stood blinking, silently, as chagrin crept up through him.

"You can't read, can you?" Ross asked bluntly.

Abashed, Gar shook his head.

"It's a shame," Stephens admitted, "but it ain't nothing to be mortified about. Plenty black folks can't read. When you was growing up down in Texas it was against the law to teach any-body black to read."

"Some folks learned anyhow," Gar grunted self-accusingly.

Ross Stephens shrugged. "Your warrant is for a gunswift named Clay Missouri, alias Neosho. He's supposed to be a cow-puncher, but more recently he killed a faro dealer in a gambling tent at a place called White Bead, a long ways from here—down where the Sante Fe is building track into Texas."

"I'll fix what it says in my mind," Gar assured him. "My boy will help me." He cogitated awhile. "I can pick up those pris-oners at McAlester's store on the way back."

"No," Ross disagreed. "The judge wants you to stop for them on the way down. It's a pair of robbers tried to break into his store at night. McAlester woke up, got down his shotgun, and caught them red-handed. Now he's afraid they'll break loose and kill him and his wife in their beds."

Gar kept on cogitating. "Maybe I ought to take my dog. That cowpuncher fellow bound to be on the run. I'll likely have to trail him. Ol' Blue mighty good at that." He shifted his weight thoughtfully. "I expect he's a white man?"

"That's what the warrant says."

"Well, I guess ol' Blue won't be uppity about trailing a white man. C'mon. Let's follow this parade on down to the picnic grounds. You can meet my family."

They rode to encounter Bernice. She was at her agreeable best, still helping to clear up after the noon feast. "We would have been finished, but we stopped to watch the parade, letting the ants get a foothold. So we finish up having to throw away some leftovers we could have saved. But not much."

Gar saw the Queen and her retinue, standing dismounted

under a towering shade tree not far distant, cooling off after the parade in the hot August sun. Gar shouted at P.S., his booming voice carrying to the far reaches of the picnic grounds. He saw the boy detach himself from the group reluctantly, and come toward them.

"Gar!" Bernice chided. "You shouldn't yell at Phenunda like that. He is with his friends. You'll embarrass him to death."

"I want him to speak to Marshal Stephens," Gar explained. With something like gratification he added, "You can't read either and," Gar lowered his eyes, looking away apologetically, "Ross has a warrant I want the boy to help me memorize."

Stephens began, "I could have done that—" but Bernice cut in again, this time with agony in her voice.

"Gar! You're not going off again? I hate this life you've gotten yourself into. You're going to get yourself killed, chasing out after some bad man."

"It's what I hired out to do," Gar argued phlegmatically. "I can make better money catching runaway outlaws than I can cultivating cotton on land I can't even own."

"I worry myself sick—"

"I'm sorry you worry, Bernice, but you don't have to. Worrying is no more good than trying to scoop up smoke."

Ross, shielding his movement from other groups around the picnic grounds, pulled a brown paper packet from his pocket. "Speaking of money," Stephens said, "it looks like we're not going to find any real private place for me to give you this." He handed the packet to Gar.

Gar opened it. Not counting its contents, he took out a few bills of the greenback specie it contained, stuffed them in his pocket, and handed the rest to Bernice.

"Put some of it in a safe place, if you can, woman," he urged her.

P.S. came up to say, "Papa, some of those folks want to see you shoot." He seemed, momentarily, to have put the competition for Queen Etta's attention out of his thoughts and acknowledged the presence of Marshal Ross Stephens. P.S. read Gar's warrant aloud to his father. Gar stood with his eyes closed, moving his lips as he did his memory work, and as P.S. finished reading the paper he said, with fear coloring his voice, "This is another white man you're going after, Papa."

"Gar! You're going to get yourself lynched." There was plain fear in Bernice's voice, and she took hold of Gar's arms, pulling him toward her.

"No, I ain't going to get myself lynched," Gar resisted gutturally. "Maybe I might have to run. But I been outrunning an' outfighting white men all my life. Ain't no reason I can't keep on doing it."

Ross Stephens put in abruptly, "I've got to get on up north to Tulsa. You folks need to say your goodbyes in private."

"Ain't going to be no goodbyes," Gar declared. "I'll burn a little powder here for entertainment purposes, then I'll be heading south."

Ross Stephens mounted and rode away to the north, unhurriedly, his pace geared for long distance rather than speed. At the firing range, the amateur competition proved inadequate for Gar. He had learned to shoot during the Civil War years when he was on the scout and there was never a spare ounce of powder or a ball to waste.

His rifle shots, with pinpoint accuracy, penetrated the bull's-eyes of the rifle range targets so consistently that Gar offered to eliminate himself from the competition. His offer was gladly accepted, and the crowd of spectators for the shooting grew.

Gar's seemingly careless shots with his shotgun put by far the greatest concentration of shot in the crosshatched area of the turkey-shoot targets, and again Gar took himself out of the competition. The spectators became more interested in watching Gar shoot than in determining who won the competitions.

So what started as a competition concluded as an exhibition, with Gar pistol shooting his own brass .45 cartridges, tossed high, out of midair. He listened to admiring compliments and responded cordially to the crowd's adulation until he was surfeited, then said quietly, "Bernice, son, I'm going over to the house and pick up my traps. You stay here and keep the party going just like I was coming right back. This day's almost over. The Yahola, Tullahassee, and Choska folks will be heading home before sundown. It's too late for heavy trouble to be likely."

Gar, walking and leading the copper dun horse P.S. had fetched for him, started off. He turned in parting to say over his shoulder, "Oh, yes. I'll be taking ol' Blue with me. So when you get home an' miss the dog, he ain't lost."

Ol' Blue found the wagon on the river as facilely as if he had been doing it every day. Leaving Pleasant Hill, the hound had picked up Ross Stephens' trail where Gar had met him along the parade route, back tracked him, and by the time they were heading down into the big river bend near Yahola the dog was running full speed. It was all the copper dun horse could do to keep up.

Jake Hesse was not pleased at what happened after the dog found him. He had been taking his ease, fishing from the trunk of a fallen cottonwood tree, scorched and tumbled by lightning. It lay out into the river current, having lost its leaves and bark, a sun-bleached and gnarled giant.

When Gar saw Hesse he was standing scared and erect on the trunk of the fallen tree and Blue was baying at him loudly from where the dead tree's roots were still embedded in the bank. Hesse was palpably frightened, not knowing whether to retreat further out where the tree trunk narrowed and its dry, broken branches thinned over the deep river current.

The terrorized wagon master certainly had no intention of approaching any closer to the barking hound that had him treed, its front paws up among the tangled, washed-out roots, its hind legs trying to find a foothold sufficient to claw itself up and out on the log.

Hesse's cane fishing pole floated awry, midway out in the stream, the only thing that had kept it from being carried off was its line, entangled among the barren branches reaching down into the water. It moved about erratically, almost like a live thing in the turbid, muddy current.

Gar rode up fast, shouting, "Ho! Blue! Come off that!" He slid the copper dun's haunches in the soft riverbank leaf mold, calling out again to silence the dog. When it was quiet he said gruffly, "Evenin', Mistuh Hesse."

Blue was panting, his long red tongue lolling and dripping saliva. He came to sit by Gar's stirrup, looking up eagerly at his master as if expecting commendation, or instructions to attack.

Hesse approached the bank-rooted end of the tree angrily and reluctantly. "Good afternoon! That dog's vicious!"

Gar dismounted and scratched Blue's ears. "No, he ain't. He just enthusiastic. Let's get hitched up, Mr. Hesse. We got a long ways to go."

Following down the Texas Road they reached McAlester's store after two and a half slow days of travel. The storekeeper's prisoners were a pair of Indian boys who had been out on a lark hoping to steal some tobacco and a little spending money. McAlester had them chained to a tree in the open, out in the weather, like a pair of performing bears.

Gar asked, "You believe a couple nubbins like this could break that log chain and kill you?"

McAlester was a hardened frontiersman. He declared, "Don't let these redskin boys fool you with their smooth-faced innocence. They'll kill you as soon as look at you."

Gar opened the padlocks, taking the pair away from the stench and flyswarm of their own excrement. They appeared to be mighty glad to get away from the tight encirclement of summer heat that had been their prison for more than a week.

The marshal had Hesse stop at the first creek they crossed to allow the boys to wash themselves. Then he leg-ironed them in the wagon bed and ordered, "Let's go. We got farther to travel than we already come."

Gar did not hurry Hesse. Moseying west, camping, eating, sleeping, the changing moon had waxed almost full by the time they finally struck the Santa Fe right-of-way above Pauls Valley.

Gar, leaving his prisoners with Hesse and the wagon, rode on south across the lush valley of the Washita.

Intending to travel light, he left all his armament except for his Colt's revolver with the wagon. He did not even wear the six-shooter but, like a drifting cowboy, wrapped it in his war bag and tied it behind his saddle.

White Bead was no more than a water, wood, and coal camp on the Santa Fe right-of-way. Beside its roughly fresnoed grade were ricked cords of wood, haystack-high heaps of glistening coal, piled stocks of new creosoted railroad ties, a wooden tank tower leaking water, a racked supply of dully gleaming new iron rails, a ragtown of sleeping tents for the workers, and the gambling tent.

Over it all hung the acrid smell of coal smoke. The circular gambling tent, far bigger around than any corral or stock pen Gar had ever seen, stood on a broad knoll not far from the temporarily spiked-down work track. The tent's canvas sides were rolled up, making it a wide-open outdoor saloon.

As Gar rode in from downwind, the stale smell of sweat, beer, and whiskey floated down from it, cutting into the coal-smoke stench and finally replacing it with the strong miasma of, to Gar's mind, sin. With the overwhelming smell of strong drink came the tinny, discordant sound of fiddle and honky-tonk piano music.

Gar could see a scattering of floozies circulating among the customers of the off-work shift. While Gar pulled up, watching, the girls gathered to sing and dance on a rickety stage behind the piano, then scattered out again to work the crowd. Gar saw, halfway around on the far side of the tent, an elderly Negro porter. He was gathering up spittoons. Gar dismounted and, leading his horse, circled to intercept him.

The aged black man came promptly out to meet him. Gar pulled his badge from his pocket, hiding it in his huge palm, and opening his hand only enough for the elderly man to see its insignia.

The porter saw. "Oh, oh!" His grizzly head gave a negative shake. "You *are* looking for trouble."

Gar asked, "How they call you, friend?"

"Tully Mills."

"Mr. Mills, I'm Deputy Marshal Rutherford from Fort Smith, and I ain't looking for trouble except maybe as it concerns a puncher named Missouri. I heard they call him Neosho."

"Puncher?" It was an exclamation. "You mean that gunslinger that killed Three-Finger Jack in here awhile back? I heard him called Neosho, but he ain't no cowpuncher."

"Whut he look like?"

"Curly-headed fellow. Mighty fine looking. Stocky. Weighs maybe a hundred and eighty. Cow waddy clothes, all right. With fancy high-heeled handmade boots. Fast, oh, I say fast, with his six-gun!"

"What kinda hoss he ride?"

The porter nodded. "Palouse hoss. He, Neosho, got a little limp, I hear from a bullet took in the foot during a gun fight, but it don't slow him down none. He off an' on that Palouse hoss like a jumping jack. They say he got 'leven notches cut in the butt of his six-gun."

The six floozies were getting together again for another turn on the frail stage. A derby-hatted Irish bouncer came ambling across the tent toward Gar and Tully Mills. He reached them, rolled a toothpick across his wide mouth and asked,

"What are you doing here, boy?"

"Just a wandering cowboy, looking for work," Gar said gently. "I stopped to listen to the music."

"Then keep on wandering," advised the bouncer. "The music is for the boys who come to spend their money—and we don't want yours."

"Haven't got none nohow." Gar grinned malevolently. "Thank you. I'll be ridin' on."

"That your dog?"

"Yas, sir. Best cowdog ever chased a lost heifer."

"Well, be sure to take him with you." The derby-hatted bouncer glanced at the stage. "These heifers get a-plenty chousing from Santa Fe gandy dancers."

Gar stepped up across the copper dun horse. He leaned down from the saddle. "You don't know where a hard-up colored cowboy might look for work around here, do you, sah?"

"You might try Billy Jefferson's spread down in the mountains," the bouncer offered. "They ought to be hiring hands for fall roundup before long."

"Thank you kindly." Gar whistled up ol' Blue. Turning to ride away, he pulled up in afterthought and put a hand on the dun's rump. "I used to rodeo with a curly-headed waddy called Neosho. Heard he was down this way. I'm a pretty fair bite-'em-lip bulldogger myself."

The bouncer studied him carefully. "Skinny fellow?"

"No, suh. He kind of stocky. Walks with a limp."

The bouncer grinned enigmatically at the porter. "Seen anybody like that, Tully?"

Mills suggested tentatively, "Seems like they was a fellow like that. He might be hanging around Mistuh Jefferson's store down there in the Arbuckles."

The bouncer turned and walked back under the tent. Tully Mills followed Gar out a few steps and laid his hand on the horse's copper rump. "I don't think they'll aim to let you take him," he said softly.

Gar lifted his hand in parting salute.

The porter slapped the copper dun's hip gently. "Be careful, brothah," he cautioned.

Gar cantered off toward the blue shadows of the distant Arbuckles, the hound trailing at his horse's heels. He took his time. If there was a grapevine telegraph running into those mountains there was no use trying to beat it. Better to confound it by poking along, by making it appear he really was a cowpuncher on the drift, and in no way a hunter, or in a hurry.

Gar let a full day ease by in his approach toward the low

mountains, even taking his own sweet time about getting up and started out on the second morning. It was late August and the first feel of early autumn was in the air. He could see it in the sumac leaves, turning bright red.

He could sense it in the cool anticipation, the scent, the very weight of the air through which he traveled. The oppressive heat, the steady afternoon racheting of the midsummer locusts, was behind him now. The locusts sounded different, as though fading into a weary distance. The midday summer air grew heavy, humid. The leaves of deciduous trees would soon begin to turn, but the country through which he rode was predominantly evergreen. Giant blue cedars towered along the water courses, making the still pools of water beneath them seem dark and deep.

The incline of the trail up into the Arbuckles began to rise, and Gar let the copper dun horse choose its own pace in the gravelly footing. Switchback followed hard on switchback as the trail elevated. He climbed on through the day, following along the narrow slanting ledges of limestone until time came to ascend to another level, whereupon the trail became a steep caliche of loose and crumbly travertine, rough stones pitted and round from the untold succession of centuries that had made the trail, following always the line of least resistance.

First a game trail, Gar figured, for deer, elk, and antelope. For the crusty pads of bears and mountain lions. Indians afoot. Then Indians on horseback. Then white men and black men. Now men and the cattle they moved from summertime pastures to lowland winter graze. In turning it into rangeland, ranchers like Billy Jefferson, probably a Chickasaw squawman, had grown rich fattening their herds on these nutritive limestone grasses.

The switchbacks flattened and leveled off a little just before reaching the summit of the Arbuckle range. His hound had begun the day ranging out ahead of him in excited forays. Now, his tongue hanging out, he trailed along not far behind. Gar came out on a rocky flat high enough to be shrouded with moisture on a cloudy day. It was significantly cooler up here. The rocky flat of the summit was manmade. Graded down by the fresnos and mule teams of the railroad crews, Marshal Gar Rutherford guessed, in exchange for rancher Billy Jefferson's various cooperations with the railroad being constructed through the valley beneath. Jefferson had doubtless guided them to the mountain pass they would use and given his blessing to their use of it—a permission he really did not have the right to grant.

But it took all kinds of cooperations for the big money moguls to get along, Gar knew, and these flat, rocky acres here on the summit would surely be one of them. In the middle of the broad spread of barren rock stood the store that Gar assumed he was looking for. It was a low, square building, set on a foundation of piled-up native stone. Its walls were made of slab cedar.

There was a sign on the storefront which Gar studied. Since it consisted of three words, the middle one the longest, he took a wild guess that they said *Billy Jefferson's Store*. Beneath it was another sign made up of two words that he could read, for his son P.S. had taught him to recognize those two words. They meant *Post Office*. There was a fairly new United States flag flying from a cedar pole above them. The other signs on the storefront didn't take much reading.

One of them showed a dark twist of Three Star burley chewing tobacco. Another pictured a big patent medicine bottle—bitters, Gar figured. Beneath it, to the right of the store building's single front door, was a colored drawing of beer being poured from a bottle with elk horns on the label. The brown brew was foaming and running down the sides of the stein. It looked refreshing and inviting. On the other side of the narrow door was a tin panel with a Bull Durham sack half as tall as a man painted on it.

Under the store's shallow, overhanging porch roof was a pair of rustic wooden chairs occupied by two men who sat with their chairs leaning back against the words on the Bull Durham sign.

They were both whittling, and one of them folded his pocket knife, arose slowly, and went inside the store. Gar did not hurry. He sat still on the copper dun horse, looking over the country-side.

The rocky flat of the summit sloped off into rocky, high mountain pastures. The store was well located to serve all this mountain country, as well as drovers who, with their herds, ascended the switchback trail from the plains below. Gar did not know this country. His running ground had always been in Texas and the eastern Indian Territory. He felt a little ill at ease here, and cautious.

Far off to his right, across an intervening valley, he could see a waterfall. It seemed toylike, miniature at this great distance. Probably six or eight miles to the west for an eagle in flight, through descending country impassable to man. They were so far that no sound of the considerable roar such a cascade would make reached his ears.

Gar touched his spurs to the horse and rode on up to the store.

"Afternoon, suh," he greeted the remaining whittler.

The seamy-faced loafer spat, but did not return his greeting.

There was no hitchrail before the store. Instead, one ran empty down the store's west side. Five horses, taking advantage of the afternoon shade, were tied to the hitchrack running down the east side of the store. Gar eased his dun around to leave him racked there among the other horses. The bluetick hound followed along to lie down in the shade, against the cool side of the building. Gar dismounted to climb the limestone slab steps up to the porch.

This store stood on what was bound to be a major north-south trail through the Territory. A route frequented by passing strangers, most of whom would stop to pass the time of day and give the little store their custom. Gar acted like he was one of them. He made no further overture to the front porch whittler. He went directly to the store door, turned its knob, and entered.

Its low roof made it seem even smaller on the inside than it had appeared from the outside. It was a dark room, lighted only by open windows on either side. A cool breeze circulated through, coming from a closed-off rear area apparently used for storage, and blowing out both open windows. The place was cluttered, redolent with store odors, a counter running along its west side to terminate at the post office cage in the southwest corner. Four men sat at a square table on the west side casually sorting and slapping down dominoes in a game of moon.

The fifth man leaned against the store counter watching the game. He was the other of the whittlers who had been sitting out on the front porch, the one who had gotten up and come inside upon observing Gar's arrival. Though he wore no apron, it occurred to Gar that he might be the storekeeper. Perhaps he had got up and come in, not to announce Gar's approach but because he had assumed that, in Gar, he might have a new customer to wait on. So Gar addressed him.

"Yas, suh. I'd sho' like to buy a bottle of that Elkhorn Beer you advertisin' outside."

The storekeeper eyed him levelly. "You'd have to take it outside to drink it," he said flatly.

"Yas, suh," Gar agreed.

The four moon players had paid no more attention to Gar than if he had been a fly crawling on the wall. Intent on their game, they shuffled and mixed the clacking white dominoes, made dilatory talk about the hand just played, drew fresh hands, and began arranging their dominoes before them. Gar looked over the four. Cowhands, range riders, all of them, except the one with the kinky blond hair who sat with his back to the west wall.

That would be Neosho—Clay Missouri—or whatever his right name might be. A stocky, blond man, less than thirty, tan-faced and handsome, with no work calluses on his blunt-fingered hands. Instead, Gar could see a pair of kidskin gloves thrust in his belt, the trademark of a man who meant to keep the skin of his hands smooth, not hardened by knotty, slick calluses that might deter his draw and make him awkward in gun handling.

Plainly a man who meant to make his living by being good with a gun. Slung beneath the belt in which the gloves were thrust, Gar saw another belt, a low-riding cartridge belt looped through an open holster from which the well-notched handle of a .45 six-shooter thrust up handily.

Gar backed away and followed the storekeeper toward the store's back partition, where he received from him a bottle of beer, dripping wet from the vat of water in which it had been cooling. He kept his eyes fixed on Neosho. Sure enough, the holster was tied down by a pair of leather thongs encircling the gunman's muscular thigh.

Gar got out his money to pay for the beer and asked, "Suh, you sho'ly don't happen to have one of them stein glasses I could po' it in, do you? That sign do make that look appetizin'!"

The storekeeper stepped behind the counter with reluctant ill grace to pick up a heavy glass stein from the pile there and handed it across. Gar surrendered his money. He turned back to the moon game and began pouring the beer in the stein.

"I told you you couldn't drink that in here," the storekeeper snarled.

"Yas, suh. You said to drink it outside. I'm just a-pouring it in heah."

He finished pouring it, with patient, deliberate slowness. Ignoring the rising fury in the storekeeper's face, Gar handed back the empty bottle. With a smooth, continuing motion then, Gar reached into his shirt's right front pocket, lifted out his badge, and carefully laid it on the bone pile of white dominoes accumulated near the center of the table.

"I'm Deputy Gar Rutherford—U. S. Court for the Western District of Arkansas," he said. "Mistah Neosho, I have a warrant for your arrest."

Neosho did not even glance up. Instead, he went for his gun. Gar was clearly unarmed. His gun was still wrapped in his poncho, inside his war bag, tied behind the saddle of the copper dun horse outside. But Neosho had paid Gar no obvious attention and may not have noticed that he carried no gun. At least he had visibly decided to take no chance now. As his gun cleared the holster Gar leaned across the square table to pour his beer down Neosho's forehead.

Then he hit the gunswift on his kinky blond head with the empty stein. The stein was heavy and blunt and the force of the blow rocked Clay Missouri back in his chair. Apparently too dazed to try, he made no attempt to bring his six-shooter to bear.

Neosho rocked his chair back against the open window, and rolled out of it. He hit the ground on his hands and knees, scrambled up still holding his gun, flicked his horse's rein loose as he ducked under the tie rail, jumped into the saddle, and was gone.

Gar dove headlong across the table, scattering dominoes as he slid out the window. Grabbing the tie rail he swung to land on his feet and ran to the copper dun standing slip-tied at the end of the line of horses. His swinging aboard startled the horse into motion. Neosho was already riding out of sight over the edge of the flat graded lip of the summit toward one of the open pastures.

Gar stripped loose the thongs lashing down his war bag as he took up the pursuit. Neosho came in sight again, riding hellbent across the high pasture spreading off to the south. Gar dug down into his war bag, came up with the poncho, and flung everything else aside. He unwrapped the holstered pistol, strapped it around his waist, and threw the poncho on the blurring brown earth over which he rode. The copper dun plunged down off the summit grade onto the limestone pasture. Neosho was shrinking small in the distance, riding for a motte of mountain ash. Gar could hear ol' Blue now, baying beside him.

It was hard and dangerous riding. The limestone ridges here had been canted awry by some ancient earthquake and came thrusting up out of the earth as if the ledges had been planted in long rows, growing a foot or more out of the ground. Gar ran his horse with full-out abandon through these rows of rock with the certain knowledge that one misplaced hoof meant broken legs for the copper dun horse and a spill that would surely kill him.

Gar thought, *We s'pposed to have hard heads. I'll find out if I bash my brains up against one of them rows of white rocks.* His horse was courageous, and a racer. Gar was gaining on Clay Missouri. The gunman turned in the saddle to fire. His bullet tore at the brim of Gar's hat, ripping it from his head. Gar drew his own gun. *If he can shoot that good a-riding hard,* he thought, *I'm going to have to do better.*

Neosho was unloading from his horse. He dismounted smoothly, and turned to face Gar, planting his feet and raising his six-shooter, steadying it with both hands as he prepared to shoot. Gar flung himself out of the saddle. As he did, Neosho shot. Gar's coat was flung open by his own trajectory through the air. One of its buttons splintered into a myriad of flying pieces as Neosho's bullet hit it.

Gar hit the ground running toward Neosho with all the hard momentum of his leap off the copper dun stallion. Neosho's six-gun still pointed dead at him, held at arm's length in both the gunman's hands. Neosho was ready to shoot again. *I'm going to have to kill him,* Gar thought. He thumbed back his gun hammer, aiming the weapon like a pointed finger at the blond gunman's chest. As Gar slowed and brought himself to a halt, he fired.

Neosho lost his gun and turned, grabbing with both hands at his brisket. He sat down. Gar was instantly hovering over him, ready to shoot again. But it was not necessary. Clay Missouri's face was bleached, paste white, and blood was leaking out through the fingers he clasped over his breast.

Gar helped Neosho to lie down, watching the contorted wrenching of his face, sharing with the gunman the shock of death. Clay Missouri was trying to speak.

He said, hesitantly, "You came in after me without a gun, didn't you, black man?"

"Yas, suh, Mistah Neosho," Gar admitted. "I doubted how

them Billy Jefferson cowboys might take to a armed nigga walking in amongst 'em."

"Well, Rutherford, you are a damn brave man." Missouri
exhaled a short, bubbly gasp. "Here," he said. Removing bloody
fingers from his wound he fumbled with the buckle of his cartridge belt. Unfastening it, he felt around in the pasture grass,
retrieved his dropped weapon and stuffed it, bloody-handled,
back in its holster. He handed both shell belt and holstered revolver to Gar. "Here," he repeated, "I want you to have this."
And he was dead.

Gar took the holstered gun. He touched the drying blood on
its notched, walnut handle and stood up to look down at the
man. "Mistah Clay Missouri, you wasn't any piker yo' own
self," he told the dead body. "And I expect that faro dealer you
killed back at that gambling tent was."

Blue, sitting on the grass at Gar's feet, whimpered and looked
to the rear. Gar strapped Neosho's gun around his waist opposite
his own, and turned around. Arranged in a tight semicircle,
twenty-five yards behind him, he had an audience. The three
Billy Jefferson cowboys, the storekeeper, even the old-timer Gar
had left whittling on the store porch, were sitting on their
horses, motionless, observing.

Gar watched them. Perhaps the black marshal, standing as
broad, and taller than, his own horse, two guns crisscrossed
about his waist, a dead man at his feet, dismayed them. They
remained motionless. No one spoke. Gar mounted the copper
dun. He rode back to pause beside the storekeeper.

"See that man gets buried," Gar ordered emotionlessly. "See
has he got something on him that says who ought to get his
horse and anything he has worth keeping. Then write to Judge
Parker at Fort Smith and tell him you did it."

Gar cantered back across the rocky plain, stopping to pick up
his poncho and the garments scattered from his war bag. Wad-
ding them against his saddle horn, he headed down out of the
mountains toward Pauls Valley.

CHAPTER 5

On reaching the Pauls Valley camp, Gar had commented pleasantly, "I didn't even need ol' Blue."

"That dog is as worthless as tits on a boar hog," Hesse growled.

Gar shut up and told him no more whatever of what had happened at the gambling tent, now three days ago. Or in the Arbuckle Mountains beyond the railroad camp the following noon.

They broke camp and began the trek back to Fort Smith. Near dusk, a few miles south of Sasakwa, crossing a creek branch near its junction with the Great Canadian, Gar offered gently, "I reckon we might as well stop here for the night."

One of the Indian prisoners urged, a little timorously, "This is a kind of spooky place." Some yards upstream from the trail crossing, gas, seeping up through the bed of the creek, broke the water with intermittent stuttering noises not unlike a frightened human, trying to speak, just out of sight in the shadowy, darkening timber.

"Those are the spirits," said the other Indian boy. "They are warning us not to stay here. We got a creek like this down in our country. We call it Bok-túk-alo. One night some women out hunting possum grapes camped there. The next morning they were all dead."

Gar knew about Bok-túk-alo Creek. The gases escaping from its bed were indeed noxious, poisonous smelling, and he had often avoided camping there. But there was much greater gas seepage along Bok-túk-alo than here. Bok-túk-alo ran through the Choctaw bottoms so low that, on a night when the spring air was heavy, about possum grape ripening time, Gar figured it would be possible for the gas to accumulate in a pocket of sufficient density to be fatal.

Here the gas seep was minor, only enough to give the air a faintly sour, sulfurous odor, and the autumn wind was gusting sharply, blowing the gases away.

"We'll be all right here," he assured his prisoners.

Hesse had already set about preparing supper. Fatback was frying noisily in his big iron skillet. Gar took a bucket and went off upstream, well above where their crossing had riled the water. When he returned, Hesse complained, "Sure takes you enough time to fetch a bucket of water!"

"Call of nature," Gar explained shortly. He had stripped to the waist, washed himself, and was drying his dark chest with his undershirt.

As they ate their fatback and beans the night's obscurity intensified, and a new sound joined the stuttering and popping of the gas bubbles upstream along the creek branch. At intervals, a heavy, thudding clunk echoed among the dark, specterlike upstream tree trunks.

The Indian boys ate greedily, gobbling their beans, guzzling their coffee, before one of them asked with some return of trepidation, "What is that racket?"

Gar paid him no mind. The fire was dying. The two boys sat across from him on the opposite side of the fire, half obscured in the dimming flickers of its light. They were leg-ironed to one of the wagon wheels. *They just look like a pair of scared and lonesome kids,* Gar thought desolately.

Then the other one asked, "What is making that noise?"

Gar brooded over the guttering fire. Disconsolately, he thought to himself, *Here I am in the big middle of nowhere with two guilty-feeling, scared Injun boys and a mean white man who is sorrier company than the boar shoat he says Blue as wo'thless as.*

With evil malevolence, Gar told the Indian boys, "That noise is old hangman George Maledon, a-practicing. One of these days right soon, if you don't change your ways, that *clunk* is going to be you two, falling through his hanging trap, with your feet fetching up short of hitting the ground. His hangropes are going to break your brownskin necks!"

The boys stared at Gar, in owlish, stone-faced stoicism.

"You think I'm fooling you?" Gar asked.

"Build up the fire," urged the taller one of the boys. "Maybe it will show far enough up the creek so we can see what is making that noise."

Gar listened to the echoes of another of the dull thuds. He threw a dead cottonwood branch, dry leaves and all, across the fire and it flared up fitfully. Both boys leaned out from the wagon wheel to which they were chained. They stared up the creek branch. Another thud sounded up yonder, and as its sound died, a flash of white glistened in the dark timber.

"I guess I had it wrong," Gar said. "Ol' Maledon ain't practicing now. That time he hanged somebody. I done seen the dead man's ghost a-skittering through the timber."

For a while, as long as the fire remained high, Gar could see an occasional flash of white in the gloom of the pitch-dark woods. The hollow thuds, separated by long, tense minutes of waiting, kept on.

Gar said, "That Maledon having a busy night. I expect he hung eight or ten boys your age by now."

Neither boy even looked at Gar. Both stared intently into the upstream darkness from whence the dull thuds came, and where an occasional glimmering of white flashed among the trees. The tall boy sat grimly stoic; the jaw of the short one hung slack. In spite of the cool of the evening, a sheen of sweat glossed the faces of both of them.

"You boys can set here an' watch them ghosts till Mistuh Maledon finishes his chores if you want to," Gar said. "I'm going to bed."

Hesse had already cleaned up from supper, and had turned in. Gar could see the top of Hesse's head with its straw-colored hair, thrust out from the top of his bedding, between a couple tree trunks on the far side of the creek. A spare blanket lay beside him on the ground, ready for the chilly early morning hours.

Gar chose a convenient tree trunk, walked to stand against it, and began to unbutton his fly. Then, as if unwilling to expose himself in the plain sight of the two Indian boys, he stalked off into the timber.

He circled around upstream to the place where, earlier in the evening, he had dipped up his bucket of water. The fire, downstream from him now, was guttering again and he stood in stygian blackness.

Reaching up to the branch above him, he unhooked the white shirt he had left hanging there to catch the reflection of the firelight when whipped up by the gusty wind. He knelt then to unwire the water-hollowed stone he had balanced beneath the flow of a small spring gushing down into the creek branch.

One outreaching arm of the slender limestone slab, hollowed by centuries of the swirling water to create a shallow basin, would fill with water until weighted down. Then, like a millwheel bucket, it would lower and dump itself. Whereupon the other end of the balanced slab would fall back and strike the rocks of the creek bed with a hollow thud. Gar rolled up the piece of rusty barbed wire he had found to secure the balanced rock in place. Tossing the wire into the timber, he went back to turn in.

In the morning he began working to establish a friendly relationship with the two Indian boys. He ragged them about being afraid of spirits, but did not reveal the mechanics of the ghostly spook he had created the night before. He prized at them to learn their names, and after giving him a variety of unlikely aliases, the taller one revealed that his name was Tukefelélesku —Bat. The shorter one was called Svkco—Crab. Both of them were full-blood Choctaw.

"All right," Gar nodded. "Tukefelélesku, yo' name is too long, an' I cain't say Svkco. So I'm going to call you Bat an' Craw-dad."

As they sat around the fire that night, Gar recited doggerel he had made up during the day to entertain them. He said,

> I's talkin' 'bout Squire Satan.
> With his pitchfork he's a-spadin'
> Hot fire coals, you to cover.
> Them coals'll sizzle while he hover
> Huntin' for the hottest one
> To scorch yo' fraidy eyes out, son.
> You'll be sorry. You'll sho' quiver
> While he's fryin' up yo' liver.
>
> Bettuh change yo' ways, boys
> While they still is time.
> Now you Satan's toys
> Whilst he yo' souls destroys.
> Less'n you all minds the morals
> Preached here in my rhyme.

Hesse drew Gar aside.

"Marshal, you're making a big mistake, trying to be kind to these worthless young fellows," the white wagoner castigated Gar. "The storekeeper, McAlester, plainly told me that he and his wife were afraid these heathens would get loose some night and slay them in their beds. If that hound dog of yours is any good at all you ought to set him to guarding them. Indian bucks are conscienceless thieves and skulking killers. If your dog here could be taught to set up a barking if they try to creep . . ." He drew back a foot then as if tempted to kick at Blue who had come fawning up to Gar's side. Hesse turned away, visibly sickened, when the dog licked Gar's black hand.

In camp that night Gar unlocked his prisoners' chains and in the greatest sincerity, in his deep voice, quoted for them the first psalm:

Blessed is the man that walketh not in the counsel of
    the ungodly,
Nor standeth in the way of sinners,
Nor sitteth in the seat of the scornful.
But his delight is in the law of the Lord;
And in his law doth he meditate day and night.
And he shall be like a tree planted by the rivers of water,
That bringeth forth his fruit in his season;
His leaf also shall not wither;
And whatsoever he doeth shall prosper.
The ungodly are not so;
But are like the chaff which the wind driveth away.
Therefore the ungodly shall not stand in the judgment,
Nor sinners in the congregation of the righteous.
For the Lord knoweth the way of the righteous;
But the way of the ungodly shall perish.

Then, line by line, he had them repeat it after him.

Hesse complained again, this time vociferously. "Rutherford,"
he blustered, "your preaching to these rapscallions is going to
come to no good! All you're doing is lulling them into thinking
we're tenderhearted!"

"Them boys need to exercise around," Gar said stubbornly.
"Their blood got to circulate or they arteries going to harden."

"Once they're convinced we're soft in the head they're going
to rush us! Then it will be too late! You're responsible for getting them to Fort Smith, not through the pearly gates! Use some
sense!"

But Hesse's warning produced no rebellion, and no attacks.
Instead, it was Hesse who went berserk. Camped outside Fort
Smith on the fourth night, Gar planned to take his prisoners in
the next day, collect on his vouchers, and pay off his wagoner-
cook.

Blue came sniffing around the fire while Hesse was cooking
supper. A pan full of venison liver frying in bacon grease was

chatter of departing churchgoers, and he had to reach far up to touch her tan fingers. He backed down the top step, thinking, *This girl is looking down her nose at me,* but he smiled—reservedly.

She was overdressed for churchgoing, he thought, and her clothes fit too tight. Gar scanned her bracelets, beads, and rings. P.S. was wiggling like an overeager puppy and Gar squeezed against his son to whisper, "Boy, if you had a tail it would be wagging so hard you'd be hitting people."

The boy's face clouded.

Bernice was saying loudly, "You young folks don't forget. You're coming to our house for Sunday dinner now."

The heavy press of people thinned in descending the church house steps and Gar said to Bernice, "It appears to me that the harness may be worth more than the hoss."

She pinched his arm, hard, and hissed, "Shhh!"

When they were completely clear of the crowd, Bernice said, "Gar Rutherford! Your voice carries like a bullfrog croaking on a July night. Everybody heard what you said!"

"Ever'body don't know what I mean," he contested.

"Glowering like you do, anybody can guess," she said.

They walked on toward home, disputing.

"She says her father is a fine guitar player, down New Orleans way," Bernice informed him. "He grew up on a French Creole plantation. That's how they come to be named LaPlace."

"Your church-lady friends won't approve of no man who picks a box."

Bernice ignored this. "Her father is part white," she said, "as I'm part Creek."

Gar persisted, "A Frenchy nigga who plays on a box. Where? In some New Orleans house of joy?"

He felt the hard edge of her shoe hit as she kicked his ankle.

"No," she ejaculated. "When we get home you be polite to that girl! Heah? Phenunda Sterling has got his mind set on her, I think."

"*He* better take a little time to think. Give me time to make up my own mind. Then listen to me."

"She has been elected Emancipation Day Queen, I hear. If you're going to be law and order man on the grounds, you're going to have to make way for her tomorrow. You'd better be ready to do it!"

Gar had arisen with apprehension. He had dressed anticipating trouble, and ridden the copper dun to the east edge of town, tying him there so folks would think he was patrolling there. Then he had walked across town to do his scouting around the west side. There was bound to be some drinking.

It was early, but most everybody was up and out, wandering around, visiting in pairs and bunches, getting ready for the parade, claiming picnic areas under the trees to serve as gathering places for family reunions. While white folks in Territory communities celebrated July 4th as Independence Day, black folks celebrated August 4th as Emancipation Day.

Past midmorning, Gar heard the cannon near the flagpole go off for the first time. He moved toward the center of town to watch the Yahola clan ride in. They were mostly half-bloods, Creek-Negroes from Bernice's old settlement. She would have many friends and relatives among them and her day would really begin now as she gathered with them to talk and visit.

Gar went on across town to untie his horse, ride through town, tie the copper dun on the west side, then walk slowly back to scout the east side. He thought about Sunday dinner yesterday, its strained atmosphere, and the interminable afternoon that had followed it.

He had tried to be friendly with P.S.'s fancy girl. But she wouldn't have it. Etta LaPlace was beautiful, haughty, unsmiling, expecting others to pay court to her but giving nothing in return. P.S. seemed satisfied with that. Every time she gave her long, dark tresses a toss, P.S.'s eyes rolled like marbles in a game for keeps.

too tempting to resist. Hesse kicked at Blue, yelled at him, and when that did not drive the hound away grabbed up the scalding hot spare bacon grease he had just poured out of the skillet and threw it on the dog's back.

Ol' Blue went howling off into the timber, chasing himself in circles, trying to lick his scalded back, wild with pain. The Indian boys caught him. Gar ran to the wagon and pulled a bottle of vinegar and a can of lard out of the chuck box. They poured vinegar on Blue's wounds and coated them with the soothing hog lard, then Gar walked up on Hesse. He grabbed the cook's shoulders, shook him, then knocked him sprawling on the ground.

Gar knelt beside the dazed Hesse and turned him over on his belly. Planting a thick knee on Hesse's butt, Gar ripped the shirt off the cook's back. He reached for the cup of spare bacon grease and trickled some of the hot fat out on Hesse's pale flesh between his shoulder blades.

"How that feel like, white man?" he demanded in fury.

The first trickle of the burning grease aroused Hesse out of his semiconscious stupor as sharply as if it had been a dash of ice water. Now he shrieked with pain, threshing galvanically, trying to break the power of Gar's hold. There was no use. Gar had him locked to the ground in an iron grip.

"Bring that vinegar an' grease," Gar told the two boys. He had Bat pour the bottled vinegar on Hesse's burns, then Crawdad smeared them with lard.

"Come on, you two," Gar told the boys. "Git yo' traps. We going to spend the night in town."

Leading the copper dun horse and the bluetick hound on opposite ends of his catch rope, leaving Hesse behind, they walked on into Fort Smith and spent the rest of the night sleeping on the courthouse grounds. When morning came, Gar tied his horse and dog and took Bat and Crawdad with him into Judge Parker's courtroom. It was an impromptu arraignment in which Gar tempered his charges against the two boys.

"They ain't really guilty of nothing much, yo' honor," Gar insisted, "except having a bad idea. They didn't steal nothing from McAlester's store. Just looked like they was a-fixing to."

Judge Parker questioned Bat and Crawdad severely and at some length, and began rendering a guarded judgment.

"I presume that if you took nothing . . . The marshal states that you had no stolen property in your possession when he took you in custody. Is there a charge of breaking and entering, Marshal Rutherford?"

"No, suh, yo' honor. Storekeeper McAlester caught them before they got inside."

The overweight, apoplectic Hanging Judge shrugged. "In that case, I guess you boys are free to go. Stay out of trouble!"

Bat and Crawdad scurried out of the courtroom. Gar turned back to the judge. "Yo' honor, I wonder if you could tell me what happen to the first prisoners I served warrants on? There was a Indian fellow named Vkéeē, two black boys named Cabot from down by Bokoshe, and a white man named Eads."

"Marshal Rutherford." Parker's blotchy face was flushed, his voice testy. "First, I would appreciate it if you would, on future forays, not bring your prisoners to my courtroom and come bursting in here before I've even convened court. We employ a clerk for these preliminary matters, from whom you can solicit information. Since you are here, however, let me also say something about the Vkéeē matter.

"For you to bring a man to this court with evidence of 'witchcraft' is intolerable. This is Fort Smith, not Salem, Massachusetts. The court has a jail, and a gallows, but no dunking chair. If you remand another prisoner on an accusation so bizarre as 'witchcraft' you will be the one charged—with false arrest!"

"Then I expect you turned him loose," Gar said petulantly. Some extrasensory perception intervened to prevent him from suggesting to this crusty judge that Vkéeē had witched him, the arresting officer, however well Gar knew that he had. There were some things white folks just did not understand. The judge's look had altered to become a scowl of perplexity.

"As for those two black fugitives, the Cabot boys, they have been spirited away. It is a mysterious matter. There is no evidence of how they escaped. They were here at sundown one night and gone at daylight inspection the next morning. How or when they were delivered from the cell block remains a mystery."

Gar could have explained to Judge Parker that his first guess was likely. They had been "spirited" out, but good judgment blocked his suggesting that, too. Gar just stood, thinking of Old Winged Trudy sitting there in the dogtrot with her spells and potions spread out before her, while he considered Judge Parker's discourse on witches, and listened to the fate of the white man, Eads.

"Frank Eads has been charged with grand larceny, has made bond, and is free on bail," Parker reported. "He has secured the services of the Arkansas attorney who has been most successful in circumventing the work of this court, Lawyer Hoggat of Van Buren—"

The hall door at the rear of the courtroom burst open to admit a violent disturbance. It was Jake Hesse, shouting and accusing. Judge Parker reached for his gavel but before he could fumble it into hand and bang Hesse into silence the camp cook had delivered himself of most of his tirade.

"How is it," demanded Parker when Hesse paused, "that you people have the effrontery to come in here, overwhelming me with your problems before I have even a court clerk or a bailiff here to assist me? I will learn better than to come to work early!"

An elderly, somewhat heavyset marshal had followed Hesse into the courtroom. Gar knew him to be Dan Wells, the Fort Smith court's oldest marshal in point of service, and Parker's chief marshal. "Uncle Dan" Wells, hanging back to maintain a considerable distance from Hesse, was also carefully observing Hesse's irate behavior, presumably in case Hesse decided to attempt something more threatening than shouting. He came forward now to stand between Gar and Hesse.

"I say, yer honor," Hesse repeated insistently, "that this nigger marshal of yourn jumped me an' attacked me, *bodily*. I ought to have beat him to a pulp, but he got the drop on me—"

Parker banged his gavel again.

"I assume," Parker said to Wells, "that you must have some knowledge of what this man is shouting about, Marshal Wells. Otherwise you would not be here."

"Yes, sir," said Wells. "I think I do." He walked to the tall double windows over the jury box. Both windows were wide open to admit the morning breeze and, through one of them, Wells whistled shrilly. "I was talking to those two Indian boys out there," Wells said as he returned to the judge's bench. "What they say don't agree with what this cracker Hesse is claiming."

"What is he claiming?" Parker demanded.

"I can speak up for myself, judge," Hesse stormed. "This Gar Rutherford threw down on me with his gun." Hesse stripped off his shirt. "I thought he was going to murder me," he turned to show the grease burns between his shoulder blades. "Now it ain't no sin for a man to defend hisself against a dog that is trying to bite him . . ."

Bat and Crawdad came in through the courtroom doorway, leading ol' Blue.

Parker pointed his gavel at Hesse. "Sir, you will remain quiet until I ask you to speak! Marshal Wells, will you please continue?"

"Yes, sir," said Wells. "I've known a few dog haters in my life, and more than a few self-proclaimed nigger haters. I think the fracas was the way these two boys tell it, and you can see there, judge, that all the hair is burned off that dog's back."

Hesse interrupted, "I have been working as this so-called marshal's wagon master for several weeks now, and he is the poorest excuse—"

Parker whanged his gavel in desperation. "Sir, I have not the time, nor is it my place, to sit here and listen to this sort of diatribe. Do you have reimbursement for services coming to you?" The judge looked questioningly at Gar.

"Yes," Gar admitted. "He does."

"Very well. Go through that door," the judge ordered Hesse, "to the court clerk's office. File any claims you have. The clerk will tell you how to prefer charges, and they will be heard in the proper time and in the proper way. Now clear this courtroom. All of you. Take that dog with you, so I can get into my docket of this day's hearings."

Outside, Gar took custody of Blue, and sent the two boys on their way. They headed willingly for the river, departing for Choctaw country.

Dan Wells suggested, "Let's go get something to eat, Rutherford. I think Hesse is a redneck who got his hackles up for no more reason than that your dog likes you. Maybe we ought to talk about it anyhow." He leaned to examine Blue's back. "Looks like he's going to heal up now without too much trouble."

"That's Bat and Crawdad's doing," Gar credited. "They got that vinegar and grease on there mighty quick. Where we going to find a place where a black man and a white man can eat together?"

Uncle Dan Wells grinned, his white handlebar mustaches twitching. "We'll go over to Poligamino's place. That is, if you think you can eat barbecue, beans, and drink beer this early in the morning."

"I can eat Poli's barbecue most anytime," Gar agreed politely. "But ain't a white marshal going to feel uncomfortable in a black folks' barbecue joint?"

Wells's roguish grin spread wide. "Parker's marshals, us white ones anyhow," he said, his grin was almost predatory, "feel about as comfortable one place as another. We go wherever our business takes us. Come on."

Gar retied Blue beside the copper dun horse and Uncle Dan Wells prompted him, "You had a warrant to serve down south of Pauls Valley, didn't you?"

As they walked the intervening blocks between the courthouse and Garrison Street, Gar told the chief marshal of his encounter with, and the killing of, the gunman Clay Missouri. Reaching Poligamino's famous creole barbecue establishment, Gar said, "I've still got the gun he gave me. All bloody-handled and wrapped up in my poncho. What ought I to do with it?"

"I'd take that gun home, clean it off, and put it in the farthest back corner of a bottom dresser drawer. The less you think about a man you've had to kill, the better off you are."

They opened Poligamino's rickety screen door, and passed back through the semidark interior to slide into the wooden seats of a booth. Wells asked for the warrant for Neosho's arrest, which Gar was still carrying. Across the face of it the chief marshal wrote, saying the words aloud as he wrote them, *"Killed resisting arrest, while firing at the arresting officer."* "I'll turn this in to Judge Parker," he said.

The restaurant and the high-backed booth they had chosen were redolent with the odors of spilled beer, cooked meats, and the fragrant hot sauce that sat bottled on the table between them. Before they could renew their conversation, Gar found himself listening to the talk emanating from beyond the tall wooden back of the booth.

Whoever sat in the booth behind them was saying, "Etslay obray orestay ownday atay orbergnay."

Marshal Wells opened his mouth to speak but Gar silenced him with a wave of his big hand, and kept on listening.

"E'llway ogay onay eartay atthay illway akemay otheray angsgay ooklay ikelay undaysay oolschay eacherstay. Oingday anyay ingthay eanmay ustjay ecausebay itsay eanmay." The gruff voice finished and a companion in the booth responded with a laugh that sounded near half-witted.

There was foot shuffling and the sound of rough ducking pants sliding across the wooden benches as the occupants of the booth got ready to leave. Gar gave them covert attention as they walked past the booth in which he sat with Wells. There were only two of them, both Creek Negroes, Gar decided. The one who led out was middle-aged, a man looking more black than Indian. His follower was much younger, short, obese, and as half-witted-looking as his laughter had sounded.

Both wore long black braids tied with wool, and broad-brimmed, black, uncreased, high-crowned hats. As soon as they were out of earshot, Gar asked Dan Wells, "You reckonize either one of them fellows?"

Wells asked, "They the ones that was talking that mumbo-jumbo gibberish in the booth there behind you? The first one was Rufus Fowler. He just got out of the federal jail, serving time for rape. I hear he was a model prisoner and got time off for good behavior. I don't know that short fellow."

"They ain't planning no good behavior now. They was talking pig latin." Gar translated, "They aim to rob the store down at Norberg. One of 'em said a good deal about doing mean things just to be mean, and that they was going to make other outlaw gangs look like a bunch of Sunday school teachers."

Dan Wells sat quietly for a moment. "What they were saying didn't mean anything to me at all. Maybe we ought to trail after them. Do you think they were serious, or just mouthing off?"

"I expect Poli's good barbecue ought to wait for awhile," Gar evinced. "We could kind of see where they're going, then come back after bit."

When Gar and Wells left the restaurant they could see Fowler and his short partner walking down toward the Arkansas River.

"Let's go get our horses," Gar suggested.

They hurried back to the courthouse. Gar untied the copper dun and said, "I got to find someplace to leave Blue. He ain't up to no hard traveling till his back gets well."

Dan Wells frowned thoughtfully, then answered, "Leave him with George Maledon. I'll ease around to the stable and get my horse."

Gar led ol' Blue over to the gallows. The gaunt hangman seemed pleased. "I like dogs," he declared. "Here, we'll tie him right here to the scaffold. I'll feed him well."

Uncle Dan came riding up from the courthouse stables. "Don't feed him any of your victims, George," he cautioned.

Maledon's hollow eyes sparkled brightly. His laugh was a cadaverous rattle. Dan Wells and Gar rode down to the Arkansas ferry and Uncle Dan described Fowler and his companion to the ferryboat operator.

"They forded the river, downstream, less than half an hour ago," reported the ferryman. "Looked like they was headed for Moffet."

Uncle Dan had accumulated sufficient years to slow his traveling a little but they reached Moffet in time to see Rufus Fowler, his short friend, and three more friends, riding toward the far end of that tough little border town's main street.

Uncle Dan, chewing the ends of his mustaches, speculated, "they sure could be drifting in the direction of Norberg. It's southwest of here."

"Wisht they was a short cut," Gar stewed.

"They're going to have to skirt around the edge of Cavanal Mountain," Wells said thoughtfully. "Doesn't make much difference if we circle it to the left or to the right."

"Then let's just follow along after 'em, and try to keep out of sight," Gar urged politely.

There was no problem in keeping out of sight. Uncle Dan's avoirdupois overflowed his saddle in places and frequently reduced his horse to a walk, while the five cantering horses up ahead soon disappeared along the wooded trail bending west toward Cavanal.

Marshal Wells worried, "They're going to have plenty of time to get to Norberg before we do."

"I could ride on ahead," Gar offered.

"If they've seen us, and decide to stop of a sudden to find out who we are, you could run right in amongst them and have some hard explaining to do. They might decide you'd be less trouble knocked in the head, or shot. We're not going to lose their tracks. Let's stay together. We might get lucky and reach Norberg while they're still holding up the store. Then we'd have them, guilty without argument."

They continued plugging along.

Uncle Dan's overloaded horse began to suffer some and there was no choice but to stop. They dismounted, hunkering down at the timber's edge, and Uncle Dan broke out his pipe. Smoke curled off through the trees while the overtaxed horse and his over-age rider rested.

They did not lose the tracks of Rufus Fowler and his four companions, but it was almost noon, with Cavanal looming big before them, when they rode around a narrow trail bend and encountered the wagon turned awry in the trail. A woman, her dress torn and mussed, sat in the dirt beside it, crying. A young boy stood beside her, embracing her and trying to comfort her.

Gar and Uncle Dan pulled up and got down. She was a pretty woman, thirtyish, her hair matted with twigs and dry leaves from the timber mulch into which she had evidently been thrown. The boy was no more than ten or eleven, and he explained tearfully, "Some men came and hurt my mother."

Wells knelt beside her.

"They—tore my clothes—they were—" she broke off, trying to add more.

"You don't have to explain, ma'am," Uncle Dan said softly. "I reckon we know what happened here. There were five of them, one of them likely a part Indian black fellow called Rufus Fowler."

She nodded.

"Did they say anything that might help identify the rest of them?"

"They called each other by names; Sim, Lucky, Hector," she sobbed. "I never heard them name the fifth one. But he didn't—"

Marshal Wells said, "Along with Fowler, that would be Sim Davis, Lucky Sampson, and Hector March."

"The other one seemed almost feebleminded. He took Jimmy off somewhere."

"Just back down the trail apiece," the boy said. "I know his name because he said, 'You ain't a smart enough young'un to get away from Bennie Gault.' He kept hitting me and knocking me down." There were bruises on the boy's face.

"I am a widow woman," said Jimmy's mother. "We are moving down to Pocola where I've been offered a job cooking. Our name is Austin. Jimmy and I loaded the wagon with our household goods yesterday and started out from Skullyville early this morning."

The spring wagon, drawn by a team of indifferent mules, was loaded with furniture and stood crossways of the trail as if Mrs. Austin and her son had tried to flee and the team had been caught and dragged to a halt.

"Do you feel like traveling, ma'am?" Dan Wells asked with compassionate sympathy.

"We've got to go on," said Mrs. Austin.

"Well, get back in your wagon, ma'am. Can you still handle your team?"

The boy declared stoutly, "I can drive. Good."

"Then let's go. Marshal Rutherford and I will ride with you."

Uncle Dan helped the harried woman to her feet and, beckoning Gar to follow, walked around to the head of the mule team. As Dan hauled on the off-mule's bridle, realigning the team in the trail, he said quietly, "Gus Phillips' ranch is just ahead a piece. Maybe we can get help for her there."

Gar moved out in front, riding alertly, and Uncle Dan brought up the rear. In their cautious passage Gar kept careful watch for any sign of the outlaws' doubling back. With five to two odds, an outright attack or ambush would be hard to handle. The tracks of the Fowler gang's five horses went forward steadily.

Gar eased his vigilance as they rode into the Phillips ranch yard, only to bring himself up short in greater tension as a rifle, fired from one of the ranch house windows, sent a bullet singing

over his head. It was either a warning shot or the outlaws were
holed up there.

Uncle Dan came riding up beside him to shout, "Ho! The
house! Gus Phillips!"

The rancher came out on the porch of the low pine-slab
house with its peeling brown paint. He was a thin, jaundiced
man with a shaggy, overhanging mustache as generous as Uncle
Dan's handlebars. Phillips held a heavy caliber rifle across his
chest.

He shouted back, "Is that you, Dan Wells?"

"Me an' Marshal Rutherford," Dan replied.

"You're a hair too late," Phillips yelled. "I've had visitors."

"Rufe Fowler's gang?" As he shouted his query Dan beckoned to Mrs. Austin in the wagon. They pulled on up toward
the porch.

"Five of 'em," said Phillips. He lowered the rifle, leaning it
against his homespun britches.

Dan called back, "Rufe, Sim Davis, Lucky Sampson, Hector
March, and a sadist kid who calls himself Bennie Gault. Did
you run them off?"

"I come almost inviting 'em into the house, then I saw it was
a bunch of niggers an' Indians." Phillips glanced apprehensively
at Gar. "If they'd a-knowed I was here by myself, they'd a-come
on in anyway. Way it was, I was able to git back in the house
an' start shooting afore they throwed down on me. They shot
my house full of lead and emptied my horse corral."

Now they got fresh horses, Gar thought somberly.

"Did you hit any of them?" Uncle Dan asked.

"They was ducking in an' out from behind the barn and
swarming like a bunch of horse flies. I couldn't hit nothing. I'll
take after 'em with you boys now. We're bound to come up on
'em sooner or later."

"We can't do that, Gus," said Dan. "We've got to leave Mrs.
Austin and her boy here at your place and send a doctor back
out. We sure can't leave them here by themselves."

Mrs. Austin put in, "No, you can't. You can't leave us here at all. I'm feeling better. If this turns out to be a long chase I can cook for you men. We have all the vittles that were in our pantry right here in the wagon."

Gar exclaimed in surprise, "But, ma'am, are you sure—"

"I'm positive," said the woman. "Seeing those hoodlums caught seems very important to me."

"All right," Dan Wells agreed reluctantly. "Gus, you got a horse left?"

"There's a fast-stepping little rose gray mare out in that pasture just over the hill from the barn. Normally I wouldn't want to ride a mare but I ain't got any choice, and right now I'd be willing to ride a stick horse to get after those owlhoots."

"I'll go find your mare," Gar volunteered.

It was beginning dusk by the time Gar ran the frisky little mare back into the empty corral where Gus Phillips stood waiting, holding his saddle and bridle.

Gar said, "Took a while to find her." Uncle Dan came riding into the corral. Gar said to him, "Pretty soon it's going to be too dark for us to see those tracks."

The elderly lawman leaned on his saddle horn to consider. He looked tired, but he suggested, "We could just head on down around the mountain to Norberg."

"Whut if they takes a mind to turn around and come back on us in the dark?" Gar asked.

"I'm not sure they even suspect that we're following them," Marshal Dan Wells speculated.

Gar nodded. "That may be. They've had plenty chance to see us. But they're just going from one thing to another. Their plans ain't no more permanent than a tumbleweed blowing across open country. If the wind changes direction they change their minds. What if they decide to go off someplace else instead of Norberg?"

"Sounds like he's making sense," Gus Phillips agreed.

"It is near dark," Wells reflected.

Gar suggested, "Why don't we just fort up here for the night? Take out after them in the morning?"

"That would give Mrs. Austin a night's rest," Uncle Dan said, looking like a little rest might be welcome to him, too. "Looks like it's going to be cloudy tonight. Not much moon. Gus, could you put her and her boy up in your house? Gar and I'll sleep down here in the barn—" he hesitated a moment, "that way we can whipsaw Fowler's bunch with crossfire between the house and the barn if they come back here."

Gar guessed that this, mainly, was just a kindly device on the part of Dan Wells to keep Phillips from objecting to a nigger sleeping up in the house with the white folks. For once, instead of being resentful, he was grateful to avoid the tension, but when Phillips handed him his saddle and bridle and said brusquely, "Here, Rutherford, hang these back over the stanchion in the barn," Gar felt himself growing resentful again.

They set the watch, Gus Phillips to stay awake until midnight, then walk down to the barn and awaken Gar. Gar would take the watch until three, then wake up Uncle Dan.

Dan awakened them all at daybreak and, trying to shake the sluggish aches and pains of not enough sleep, they took the trail again. They had followed only a few miles when Gar saw a man up ahead.

He was limping painfully, doggedly, making slow progress. By that time Gar was nearly alongside him, and Mrs. Austin and her mule-drawn wagon were not far behind.

The walker, with Gar riding down on him, turned, cowered, and took to the brush. Seeing Mrs. Austin on the wagon seat then, he paused in his lame, sore-footed flight.

"You been troubled by some outlaws?" Gar called out.

The lame walker stopped, timorously, still poised on the brink of flight. "They took my horse, saddle, bridle, watch, my sample cases, even my boots, and five hundred dollars."

Gus Phillips came riding up. "You're lucky they left you your life."

"The truth is they left me for dead." The man afoot exhibited the matted blood and hair over his right ear. "Big devil. Almost as big as this black man of yours. He hit me up the side of the head with his gun barrel."

"Whoa!" Uncle Dan rode up to interject, "That would probably be Lucky Sampson."

"Whoever it was, I went down like a poled ox and lay like a dead man until a few minutes ago. When I recovered consciousness, everything was gone—my whiskey samples—"

"Your what?" demanded Wells.

"I'm a whiskey drummer," came the reply. "Not selling anything, you understand. I know the law against selling alcoholic beverages in the Indian Territory. I was just passing through on my way to Texas."

"Now they've got whiskey and fresh horses to boot," Gar bemoaned.

"They must have been camped within five miles of my house last night," lamented Gus Phillips.

"Maybe, but no matter," said Dan. "We might have gone right by them in the dark."

"When I saw this big black fellow of yours," the whiskey drummer laughed shakily, "I thought they were upon me again."

"This is Marshal Gar Rutherford," Wells said, his voice impatient and flat. "I'm Dan Wells. We're both federal marshals out of Fort Smith."

The drummer looked chagrined. "Well. I've never encountered a black marshal before."

"What time did they jump you?" Gar asked.

"About sundown. I guess I laid unconscious most of the night. The morning star was clear on the horizon when I came to."

"They could have ridden on, been riding all night. If that so, they's long gone," Gar speculated.

"Unless they've been up to some other devilment," Dan suggested.

Gus Phillips said, "Dave Jordan's ranch is between here and

Norberg. It's just a couple miles west of the trail. Maybe we ought to look in there."

"Fowler said they'd be doing whatever was mean, just because it was mean," Gar reminded.

"Let's ride on," Wells ordered curtly. "Mister, you can climb up in the wagon here and help Mrs. Austin's boy with the driving."

As the drummer climbed up on the wagon seat beside Jimmy Austin, Gar heard him say, "I certainly appreciate this, ma'am. My name is Hiram Mercer." He began picking cockleburs out of his torn and ragged socks as he told Jimmy, "I'll take over those reins, son, in just a minute."

Gar fretted at being held up by the slow progress of the wagon, but he knew better than to suggest that they hurry on ahead, and leave a woman, a boy, and an unarmed drummer to the improbable mercies of the Fowler bunch. Surely the ranch would be better able to defend itself unless, like Gus Phillips, they caught the rancher alone, on another of the hardscrabble, isolated homesteads common to this rough frontier.

They kept to the trail for four more long, slow, miles, until they reached the Jordan ranch road. Here they turned west and crept another careful mile before Gar smelled smoke. The wind, out of the southwest, was mild and dry, stiff enough that when it slackened it was no longer possible for the acrid scent of the smoke to drift its way to Gar's sensitive nostrils.

He took a chance, leaving Phillips to ride alone in advance guard, while he circled around behind to tell Uncle Dan, "They're burning him out."

"How do you know?"

"I smell smoke."

"By golly! Now that you mention it, I do too."

They rode on in silence for a moment.

"How do you think we ought to handle this?" Dan Wells asked.

"There's three of us can fight. Either four or five of them, depending on how you figure that Gault boy. He could be as bloodthirsty and dangerous as Rufe Fowler himself. We could scatter an' try to come in from three sides, but if one of us gets caught out alone, he is a dead duck."

Uncle Dan stared at the wagon, with the woman and small boy sitting beside the citified drummer in his bedraggled, rumpled townsman's suit.

"We'll hang together," Dan Wells decided.

Gar spurred the copper dun horse, passing the wagon to rejoin Phillips, riding advance guard in front of the procession.

CHAPTER 6

The smell of smoke was strong now. Gar could tell that it was difficult for Phillips to keep from breaking his horse into a run up the road to his neighbor's house. His own copper dun was caracoling and prancing impatiently. But they held fast. When the house came in sight it appeared that the whole of it was burning. Two men were fighting the fire.

Gar did touch his spurs then, releasing the copper dun to charge the house, for he could see that only the porch was on fire. The wind, gusting around the corners from the rear, brushed the flames upward. The pair of men fighting the fire were filling their buckets at the yard pump, then running up to throw water on the flames.

It was a losing battle. Phillips rode to gather a couple more buckets from the barn, and they formed a bucket brigade. The fire was eating its way back from the edge of the porch. The wind was in their favor, though it swept the flames upward making it appear larger than it was. The two men fighting the fire had obviously, at times, been almost able to extinguish it.

"How long you been at this, Dave?" Gar heard Gus Phillips shout.

"Seems like a long time," came the answer.

"How long they been gone?"

With eight now passing up water to splash on the fire, they were beginning to contain it. The rancher finally replied, seeming to have had to think about this. "No more'n an hour, I reckon. They stayed all night. Drank up two suitcases full of little bottles of whiskey. God knows where they got them!"

Jimmy Austin ran past, grabbing up empty buckets from the

head of the line, carrying them back to thrust them under the pump spout where Dave Jordan pumped frantically filling them.

Jordan shouted as he pumped, "They had a hell of a time! Ever'body got drunk. They made Everett an' me put on a fistfight for 'em."

The line of fire across the front of the porch was beginning to falter. Gar could see that both Jordan and his hired hand were bruised and beaten.

"When they finally got ready to leave," Jordan panted, "they set fire to the front steps. They left us tied up in the front room. Told us how much they'd enjoy remembering how they left us to watch the fire creep up on us. By now, they'll figure we've fried."

The flames were dying. The line of fire was mostly smudge. The posse broke up and, with Jordan's hired hand, went along pouring cooling water on the smoking boards.

Jordan said, "It didn't take Ev an' me long to bust loose. Amazin' how strong you get when you see a fire comin' at you! We thought we might get it put out, too, but we wasn't going to make it."

They stood around the pump then, washing off the smoke and cinder smears. Gus Phillips mentioned the name of each member of the posse and told Jordan how they came to be there.

Jordan responded, "This here is Everett Krupper. I only hired him about a week ago. He'd of kept on a-driftin' if he'd knowed such a warm welcome was waitin' for him."

Krupper dashed cold water from the pump spout to his face. "Well, I don't know," he said. "How many grub-line ridin' cowhands git a offer to whip the boss after only a week's work?"

"Them sons of monkeys held their guns on us, made us prize fight for their entertainment," Jordan reiterated. "Made us jump around doin' a jig dance."

Both men's faces were black and blue, mottled with bruises, swollen from the blows they had taken.

"Gus," Jordan said to Phillips, "you an' me are going to have to get married. Raise us a passel of hard-fighting boys."

"What would we do while they was little? Let's figure out some way to signal each other when we need help. Once we get to where we can *hire* plenty help—"

Jordan said, "Yeah, we might as well stay single. Ev an' me can quit ranching anyhow." He was clearly feeling good about getting the fire put out. "We'll join up with a carnival. We can put on prize fights. Jig, an' sing—"

Gar prompted, "You said Fowler's bunch has only been gone about an hour."

"Nearer two hours now," the lean Krupper said through bruised and swollen lips. He glanced at the sun. "It's past noon now."

Uncle Dan Wells invited Jordan and Krupper, "You two want to go on with us? After your firebugs?"

Dave Jordan began nodding. Ev Krupper answered with a single word: "Yep."

They took the trail with the odds seeming better than even now. Jordan and Phillips optimistically agreed that they were surely in hot pursuit. But Gar thought in frustration, *They were only a half hour ahead of us when we left Fort Smith. We caught up to 'em in Moffet. Since then they have got anywhere up to a whole night ahead of us, and raising hell all the way!*

Here we go with five men, a woman, her boy, a bare-footed whiskey drummer. And a wagon slowing us down! Dan Wells is too old for this kind of chasing. Fine as he is, he is slowing us down, too. Getting worn out from hard riding, making do with too little rest, sleeping in a barn. Them half-breed Creek niggers an' Indians is on fresh horses, full of whiskey an' their own natural juices. What chance we got of ever catching up?

They followed on doggedly, with Phillips, Jordan, and Krupper riding on out ahead, and already beginning to complain because the wagon was slowing them down. Uncle Dan stayed with the wagon and Gar rode behind, to hustle the wagon on as best he could.

Presently Phillips came trotting back to gripe, and Gar heard

Uncle Dan insist that they could not leave the woman. "Night will be coming on," Dan reminded Gus Phillips.

The sun crept down across the sky toward its setting place. Even before nightfall, a waxing moon was riding high. It spread its light as dusk turned to darkness. They had no trouble following the tracks in the bright moonlight, but it was close to 3 A.M. when they arrived at the Norberg store.

The place stood seemingly deserted, looking lonesome in the light of the three-quarters moon. Its broad front window had been broken out, or shot out. Gar rode up to the wagon.

"Ma'am," he suggested softly, "just in case this is an ambush, maybe you and the boy ought to get underneath the wagon and wait until we scout it out."

Phillips with his rifle, Jordan, armed with Gar's .45, and Ev Krupper, with Gar's shotgun, spread far apart while Gar and Uncle Dan approached the lonely country store. They entered, without challenge, through the broken window, and Uncle Dan quickly returned to force open the front door, beckoning hurriedly to the three men waiting outside.

Norberg and his wife, both dead, were lying on the floor in the wide shaft of moonlight that flooded in through the broken window. Mrs. Norberg, like Mrs. Austin, had been ravished. Her clothing was almost torn from her body.

"Man, they just never git enough," Gar commented wonderingly.

As Phillips, Jordan, and Krupper came in, Uncle Dan lifted down a new kerosene lamp from stock. He filled it with fuel from the barrel on blocks at the back of the store, trimmed its wick, and lit it. Hiram Mercer came in, pussyfooting in his sore sock feet, then hurried back outside, retching, sickened by what he had seen.

"Let's hurry along," Uncle Dan urged. "These are desperate men and their depredations are not going to stop until we stop them. Maybe we can catch up with them before daylight."

The searchers began turning up evidence.

"The cash box has been busted open and turned out," Ev Krupper observed. It lay on the floor behind the candy counter. "Somebody's got a sweet tooth," he added. "The candy trays have been emptied."

"Tomatoes, peaches, sardines, crackers, a slew of canned stuff has been swept off this shelf," Gus Phillips observed. "Look for 'em to be carrying a gunnysack."

"They sure stocked up on ammunition." Dave Jordan pointed to spilled boxes littering the floor. He bent then to turn over storekeeper Norberg's body and found a Navy Colt's still awkwardly clutched in the storekeeper's hand. Jordan pried it loose from the storekeeper's fingers and handed Gar back his rifle. "I reckon I won't need this now," he said.

"When we catch up," Uncle Dan observed, "we'll find some of them wearing new clothes." The store's clothing tables and hanging racks had been rifled. Garments not chosen had been carelessly thrown aside. Discarded pants, shirts, suits, were strewn around the floor. Uncle Dan picked up one frayed, filthy shirt. "Fowler was wearing this shirt when Marshal Rutherford and I saw him back in Fort Smith."

"They took everything but seed to plant next year's garden." Gar leaned to use his jackknife in removing the screws from a heavy wooden box that had been left undisturbed. At first the box appeared to contain nothing but sawdust, but his prowling fingers found a wax-wrapped cylinder and half a dozen .30-30 cartridges. He put the cartridges in his pocket, thrust the wax-wrapped cylinder in his belt, and cut a length of primacord from a cardboard box nearby. "Reckon they know anybody is following them?" Gar conjectured. "How long since they were here?"

"Quite a while." Uncle Dan was wrapping the stiffening bodies in blankets taken from stock. "There's an icehouse out there. Gus, you and Jordan knock the lock off of it and put these bodies in there until we can get back."

Uncle Dan went to the door to call the whiskey drummer,

who came to hover reluctantly in the shadowy doorway. "Mr. Mercer, find yourself a pair of shoes in here," Dan Wells ordered, reaching to lift down a bushel basket from a ceiling hook. He handed the basket to Ev Krupper. "Fill this up with what ammunition the outlaws left and carry it out to the wagon."

Hiram Mercer stepped with chary respect around the blanketed bodies Phillips and Jordan were preparing to carry to the icehouse.

Ev Krupper, picking up cartridges, said in anticipation, "If those owlhoots are still drunk, we ought to be able to take 'em easy."

"I wouldn't depend on that," Hiram Mercer pulled on a pair of new gaiter shoes. "There wasn't enough whiskey in those sample cases to keep five men intoxicated very long. More than likely they've worked off the effects of it by now. If they've eaten any of the food they stole here they are certainly cold sober by now."

"Let's get after them," Gar urged. "We been here too long already."

The posse followed them into rougher country, finding where they had turned off the trail. The bandits had proceeded in the sinking light of the moon up the rocky course of a dry creek bed then, in predawn darkness, once more out onto rising ground. Uncle Dan called a halt.

"What lies beyond here?" he asked Phillips and Jordan.

The two ranchers scrutinized each other blankly. Phillips shrugged. Jordan said, "Nothing I know of but wilderness."

"No settlements?" asked Dan.

"No. They're headed into the Winding Stair Mountains."

"Any ranches?"

"No graze. Can't nothing but wild hogs live in these mountains," said Phillips.

"Any main trails?"

"Game trails," replied Jordan. "I've come down in here to deer hunt a few times. Never run into a human trace."

"Then they've gone to ground," Dan guessed.

"They're carrying a lot of loot," said Gar.

Dan Wells nodded. "They're hunting seclusion. A place to stop and divide it up."

"We can't drive no wagon up there." Gar squinted at the high, dim, sky-lighted ridge of the darkly timbered rise before them.

"No," Dan agreed. "We'll have to leave the wagon here in this dry creek branch." He told Phillips, Jordan, and Krupper, "Gar and I will go on alone. String along after us at five- or ten-minute intervals. We'll travel that way until daylight. No use of all of us blundering through that brush together."

Gar and Wells rode on quietly, climbing up through a grove of burr oak. Gar was sure he again smelled smoke. They eased on up, reaching the caprock.

"There they are." Gar motioned silently at dim glimmerings of firelight mingling with a faint dimness of false dawn, through thick timber, upwind, far off, ahead of them. Gar and Dan patiently sat their horses, waiting until Phillips, Jordan, and Krupper caught up to them. Then came little Jimmy Austin, afoot and puffing.

"What you doing here, son?" Gar asked. "Where's Mercer?"

"He stayed at the wagon to protect Mama," said Jimmy.

Dan considered thoughtfully. "Perhaps this is just as well," he said finally. "Jimmy, you stay back here. Don't come any closer. Keep that firelight in sight. We may want to send some message back to your mother and Mercer."

The mounted men eased on forward. Fowler and his outlaws came increasingly into sight. They were gathered on the pinnacle of a small knoll among the huge trunks of burr oak trees. They were dismounted and seated in a circle around a brightly burning fire. Each man's horse stood behind him, still saddled, ground tied, ready for flight.

They were sorting money, ammunition, all the loot from their gunnysacks, into piles, dividing it. All five were around the fire. They had set out neither watch nor guard.

"They think they're here all by themselves," Gus Phillips said.

The false dawn was fading toward daybreak.

"They *are* still drunk," Jordan half whispered. "They're still guzzling."

"No, those are bottles of sarsparilla from the Norbergs' springhouse they're drinking," Uncle Dan said. "I expect they have some hangovers and are aching in the head and dry in the throat. They're just overconfident."

Gar confirmed, "They feel mighty safe out here in the big middle of nowhere."

They sat still, watching two of the outlaws light up stolen cigars. The small bunch of spare horses they had been driving stood rope corralled, to one side.

"There's no use setting here till broad daylight," Jordan insisted impatiently. He raised Norberg's old Navy Colt's to shoulder height. "Let's git 'em!"

Uncle Dan touched the pistol barrel. "You might get one. The rest will scatter like a flushed covey of quail. We've got to stay quiet and use the cover of what little night we have left to surround them. Then, gents, when the first sliver of sunlight hits the tops of those burr oak trees, we'll all start shooting together. Try to take them alive, but if any one of them makes a break for the open, blow him off his horse."

In the dimming false dawn the posse distributed themselves around the knoll, leaving Gar there alone on the caprock. He was left with the best view into the camp, but in the most exposed position. The others lay in the tall grass around the periphery of the knoll on which Fowler and his thieves were gathered. Gar's shots would have a relatively flat trajectory. The others would be shooting upward, and the outlaws downward, at a sharp angle.

The first rays of the sun broke the horizon. Gar could see them strike the tops of the burr oaks but he knew that the others, from their lower angle of view, would not be able to. So he waited. From where he sat, he could see Phillips and Jordan, lying low in the high grass halfway up the knoll. Krupper and Uncle Dan were out of sight on the far side of the knoll.

With the sun creeping farther down among the topmost oak leaves, Phillips finally laid his eye behind his rifle sights and let go. The others opened up at once. The social enclave atop the knoll broke up abruptly as the desperados leaped to hide, concealing themselves behind the trunks of the big burr oaks. They left nothing much to shoot at—an occasional puff of smoke, the glimpse of a piece of sleeve, the edge of a broad black sombrero brim.

The air grew acrid with gunsmoke, at times so thick it obscured the crest of the knoll. Gar, prone behind the low sandstone barrier of the caprock, could see that the possemen around the knoll, shooting upward at such a sharp angle, were tending to shoot high. The outlaws atop the knoll, shooting downward at the same abrupt angle, were holding their sights too low. A great lot of lead was spraying the air and doing no one any damage.

Gar could not even see anyone to shoot at. The tree trunks were too thick. He fired when he could, at what little he saw, and thought he might have creased an outlaw's arm, but the shooting went on in futility. Around midmorning, Gar beckoned down the hill to Jimmy Austin. When the boy came scuttling up to the caprock Gar told him, "Go back to the wagon. Have Hiram Mercer bring up that basket of ammunition. I got a feeling this is going to last quite awhile."

The sun rose higher, climbing toward its zenith. It grew warm on Gar's back. When the ammunition arrived it was brought not by Mercer alone. Jimmy and Mercer came toting the basket, and Mrs. Austin scrambled up the caprock slope holding together the corners of her apron, which was sagging heavily with the assortment it contained of cartridges and shotgun shells. Gar sent Jimmy scooting down through the timber on the caprock hill, then wriggling through the tall grass, carrying the proper caliber of ammunition to each of the besiegers.

The sun passed its zenith and Gar was getting sweaty, hungry, and thirsty. They had been shooting all morning and were no nearer a decision than they had been at daylight. He still seldom saw any of Fowler's men, and when he did it was a fleeting glimpse, gone before he could draw a bead. This could go on till night and if it turned out cloudy, as the autumn sky looked like it might, the Fowlers would make a run for it as soon as darkness settled in.

In any kind of a heavy mix-up there was as much chance of possemen getting killed as outlaws. More, since the Fowlers would be a-horseback and running. An old fellow like Uncle Dan could be pinned down in the high grass with a couple mounted outlaws riding down on him, and then he would be a dead man. That decided Gar.

He stood up and shouted, "Looky here! I've had enough of this. Let's stand up and fight like men!"

Standing dark and broad, skylighted against the caprock horizon, Gar made a good target and immediately drew fire. The surprise of his shouting appearance momentarily saved him, for the outlaws were so conspicuously elated at having a target they could see that they were firing wildly. Bullets whistled and sung around Gar's wide body and went wheeing off in ricochet from the sandstone caprock on which he stood.

Gar pulled from his belt the wax-coated cylinder that had been poking his belly all morning and shoved the primacord fuse into its puckered end, pushing it hard into the dynamite down inside the cylinder. The passing of the word dynamite through his mind made him wonder then why the six rifle cartridges had been stored in the sawdust of the dynamite box with the single remaining stick of explosive his fingers had found there.

Then he guessed. They were dynamite cartridges. Probably hand loaded by the storekeeper Norberg himself, and left in the dynamite box for safekeeping. With them Norberg could have put up an especially threatening defense of his store. The Fowler gang had surprised him somehow and deprived him of the chance to use them. Gar checked the fuse in the stick of dynamite he held in his hand to make sure it was stuffed in tightly.

He made no foolish attempt to light the primacord with a match. Rather, he lifted his .45 to measure off the amount of fuse he figured would be necessary, and shot the fuse in two. The white hot flash of exploding gunpowder set the dynamite fuse to burning. It fizzled tentatively and Gar lifted it to his face to blow on it. The fire took hold and the fuse hissed as threateningly as a coiled rattler ready to strike.

Gar cocked his arm. He hurled the fused stick of dynamite in a high, rocketing arc. It lobbed across the dipping swale between the caprock and the knoll, falling toward the grove of burr oak trees, and exploded prematurely. He had shot the fuse off a fraction too short. The dynamite blew tree-top high, sending off a shower of torn-away greenery, leaves, twigs, and fist-sized acorns, driving the outlaws flat on the ground, then leaping up to run out into the open.

The possemen were shooting but, overstimulated like the outlaws by the explosion and the sudden sight of live targets to shoot at, they, too, were shooting wildly. Gar took one of the dynamite cartridges out of his pocket, opened the breech of his rifle to extract the gunpowder cartridge already in place, and thrust the dynamite cartridge into the chamber.

It might blow the barrel of his rifle up in his face, but he was determined to take the chance. With the outlaws heading back for cover among the trees, there was no other way of keeping them out in the open. Gar nestled the rifle butt against his shoulder, aimed, and fired. The explosion, close to Gar's ear, was deafening, a thunderous boom that sounded as loud to him as the detonation of the dynamite above the trees.

The bullet flew across the gap and detonated explosively against the trunk of the oak tree at which Gar had aimed it. A hail of burr oak bark and slivered wood flew out from the point of impact. Gar took another of the cartridges from his pocket, opened the rifle breech, and chambered the dynamite cartridge. But he did not need it.

The outlaws had thrown away their guns, lifted their hands, and were scattering down the slope with upraised arms. Gar advanced down into the swale toward them and he could see Phillips and Jordan standing up in the high grass with their weapons aimed.

Uncle Dan and Krupper came into sight herding a pair of Fowler's men before them. The posse bunched the outlaws in the hollow between the caprock and the knoll and shook them down. They came up with a generous assortment of knives and small-caliber firearms. Gar ordered them to line up.

Gus Phillips' exultation burst the bounds of his good judgment. "By god!" he exclaimed. "I never thought I'd see a brave nigger!" Still he did not seem to realize what he had said. "Rutherford, by god, you beat anything I ever saw, black, white, or redskin!"

Gar decided the best way out was to accept the compliment in the spirit in which it was intended. "All right," he ordered, "let's line up here." He did a little necessary pushing and shoving to get the five outlaws aligned so that they stood, slouching, with Uncle Dan, Phillips, Jordan, Krupper, and Gar arranged around them, their guns ready to prevent any sudden break.

"Now let's see who we're dealing with," Uncle Dan Wells declared. "Each one of you men speak up with your name, good and clear."

Grudgingly, the first surly young outlaw in the line said his name. "Bennie Gault." He was short, obese, in denim pants and jacket, a red bandana loosely knotted around his throat. His uncreased black sombrero, its crown crushed fore and aft, sat awry on his head. The silly, half-witted grin that Gar remembered seeing on his face at Fort Smith was gone.

Number two said, "Sim Davis." He seemed even less intelligent than Gault, and a few years older. The crown of his black hat was mashed as if he had been butting heads. His dirty red bandana hung open around his neck. His shirt had once been white. His frayed woolen suit indicated that he lacked the interest, or had not had the time, to change to the new clothes he had stolen.

Rufus Fowler, standing in the center, muttered his name. He was middle-aged and wore a new silk shirt in place of the one he had thrown away back at the store. His box-cut business suit had once, long ago, been a fine and stylish garment.

Hector March was patently Negro. He wore a once-white hat, shapeless and battered with age, a once-white shirt, bow tie, a wrinkled vest, and baggy ducking pants.

Lucky Sampson stood a head taller than his confederates and as broad as Gar Rutherford. He wore a white hat, light blue neckerchief, wrinkled flannel shirt, vest, and herringbone striped wool pants.

Gar studied their contrasting complexions. Each man was a mixture. Gault was almost white. Davis seemed Indian but was light-complected. Fowler looked Indian, but was black. March had a dark, negroid face. Sampson's broad features were Indian and Negro, but his skin was light in color.

Both Sampson and Fowler wore their pants stuffed down inside their high boots. The whiskey drummer, Hiram Mercer, stepped up to stand alongside Gar.

"Those are my boots that Fowler is wearing," Mercer said.

"You can have 'em back when we get to Fort Smith," Gar promised. "Mista Mercer, would you and Mrs. Austin and the boy go back up there on the knoll and pick up the guns these reprobates left throwed around?"

When the knoll was cleared of weapons, Gar and the posse escorted the five captives back up atop it at gunpoint, to retrieve the store's loot, for evidence.

Uncle Dan told Phillips, Jordan, and Krupper, "Boys, before you go home I'd appreciate it if you'd go back by the store and bury the Norbergs. Board the place up as tight as you can to keep it secure until the court can dispose of the property. Contact Fort Smith to find out when you'll be needed as witnesses."

It took all the handcuffs and leg-irons that Gar and Uncle

Dan could muster to secure the outlaws together for the journey
back around Cavanal Mountain to Fort Smith.

Uncle Dan Wells kicked Rufe Fowler hard in the butt as he
shoved him down the stairwell into the jail beneath the Fort
Smith courthouse.

"Let's go upstairs and process claims for Mrs. Austin's mileage, fees for her services, and the use of her wagon on this
foray," Uncle Dan said.

They put in a busy day collecting fees, filing charges, and
putting Hiram Mercer, wearing his recovered boots, on the
train back to his headquarters in Kansas City.

"My sakes, Gar," Uncle Dan speculated. "When we had that
drummer get up in the wagon, we must have started something.
That Kansas City drummer must be a bachelor. He and the
widow Austin surely appear to be making plans."

Gar and Uncle Dan stood in the depot, watching the parting
Mercer take his leave of Mrs. Austin. There seemed to be a
good deal of tenuous hand-holding, and the exchanging of
yearning glances. Standing aside, Gar and Uncle Dan could not
hear their conversation except for fragments, an occasional
phrase about Mrs. Austin "bearing up," and a promise of
Mercer to return for the hearing.

Mrs. Austin and Jimmy left, at last, to complete their move to
Pocola. Uncle Dan and Gar shook hands warmly, congrat-
ulating each other on the chase and the capture, and Gar went
to see George Maledon, to fetch ol' Blue.

He found the cadaverous hangman in his favorite haven, se-
cluded there behind the gallows, working with his ropes and
fine-tuning the rigging that operated his efficient drop traps.
Maledon seemed embarrassed, as if Gar had unexpectedly resur-
rected a matter he'd rather not remember.

"You mean that bluetick hound with the grease-scorched
hair?" George Maledon seemed vague. "The one you left here
with me a while back?"

Gar agreed that that was the dog he meant.

"Well, you know, that was a strange thing," Maledon temporized evasively. "The fact is—I sure hate to tell you this, but you know, you all hadn't been gone fifteen minutes when a rednecked fellow riding a big mule, a stubborn-faced, wrathy fellow with a provoked look on his face, rode up here and shot that dog. Killed him dead. He rode off before I could think how to stop him or holler for help. I talked to Judge Parker—"

Gar felt a hard hand on his shoulder. Primed, he turned around angrily, expecting Hesse, but confronting Ross Stephens. Gar's dandified fellow marshal was dressed in a natty new suit and growing a trim mustache. Debonair though his dress, his face was grave.

"Where do you think you are going?" Ross Stephens asked.

"After Jake Hesse," Gar replied. He had made up his mind.

"No, you ain't. Not now or ever. I talked with Judge Parker, too."

"I'm going to get that son—"

"Revenge is mine, saith the Judge," Ross Stephens declared firmly. "Hesse killed your dog, but you ain't going to kill him. It's a trouble of a kind you don't need. Hesse filed an assault charge against you, but then he shot your dog and took off. He ain't here now to testify against you. You're probably out of that. If you let him alone. The judge has specifically ordered you not to follow that man down and punish him. He says you can file a civil suit against him for destroying your property if you want to. But right now we got to go pick up them Cabot boys again."

Gar remembered Old Winged Trudy, and her hoodoo potions. He had been luckier in escaping them than he had been in evading Hesse's reprisal. He had no intention of risking anything with that old woman again.

"Huh-uh," he said.

"What you mean, huh-uh?" Stephens demanded.

"I mean I ain't going down there to Bokoshe no more. Anything I stick out in that direction is likely to get chopped off this time."

"You can't help yourself. Here's the warrant."

"Tell the judge I won't go! I ain't tangling with that hoodoo business no more."

"Gar, you're afraid of that old woman!"

Gar said nothing. He realized he would rather not admit it. Even to himself.

"You're afraid of getting witched," Ross accused boldly.

Gar stood, phlegmatic and stubborn. "I been mixed up with witching, black or Indian, for the last time."

"Parker told me. You brought in that Cherokee Indian Vkéeē for being a witch doctor."

"Vkéeē doctored that Afvc'keko girl's husband to death. He damn near did me, too!"

"I don't claim to know much," Ross Stephens said reasonably, "but I don't believe in witching."

"Then how did those Cabot boys get out of jail?"

"They bribed a night jailer. Gave him five dollars. Judge Parker finally found out, and which one, and *he's* in jail now."

"Where did they get five dollars?"

"That's what we're arresting them for. They got a habit of getting ahold of somebody else's five dollars."

Gar shifted from one foot to another, thoughtfully. "And the judge figured I'd be afraid to go down there by myself."

"You was. Wasn't you?"

"Stephens, I been afraid to do a lot of things in my life. But I done 'em anyway."

"You said you wasn't going to do this."

The compactly muscular and dapper black marshal had Gar without an easy answer. So he said nothing.

"Anyway," Ross said, "the judge says we can ride over through Yahola and Pleasant Hill on the way down to Bokoshe. It's been a while since you've seen your family."

Pleasant Hill was going about its quiet business when Gar and Ross Stephens rode in. They went directly to the Rutherford house. It was quiet, too. The front door was locked. *Don't she never stay home,* Gar thought in irritation, searching for his key. A neighbor woman, half a block away across vacant lots, came out on her stoop to stare at them with hand-shaded eyes.

She came walking across the weed-grown empty lots then to call out, "I believe you'll find her at the preacher's house, Marshal Rutherford. They's making plans for the wedding."

Plans for what wedding, but Gar did not ask. He stepped across the copper dun horse once more, and leading out, directed their course toward the Reverend Haworth's house. They received a warm welcome. Reverend Haworth came out to greet them.

"Come in. Come in, gentlemen. We was just a-wishing you were here, Marshal Gar."

"This is my friend, Marshal Stephens, Preacher Haworth," Gar did the honors. They went inside to find Bernice, Gar's son P.S., the girl Etta LaPlace, and the preacher's wife Vinnie sitting in the parlor.

Bernice got up to give Gar a peck on the cheek which he recognized with a one-armed hug.

"We're glad you could find some time to come home," Bernice said. "After so long."

Gar introduced Ross to Vinnie Haworth and Etta LaPlace. They sat down. "What have we interrupted here?" Gar asked blandly, like a stud poker player lifting the edge of his hole card to take a peek.

The Reverend Jesse Haworth said mellifluously, "Your son and this lovely girl have plighted their troth. And I would hardly call your arrival an interruption. I'm certain everyone here is eager to have your thoughts incorporated in the planning for this blessing."

"When is it supposed to take place?" Gar asked.

"No date has yet been set," the preacher said, "but the young people are speaking in terms of some time before hard winter sets in. They want to have their love nest built before the snow flies," Reverend Haworth chuckled indulgently.

"We thought we'd say our vows some time next month, Dad," P.S. said, not quite condescendingly. "We're coming up on October, you know."

"How about Hallowe'en night?" Gar asked speciously.

"Gar." A chill came into Bernice's voice. "Are you trying to be amusing?"

Gar's disposition was curdling. "I think we ought to talk about whether there ought to be a wedding before we talk about when."

Bernice bridled, "I think that is up to P.S. and Etta. Who was it talked about whether we ought to get married? And when would they have talked? Fifteen years after Phenunda Sterling was born?"

Ross Stephens stood up. "Folks, I am intruding here. This is a family matter. I feel ill at ease here, and interfering."

"Keep your seat, Ross," Gar said curtly. "You ain't interfering in nothing. When you leave, we both go. We got a warrant to serve."

"It's been a while since you've had anything *but* warrants to serve," Bernice accused. "Don't your family count for nothing in your life?"

"Now, now," the Reverend Haworth tried to soothe, "I'm sure we can discuss this without acrimony."

"I don't think there ought to be any wedding," Gar said bluntly. "Does anybody here want to know why?"

Shock filtered into the room. Everybody sat stunned. Bernice opened her mouth, closed it, and opened it again, but seemed lost for any words to force out through it. The doll-pretty Etta LaPlace stared at Gar with a small, worried frown between her nymphlike eyes. Ross Stephens' face was dark with embarrassment. The Reverend Haworth moved in his chair, leaning forward, but even he delayed speaking, and Gar felt a passing tinge of remorse. Perhaps he had gone too far.

So he spoke again, this time tempering his remarks with a little mildness. "Leastwise, there hadn't ought to be any wedding till I've had a chance to have a private talk or so with my son, and maybe even a chance to visit with this young lady a little. Preacher, have you talked with these young folks about what it takes to make out a married life?"

The Reverend Haworth replied rather lamely, "Well, no, fact is we haven't, not yet. But we're a-fixing to. In a sense, of course, that's what we're doing right here."

Gar got out of his chair with stubborn determination. "That won't do. There's got to be some thinking and some talking done before I'm satisfied. Marshal Stephens an' I have got to ride down to Bokoshe and serve this warrant. I'll be back as soon as I can. Go ahead, Ross."

CHAPTER 7

As they rode toward Bokoshe, Gar spilled out his doubts and concerns to Ross.

"P.S. is too young to marry," Gar protested. "He ain't really growed up yet. He thinks mostly about hisself. He ain't ready to be responsible for no girl an' her young'uns. He thinks that it's all going to be a big fun time. Besides, that girl is a flirt. I've seen her working at it. She'll be trying to keep P.S. in his place. I think they ought to take a good long look at how cross-grained a time Bernice and I have trying to get along with each other. They ought to do some serious talking themselves."

"Maybe they already have," Ross countered.

Gar thought about that. Maybe they had. He hadn't asked them. He had only asked the preacher if he had talked to them. Marshal Gar Rutherford began to feel a little guilty. *God knows I'm never home,* he told himself. *I hardly even know what's going on there.* His guilt swelled, causing him to wonder if he had not blown it again. Probably ruined P.S.'s chance to marry a very pretty girl. *For no reason besides my own contrariness. Shoot from the hip with a hair trigger,* he thought. *All my life, I've ruined everything.*

In his remorse, he began to accuse Bernice. "That woman of mine could write me some letters about what's going on at home," Gar complained.

"Where would you get the letters?" Ross asked.

"At the courthouse in Fort Smith, whenever I bring in prisoners."

"But you can't read."

"I could get somebody to read her letters to me."

"Then everybody would know your personal business. A wife is going to put some intimately personal thing in her letter. Who, around that courthouse, are you going to get to read those letters who would keep a secret?"

"You."

"I'm not there any more than you are. No, you'd get a letter when I wasn't there, and get someone else to read it to you. It might accidently have a little sweet talk in it, the kind I hear wives write, and whoever read it to you wouldn't be able to wait till you got out of sight to start up laughing about it and talking to anybody who'd listen. You'd quick have most of the folks in the courthouse laughing behind your back. And you'd hear them laughing. You might wonder why for a while, but pretty soon you'd see to it that you knew why, then you'd have blood trouble with somebody, or you'd get to where you couldn't look anybody in the face."

As they rode through the morning, south through Oktaha and Rentiesville, Gar kept up his intermittent complaining.

"That woman got a tongue like a copperhead snake. She can't say nothing nice to me. It's always cut me down, make me feel little."

Ross Stephens rode a long ways in silence, having a significantly hard time trying to decide what to say in answer to Gar's critical remarks. Then, with manifest effort, he brought himself to say, "I seen the trouble between you and your wife. Both times I've seen you together. But that doesn't mean much to me. It doesn't mean either one of you is bad, or even to blame. Sometimes folks just have trouble getting along together."

It was Gar's turn to ride in silent thought, his mind chewing on Ross's observation.

"I think your wife is due mostly credit," Stephens went on, "and mighty little blame. You've said that boy was fifteen before you ever saw him. She had to raise him by herself. Then there was five more years of Civil War and slavery times when nothing was ever easy. She deserves a world of credit, and no blame at all as far as I can see. He seems like a mighty fine boy."

Ross ventured no more opinions, and Gar was reluctant to probe for any.

Gar remembered the two lamp globes at Judge Parker's Fort Smith courtroom. Whenever he stood before the judge, he saw two images of himself, one in each globe. It always set him to wondering. There *were* two Gar Rutherfords. The one he wanted to be, was trying to be, and the one he was—or other folks thought he was. Bernice, P.S., Hesse, most white folks, and especially the outlaws, all seemed to have a low opinion of him, and weren't hesitant about saying so. Now Ross Stephens seemed to be saying so. Gar wished he could make up his own mind that he had some merits and stick to it. But, as always, he was threshing around wondering about what other folks thought he was.

It turned into a silent ride of self-analysis for Gar. They kept on bending east through Porum, Kanima, and near dusk were approaching the grove north of Bokoshe where Winged Trudy's cabin and dogtrot stood among its apple and pear trees. Here the reluctance really took hold of Gar. But he knew better than to mention that to Ross. As they came cantering up into the grove, their horses making considerable noise of saddle and leather-rigging creaks, hoofs drumming on the dark loamed earth, bridle bit rattles, and the slobbery breathing of the two tired mounts, Trudy Cabot came out to meet them with no show of hesitation or fear.

In fact, as her eyes recognized Gar they turned catlike with malevolence and evil, but she said nothing to indicate that she knew him. Ross said nothing. Since Gar had made the first arrest, it appeared that the burden of this one was going to be on him too. He mustered up his courage, and met the humpbacked old woman's amber slitted eyes, with noticeable flutterings in his chest, stomach, and body muscles.

"We're looking for Squint and Albert," he said.

"I figured," she nodded curtly.

"Do you know where they are?" Gar asked.

"I ain't saying."

Numbly, Gar was forced to admit to himself that he was scared. Ross Stephens might be convinced that this woman was no witch. He might explain away the ease with which her two sons escaped the Fort Smith jail. But Gar could not explain away the deep inside fear that haunted him and made his muscles quiver. But he decided he had to face up to it, and try a new track.

"Trudy Cabot," he said, "folks know about you a long ways from here. I heard say that you are a witch an' I seen you working hoodoo. They call you Old Winged Trudy. They say that hump on your back is your wings folded up. That you fly up on the housetops an' cackle like a banty chicken. That you steal from them. An' when they beg you to go away you jus' laugh an' cackle at them. Is it you that is stealing from them, or is it your boys?"

The old woman laughed at him. It was a cackle, not much different from the cackle of a banty hen. But then, surprisingly, she giggled a little. "Folks git carried away," she said. "I'll agree that I'm good at cures. I don't try hexing a lot. But if I was to put your name in a dead bird's mouth an' let it dry up, you'd have plenty of trouble. If I pull a hair from your horse's tail an' wrap it in a dirty rag with a snake fang and some gunpowder, you'll die. If you'll give me some money, an' go away, I won't do those things."

Ross took a hand. "Missus," he said, "one time a witch tried to get after me by taking off her skin and leaving it in a pile on my floor. When she disappeared I picked up her skin and sprinkled pepper on the inside of it. She come back and put it on and like to have died when that pepper started stinging her. 'Skin,' she hollered. 'Quit stinging me. Don't you know I'm your own flesh?' Then she jumped on a broom and flew right out the window."

Trudy Cabot hinted, "I'm good at nightmares myself. Maybe

I'll turn myself into a mare tonight and toll off them stud horses of yours."

"Let's cut out this foolishness, missus," Ross suggested. "You might as well help us. The law is going to keep coming back after your boys until they stand trial and are either found guilty or innocent."

"Albert an' Squint is good boys," she declared belligerently. "They just don't like farming."

"They leaving you out here by yo'self a lot of the time now, I guess," Gar hazarded.

"I gits along," she said petulantly.

"Missus Cabot," Ross bargained, "if you'll help us, we'll come back here after we pick up Squint and Albert. We'll take you to Fort Smith with us and find you a place to stay close to the jailhouse. That way you can visit with your boys, see them every day."

Old Winged Trudy put a dip of snuff in her lower lip and ruminated it, mulling this over. Gar thought he saw her shoulders slump a little more, weighed down by these problems and the hump she carried on her back.

He pressed a little. "Where are Squint an' Albert now?"

"I reckon they's in Bokoshe," she admitted. "Looks like you all determined to hound those boys till you bring 'em down to the ground."

"Where in Bokoshe?" Ross asked.

"They hangs out around the Horny Toad some."

Bokoshe was a mining town. By carefully questioning the black miners of the town Gar and Ross found the Horny Toad. It was a roadhouse at the end of a narrow lane leading off from the coal loading yards of the T. & P. Railroad. They staked it out and watched desultory comings to and from it through the evening. Gar saw nothing of Mrs. Cabot's sons.

It was almost midnight when Gar suggested, "Why don't we tie our horses to that handcar standing on the siding and go in. Maybe they got inside before we come."

The roadhouse was no more than a shanty, where someone had once lived. Apparently a Choc beer joint where coal loaders from the Texas-Pacific could take respite from the heavy chores of shoveling newly mined coal from ore carts into railroad gondolas for shipment south to Texas.

Gar and Ross walked up quietly, ignoring the Horny Toad's front door, closed against the chill cold of the late autumn night. They moved on around the house to an uncurtained side window. A banjo player was beating out a tune in the small parlor. Three various-shaped hussies were dancing with their partners. Gar saw Squint and Albert sitting near the kitchen door, watching the strumpets, but taking no part in the dancing.

"That's them," he muttered to Ross.

A waiter, probably the proprietor, Gar figured, came out of the kitchen carrying a rough board. It served as a tray, laden with tin cups of brown Choc beer and a pie plate of sizzling cracklin's. He set the beer and hot pork cracklin's on a bench beside the Cabot boys.

"Ten, altogether," Ross whispered.

"I don't see no more," Gar agreed.

A short, buxom woman danced close by the window w[...] partner. Both the other women were tall, one broomst[...] The drinking had surely been going on all evening. T[...] the dancers were dull and glazed.

"They're pretty well separated from reality," Ros[...]

"Nobody paying much attention to anybody [...] served.

"They know you. Might start shooting, [...] run," Ross said. "I'll go in and pick them [...] me."

Gar drew his .45. "I'll stay here b[...] gives you any trouble I'll bust this gla[...] get their attention."

He watched Ross enter and, [...] proach the boys. Gar had no in[...] figured the boys would come [...]

would have, had the proprietor not decided otherwise. As soon as Ross spoke, Gar could see the waiter-proprietor, carrying his rough wooden board, start edging down the wall, either to exit the front door or circling to try to come up on Ross's blind side.

Squint and Albert stood up. The banjo player got up and stepped into the kitchen. Since Gar could no longer see either the musician or his board-carrying boss, he decided he had better not wait to find out what they were up to. Using his gun barrel, he broke out the glass pane, straddled the window sill, and stepped into the room.

The proprietor made a break for the front door and Gar let him go. He heard the back door open and close and figured that was the end of the banjo player. Bunching the hussies, with their dancing partners, against the back wall, Ross and Gar handcuffed the Cabot boys.

They took them to Bokoshe's rock blockhouse jail, awakened the jailer, and showed him their warrant. With the boys locked up for the night Gar and Ross went to the small boardinghouse the railroad maintained for section hands and coal loading laborers and turned themselves in for the night. In the morning, after breakfast, they picked up their prisoners and returned to Old Winged Trudy's cabin.

With the unwilling help of a sullenly petulant Squint and a grimly silent Albert they harnessed Trudy's small team of mules to her light wagon. Gar told her, "Fort Smith is a growed up town now with factories where they make things like gunsacks, cottonseed oil, twine string—if your boys have to do the time in jail for all this pilfering and burgling they been doing they can get a job in one of those places when they get out. Then they won't have to hate farming anymore."

They hauled back to Fort Smith, fording the Arkansas at the Point crossing, and returned Squint and Albert once more to jail they had bribed themselves out of. On the advice of her, Gar and Ross took the boys' mother to a rooming that catered to relatives of the inmates of Judge Parker's

jail. The two black deputy marshals paid a month's rent for her out of their own pockets.

Gar said, "You know, Ross, if we had thought, we might have looked around Ol' Winged Trudy's cabin and found some little stashes of money hid away. I'll bet she's cached enough of her boys' loot to keep her here in Fort Smith for a while."

Ross nodded shrewdly. "I'll ask Dan Wells to drift down there and look around."

They went upstairs to the courtroom, getting in on the end of Frank Eads's trial. The jury had found him guilty and Judge Parker was pronouncing sentence.

"You've stolen livestock," the judge lectured, "and it has been established in this court that much of the stock you stole is still in your possession." The guilty Eads stood, stuffy and pink-faced, trying to look righteous. "We have heard the testimony of a black woman from Polk County who identifies you as the man who assaulted and molested her," Parker said. Eads's pompous stance was betrayed by the crestfallen, sheepish flush on his culpable face.

The judge continued. "We have a merchant from Skiatook who recognized you in spite of your mask as the man who held up the post office in his store, as well as robbing him of various and sundry other items. This is a federal crime and requires me to sentence you to twenty-five years hard labor in the federal prison at Leavenworth, Kansas. The others are crimes of territorial jurisdiction. You are therefore sentenced to twenty-five years in the Leavenworth prison, and ten additional years in whatever prison may be designated by the authorities of the Indian Territory, this latter sentence to begin when you have paid your debt to society in the federal prison. Prisoner Eads, a felon of your despicable character, masquerading as an honest and upright citizen, is an unspeakable abomination on all human kind." Parker's gavel struck the desk with irrefutable authority. "This court is recessed for half an hour."

Eads's attorney was on his feet instantly, shouting, "Your

honor, I serve notice that this sentence, in its unparalleled severity, will be appealed to the Supreme Court of the land. Your despotic rule shall not forever be permitted its stranglehold here!"

Isaac Parker was already leaving the courtroom, headed for his chambers. Gar could see Eads's raw-boned wife weeping among the spectators as the bailiff came to remove her shaken, pale husband from the prisoner's bar. Gar walked over to shake hands with the blacksmith who had made his handcuffs and leg-irons in Porum.

"Blacksmith Wiggins, I think," Gar said. "You sent me out to serve my warrant on Eads last spring."

"Yes, Marshal Rutherford. I did that."

"I expect you had a good deal to do with the prisoner being found guilty here today."

"I testified," Wiggins nodded. "But they was plenty of other witnesses. Turns out Mistuh Eads had stepped on toes all over the Indian Territory, western Arkansas, north Texas, and even up into Kansas. There was plenty folks around to tell what he's been up to. You haven't been through Porum lately?" the blacksmith asked politely.

"Fact is, Deputy Ross Stephens an' me, we was through there just a few days ago, with a warrant to serve down in Bokoshe. Just didn't have time to stop."

"I'm still willing for you to swear me in as a posseman if you ever need me," Wiggins reminded Gar.

Gar felt a hand on his shoulder, turned, and started to grin warmly. It was Uncle Dan Wells. The elderly marshal's mustached face was serious.

"We just got a telegram from Muskogee," he said, "asking us to issue a warrant for an accused man named Phenunda Sterling Rutherford, Gar. Is he a relative of yours?"

"Only my son," Gar said. He felt hollow-bellied with shock at the unanticipated blow. Gar turned to Ross, his face slack and curious. He was about to suggest the obvious need for him to head for home when Uncle Dan went on.

"The Fowler trial is next on the docket here, Gar. We'll both be called as witnesses. The telegram said, *more to come.* I'll let you know when more information comes in."

The recess was over. Judge Parker was returning to the bench. Rufus Fowler, Bennie Gault, Sim Davis, Lucky Sampson, and Hector March were already being led into the dock. Uncle Dan eased quietly out the side door of the courtroom as the bailiff intoned, "Oyez, oyez! The United States Court for the Western District of Arkansas is in session. All rise."

The noise of the rising spectators subsided after they again took their seats, and the bailiff began reading the long array of charges against the Fowler outlaws. Gar's mind was in turmoil. The attorney for the outlaws rose to say, "Your honor, I ask that the witnesses who will be called to testify against my clients be excluded from the courtroom, so that they cannot hear, and thus falsely corroborate each other's testimony."

Gar was glad of the chance to get out of the stuffy courtroom. Outside in the fresh open air he was tempted to walk straight to the hitchrail, step across the copper dun horse, and ride for the river. But he knew that Ross Stephens, who walked out beside him, would protest. More, they walked directly into the group already standing and waiting on the barren, hardpan ground outside the courtroom. Gus Phillips, Dave Jordan, and the cowhand Ev Krupper stood bunched in triumvirate, waiting to testify. At the hitchrail, near Gar's copper dun horse, stood Mrs. Austin's wagon with the young mother and her son Jimmy waiting on its spring seat.

Ranchers Phillips, and Dave Jordan, with his cowhand Ev Krupper, were in high spirits, anticipating the revenge of the court's justice.

Gar said to Jordan and Krupper, "I see you all's faces are healing up from your fisticuffs," but his attention was out of focus, not concentrated on what he was saying.

Phillips asked, "Where is the whiskey drummer?"

"I doubt," Jordan replied, "that he expected the trial to come up this soon. Surely they subpoenaed him at his home office in Kansas City."

Gar moved aside with Ross Stephens. "What do you suppose that boy of mine has got hisself into?"

Stephens only shrugged. Time dragged past, and Gar searched his mind. *He's hasty and conceited,* Gar thought. *Spoiled by his mama. Thinks about nobody but hisself. Acts like I'm ignorant and got no sense. Don't try to hide that he is ashamed of me. But he is my boy, and none of that makes a reason for anybody to put him in jail.*

He gave thought to going back inside the courthouse and looking for Uncle Dan Wells to see if he had got any more information when he heard his name being called from the courtroom doorway. He was being summoned inside to testify. As Gar entered the courtroom, Uncle Dan was just leaving the witness stand, having apparently completed his testimony. Gar took the stand and was sworn in.

In a kind of haze he related hearing Rufus Fowler and Bennie Gault talking in Poligamino's café. He retold how he and Uncle—Gar almost slipped into the familiar. He caught himself and used the formal—Marshal Wells—had followed Fowler and Gault to Moffet, seeing them gather and depart with their confederates Sim Davis, Lucky Sampson, and Hector March.

He told of their finding Mrs. Austin who reported that she had been raped, of the attack on the Phillips ranch, the attempt to burn down Jordan's house, the ambush robbery of the whiskey drummer, and the murdering of the storekeeper and his wife in Norberg.

The prosecuting attorney remarked grimly, "Surely no more vicious chain of crimes has ever been committed in the history of civilized man."

"I object," cried the defense attorney.

Judge Parker ruled, "The prosecutor will leave the judgment of these defendants to the jury and confine his remarks to the presentation of evidence. The witness is excused."

Gar went back outside.

Phillips, Jordan, and Krupper were still waiting and talking. Ross had stepped off to one side and stood alone. Gar heard the lonely hoot of a train, arriving at the depot. He went over to Ross.

"Dan Wells didn't come out here?" Gar asked.

"Yes," Ross answered. "He said he'd be in the court clerk's office, where they'll deliver any telegrams."

"Let's go in there and wait," Gar said. "The bailiff will look in there if they want Wells or me for anything."

As they climbed the courthouse steps, Hiram Mercer came hurrying up from the depot. He tossed his small valise in the wagon bed and climbed up on the wagon seat with Mrs. Austin. "My dear," Gar heard Mercer call her, "the request for my presence here arrived in our Kansas City office late yesterday. I barely had time to pack a change of linens and catch the overnight train . . ."

Gar and Ross went on inside. As they entered the court clerk's office, the clerk's assistant was slitting open a yellow envelope. "I think this may be it now," Dan Wells said.

The clerk read it and passed it to Dan, who read it aloud to Gar. Gar listened, but at first his mind rejected it flatly, refusing to believe.

P S RUTHERFORD NEGRO MALE SIX FEET SLENDER EDUCATED DEMEANOR WANTED FOR KILLING OF DICK NASH ETTA LAPLACE CREEK NEGROES NEAR YAHOLA I T FLED SOUTHWARD TOWARD TEXAS BELIEVED ARMED AND DANGEROUS

"I'm heading for home," Gar said.

"You've got to stay here till this trial is over," Ross insisted. "What are you going to do when you get home?"

"I don't know."

"Then you might as well do what you know you have to do and stay here while they grind this thing down."

Gar realized he had some grinding down of his own to do. He

left the office, going out into the courthouse yard where he hunkered down under an autumn-yellowed elm tree. The tree's leaves had almost all fallen off and Gar crouched in the layers of yellow leaves, a stricken man, trying to think this through. How had it happened? Why?

It was hard for him to imagine P.S. as a fugitive from justice. The boy was a loner. Strictly alone, in the few years Gar had known his son. Gar suspected going it alone had been P.S.'s way from earliest childhood. Heading south for Texas, the wire said. That wouldn't do much good. He'd have to go farther than that.

Mexico. Maybe he could hide out there. Mexico, to Gar, at least the part he had seen, was mostly cactus desert and barren, sun-hot mountains. Yes, that would be the place. But he'd have to have help. I can give him that, Gar thought. Get him where the law can't find him. Where the federal marshals had no right to go.

That thought stopped Gar. He was a federal marshal himself. But P.S. would likely have to spend the rest of his life on the run. And me with him, Gar thought. That didn't make much sense or seem any good. *We can't get along,* Gar knew. *We'd get to fighting with each other.* The hearing inside the courtroom kept dragging on. Afternoon turned into evening and the trial was recessed for the night. The jury was sequestered.

Gar spent the night with Ross Stephens, in the rented room where Ross lived in Fort Smith in the home of a black Fort Smith dentist and his family. In the morning the trial was reconvened. Gar was not recalled to the witness stand, and all the evidence had finally been heard a little after the middle of the morning. The defense was short, consisting mostly of a summation of excuses and tenuous alibis by the outlaw gang's court-appointed attorney.

Gar went to stand under the courtroom window, listening to Parker charge the jury, ". . . among all else, these men are proven horse thieves. This is a frontier country where horse theft is still a capital crime, for a man afoot is no man at all. A man afoot can hardly hope to survive the dangers of this rough and untamed land . . ." the charge droned on toward drowsy noontime, but when it was ended the wait was brief.

The jury was out for less than a quarter of an hour. They returned with a verdict of guilty. Isaac Parker sentenced all five outlaws to be hanged. Now Gar knew what he must do. Summoning Ross to give him support, he went to the judge's chambers adjoining the courtroom.

Parker called out a muffled, "Come in," and they entered to find the slack-muscled, overweight jurist sitting at his desk with his face buried in his hands. He appeared exhausted, slumped in sheer weariness, and when he looked up at Ross and Gar his lined face sagged, his eyes were red-rimmed as if he were at the point of weeping. He seemed like a sick man.

Gar handed him the telegram he had taken from the court clerk. Parker had removed his long black robe. It lay carelessly thrown across the curved arms of a wooden chair and the judge sat in wrinkled, sweat-moistened shirt sleeves. He put on his narrow wire-framed glasses and read the telegram.

"P. S. Rutherford," he murmured tiredly. "Isn't that your son's name?"

"Yes, sir," Gar's voice rumbled. "I want you to give me the warrant for his arrest."

Parker raised the spectacles and rubbed his tired eyes thoughtfully. "I'd be reluctant to assign any man such a task. To run down and capture your own son?"

"I want to go and take him myself." Gar's inner certainty was less than the roughness of his voice made it seem.

"I see," the judge pondered. "Of course, you know him. You might be able to anticipate his thoughts and movements better than another marshal. But he may resist, even violently. You may be tempted—" He did not finish, did not say what Gar might be tempted to do.

"Send Marshal Stephens with me," Gar said. "He'll keep me honest."

"I'm not concerned about the honesty of either of you,"

Parker deliberated. "But the emotions involved here require the greatest restraint." He sat at the desk, brooding. "You are sure you want to undertake this commission?"

"I'm certain," Gar confirmed.

Isaac Parker's very weariness seemed to hasten his decision. "Very well," he yielded, handing the telegram back to Gar. "Secure the warrant from the clerk. I'll sign it. But—both of you—take care. I daily undergo the incredible strain of sending men to the gallows. I do not want to be responsible for a man killing his own son in an attempt to arrest him."

As Gar and Ross rode into Pleasant Hill, Gar snorted, "Haw! Whoever named this place ought to have give me some say. There have been mighty few times I've come back here anticipating anything pleasant. Pretty scenery. A quiet place. But pleasant? I've got to where I dread this place like a pest house."

Their horses walked into the yard of Gar's house. A dog came slinking out from under the porch. It was Blue. Gar swung down out of his saddle, staring at the hound in astonishment. "Come here, dog." He fumbled Blue's ears, scratched his neck, then said, "Look at this, Ross."

He fingered a scar pit on the bluetick hound's hard cranium. "Hesse shot him and figured he'd killed him. The dog must have crawled off somewhere to die. But he didn't. That hangman Maledon must have figured he'd die, too. Son of a gun!" Gar ran his hand down along the grease-burn scars on Blue's back. They were healed now, but still hairless.

Ross commented, "I expect won't much hair ever grow there again." He knelt to stroke the dog's dark muzzle. Blue whined and licked the hands of both Ross and his master.

Gar kneaded the loose skin and short hair around Blue's collarbone. "He likes you," Gar said. "He'll help find P.S. The boy was Blue's favorite." Gar stood up and walked in the house.

"I'll stay out here on the porch and talk to your dog," Ross said.

Gar found Bernice in bed, sick. The preacher's wife, Vinnie Haworth, was there taking care of her.

"She's wore out, Marshal," said Mrs. Haworth. "Can't sleep. Won't eat. You hadn't ought to remind her or make her talk."

"I got to know," Gar retorted in protest.

Bernice turned restlessly in the bed. "That bad man, Nash, drove a bunch of mules right through town here." She was almost whimpering. "Phenunda saw him and recognized the mules, knew their breeding, that is. He came home and told me, 'Mama, those mules belong to Mr. Butler, down at Rentiesville. That's the ones he gets from those big jacks and percheron mares of his. Dick Nash has certain stole them and he's driving them up to Kansas.'"

The sickbed odor of the room told Gar his wife was not pretending illness. The shock of the double killing had weakened her, making her the easy victim of the feverish sickness that beset her. "Phenunda strapped on his gun to go after him," she said. "Oh, I begged him not to. He caught up with the mule herd at Yahola. Nash was holed up in what's left of the old place—the same place I met you. It's just shacks gone to ruin now."

She fell silent, and Gar let her rest a while. She began crying. "Nash was camped out in Opothleyahola's old cookhouse—you know, where we started out from on a picnic one time. Phenunda hailed Nash out. He come out a ways, a-standing there in front of the door. Phenunda didn't even know Etta was in there with Dick Nash. Our boy didn't know they had been meeting on the sly. She was running away with her lover to Kansas. To sell those mules. Nash started shooting. So did our boy. There was a lot of shooting, and Phenunda killed him. Didn't even get hurt hisself. But when he busted inside the shanty to see if Nash had any helpers, there he found Etta's body. She had been killed by one of our son's bullets."

Gar felt a guilty surge of pride that his son had won the gunfight. He made no mention of that, however, asking simply, "Where is P.S.—Phenunda—now?"

"I don't know. He came by here and got a few things. Somebody said he left, heading south."

Gar sat on the edge of the bed, taking her hand, wishing he could comfort her in some way. He touched her face. It was hot with fever. Vinnie Haworth was showing signs that she wished he would go.

"I think she's had about all she can stand," the preacher's wife said firmly.

Gar leaned to kiss Bernice on the cheek, wet with her sobbing. "You stop your worrying," he tried to reassure her. "Get over this sickness and get well. We'll find him."

She sat up, grabbing him with both hands. "We? Who's we?"

"Marshal Stephens is with me," Gar said.

"Oh, Gar! Don't bring our boy back here. Not to face that hanging judge you work for! Hide him somewhere." She was almost delirious. "Hide him under the wings of the Lord—"

Vinnie Haworth touched his arm, urgently. "I'll take care of her, Marshal Rutherford."

Gar detached himself, pulling loose from her hands. He got up, backed out of the room, turned, and walked out on the porch.

"Let's go, Ross," he said grimly. "Blue!" Gar whistled to the dog as he stepped across his horse. They reined their horses around, and out of the yard.

CHAPTER 8

Blue had no trouble in picking up a trail as they rode south out of Pleasant Hill, even though it had been two days since P.S. had fled down that way. The dog seemed to understand when Gar ordered him, "Find P.S., boy! Ketch up to Phenunda Sterling." Gar always choked a little on that name, but Blue had heard it more often than he had heard Gar's abbreviated P.S. version.

"What makes you think he's following your boy?" Ross asked. "How do you know he's not just following down the road, where everybody else here travels?"

"I don't," Gar admitted. "But I don't know any other way to start right now. P.S. is probably riding that palomino parade horse his mama bought him. I don't know what kind of shoes it's wearing, what kind of stride it runs with, much of anything. There's too many tracks going down this road for us to pick up a single trail anyhow, even if we knew what to be looking for. We'll just have to go it on Blue for a while and see if we can't untangle something. Maybe we'll run onto somebody who saw him."

Within the first few miles, Blue began drifting off to the left, departing the main road. As the dog kept up his pursuit toward the southeast, Gar said, "That makes me think maybe Blue's following P.S. It figures that the boy might break off east toward the hills and rough country. Not much of anyplace to hide for a long ways due south of here."

Gar had thought that if they kept on going south through Oktaha they might pause in Rentiesville and notify old man Butler to go on up to Yahola and recover his mules before they scattered and lost themselves in the timber, but that would have to wait now until after they caught up with P.S.

"That horse he's riding," Gar speculated, "was bought for show. It probably won't have much bottom. We ought to be catching up to some fresh tracks pretty soon. P.S. an' his pretty horse'll begin to give out. If we keep crowding, we might stumble on them most anywhere, or be able to run them down."

But as the day latened there was nothing to indicate that they were catching up. There was no doubt now that Blue had chosen to follow the tracks of a single horse. Gar got down to study them, then, where the horse had run through a patch of buckbrush interlaced with tangles of greenbrier, he slowed to study the thorny growth. Gar got down again, to be rewarded when he pulled a few horse hairs from a greenbrier that had snagged the horse's rump.

"It's the palomino all right," he told Ross, showing him the hair. "That's P.S.'s horse. His shoes are in good shape, with long calks. They'll mark up the ground."

The sun made its way toward the horizon and Gar began to feel some stirring of worry. After all, it had been more than two days ago that P.S. had left Pleasant Hill. Gar had frankly expected to find the boy holed up in some brush-choked coulee, sympathizing with himself.

These fall nights were getting pretty cold. That soft, town-bred boy would be wanting a big fire to hover over. But the sun set and Gar's sense of urgency gave way to a more sensible caution. When it became dark enough that they could no longer see the tracks, Gar called Blue in.

He told Ross, "I don't know how strong that dog is after all he went through with Hesse. We're going to lose these tracks in this dark timber. Maybe we'd just better put up here till daylight."

"By then we're apt to lose him altogether," Ross averred.

"No. We still got the dog for a hole card. If we don't push him so's that he gets too tired to run."

With the coming of good light, after a night lying on cold

ground, Gar expressed more doubts. After long study of a good many tracks, he admitted, "The cutting edge of these tracks is dry and crumbly. Somehow, they're looking more than two days old. That horse is long gone an' I don't see no signs of it slowing down."

The palomino must have traveled steadily through its first night out, and Gar began to get the feeling that P.S. was pulling away from them. Maybe that parade horse had more bottom than he'd figured. They followed him on through the Cookson Hills. The trail bent slightly east.

"He's headed for the Sans Bois," Gar speculated. "He aims to travel in sure enough rough country."

They went on into the Sans Bois Mountains, and down into the valleys that separated them from the Kiamichi range. They laid out another night, cold and hungry. It had now been too long since they had eaten a real meal, but Gar knew the same had to apply to P.S. If it was going to be a matter of who wore out and gave down first, Gar Rutherford was determined he was not going to give out before his own son.

The morning's mackerel sky made him yet more apprehensive. High mare's tails of ice clouds toward dusk the previous evening had indicated the making up of weather, and it was clearly not going to miss them. It was coming on down. "I've seen these late November storms blow in before," Gar warned Ross, "and they can be boogers."

They made it through the valleys almost to the foothills of the Kiamichis before it struck. It swept in then, a blue norther with hard driving rain, pinning them against the north slope of the mountains. Rain changed to ice, freezing thickly on the barren deciduous trees, turning their branches into heavy arms of ice. Then the rain turned to sleet, coating the ground with inches of tiny, icy pellets. It is possible to make some progress through deep sand, but not through deep sleet. It gave the horses no footing. Gar and Ross dismounted, trying to lead the horses, but in the deepening sleet Gar fast concluded their strength would be better spent in making camp.

There, where a fast-running stream had cut a deeply rocky defile in the face of the Kiamichi uplift, he called a halt. Unlashing the war bags from behind their saddles they began with machete and hatchet to cut straight dogwood poles for a lean-to shelter.

Ross talked as he worked. "You knew what you was up to when you was teaching me last spring."

"Looks like you've got a good deal of practice since then," Gar noted.

"Where we going to put this lean-to?"

"Up there on that rock ledge, to turn the north wind."

"Build a fire under it?"

"Quick as we can."

"Talking as fast as we can to keep from freezing to death!"

"Fire down here in the flat would melt that frozen creek sand and we'd be resting in a puddle."

They lashed the lean-to together and the sleet and freezing rain quickly coated it, making it impervious to the driving wind.

"We want to drag in a-plenty of firewood. Knock that brittle ice off it," Gar said.

"Ought to get too much rather than not enough," Ross agreed. "It's bound to be a cold night." His teeth were chattering briskly.

Steady hard work could barely keep Gar from shaking with chill. "We'll build a fire under there where we're going to sleep till it gets that ledge rock warm, then pull the fire out so's it will be at both ends of the shelter."

"Should I go see if I can shoot a couple squirrels?" Ross asked.

"Better to keep on pulling that driftwood up from around the creek for the fire. Critters are all holed up out of the cold now anyhow. Best not to take hold of your rifle barrel with your hand like that," Gar cautioned. "That iron is brittle cold. You have to shoot it off, likely your gun barrel will burst right where your hand heated the iron. We'll boil some jerky for supper instead of just chewing on it dry."

After they had eaten, the flames of their fire, now drawn to the ends of the shelter, flared out into the mountain darkness. Gar felt the drowsiness of weariness and warmth from the fire creeping over him. Ross stretched out in his blankets on the fire-warmed ledge of rock beneath the lean-to. Blue curled up, whining, by the fire, at his feet.

"I'm starting to feel downright comfortable," Ross said to the accompaniment of the wind howling through the Kiamichi mountain slopes above them. "It must be hard, knowing your boy is somewhere out there in this storm, perhaps freezing to death."

"P.S. is a good two days ahead of this storm," Gar said. "We ain't even come close to catching up with him. By now, he has already crossed the Red down into Texas. He's been hurrying."

Gar could see an unasked question forming in Ross's intelligent face. He knew that Stephens still had plenty to learn about the differences between the ways of city life and living on a raw frontier, but his companion marshal had had more experience as a law enforcement officer than Gar had, and Ross Stephens was not stupid.

"Better draw that hatchet in," Gar said. "Pull it up close to the fire. It lays out in that ice all night, it'll bust itself on the first pine knot we chop into in the morning. We're going to be snowed in here before daylight."

Gar snugged down in his blankets to make ready for the sleep he knew would not be long in coming. He had some thinking to do, but he could get around to that in the morning.

Gar heard Ross say, "Happy Thanksgiving," and knew that his partner was awake.

"Sure enough! It is," Gar recollected. "November twenty-seven. We'll have to postpone the feast."

They had taken turns awakening during the night to keep the fires burning warmly. They were snowed in. Thick snow covered everything in sight outside the lean-to except the thawed wet ground around the fires.

"Hadn't we ought to be up and humping?" Ross asked.

"We ain't going nowhere," Gar replied. "There's a good six inches of snow out there and it's setting on a coating of hard ice. We'd have horses slipping and falling, and likely some broken legs."

"How long do you suppose we're going to be here?" the questionings were again forming in Ross's face.

"Not too long. These early storms come in quick, but they don't last. The ground is still warm. It'll be melting that ice. Looks like the sun going to come up. The wind will swing around to the south and make a chinook that'll start licking this snow off. We ought to be able to break camp and get going by noon."

"And your boy will be another day ahead of us."

"He's headed for Mexico. Ain't but one way to get there, and that's going south," Gar said comfortably.

Ross said no more, but sat up in his blanket roll, looking at Gar curiously.

"P.S. had to come down out of these mountains," Gar said reassuringly. "He'll be heading south through the piney woods of east Texas. That's my old stomping grounds. We'll catch up to him."

Gar turned over and went back to sleep. When he awakened, Ross was up and prowling around nervously. The sun Gar had predicted was high and the mountain slopes were filled with the noises of wild creatures out and scrambling for breakfast in the snowy woods. Gar lay still listening to the raucous disputing of jays and the chatter of a squirrel not far away.

He got up then, shook the remaining snow off a nearby bush, and spread his blankets out across it to sun. While Gar fooled around then, snaring a rabbit, Ross fretted, plainly chafing to be on the trail. The snow was melting in a southerly breeze turned surprisingly soft after so bitter a night, and the ice grew rotten underfoot.

As it melted off the tree limbs overhead it came crashing down in great shards and spears. Presently, their rabbit cooked and eaten, they were underway again. Making their way down through the long Kiamichi passes, they proceeded slowly along an old game trail, over muddy ground, in a generally southerly direction. They had lost P.S.'s trail completely. It had been erased by the ice and snow that had turned the earth into cold mud.

To Gar's surprise, and Ross's utter astonishment, Blue picked it up again along the lower reaches of the Mountain Fork, as the ground dried out and they approached the Red River.

By the middle of the next morning they were across the Red and passing alongside traces of civilization. Blue had lost the trail back at the river crossing, and was trotting alongside the horses contentedly.

"I hear there's a town called Texarkana over there now," Gar said. "Wasn't nothing but a Caddo village when we was running the plantation. This was John Douglas's country."

"Your boy is likely to be riding around any towns," Ross suggested.

Gar nodded. "Ain't no need for him to do otherwise. This is a good country. The river is full of fish an' the woods is full of game. Good place to travel easy, and live off the land."

"Like you said, P.S. is hurrying," Ross urged. "We ought to be hurrying, too."

Another recollection came to Gar's mind. "Used to be a outlaw named Cullen Baker around here," he said. "Claimed to be a Confederate guerrilla, but after the war black folks started giving him trouble. He shaved off his whiskers, disguised himself so none of 'em would know him, then got together a posse of black men to go hunt his own self. Fixed them up with guns that wouldn't shoot. Led them right into an ambush of his own outlaws. Every black man in the posse was shot down and murdered."

Blue, ranging out ahead, came to something that interested him. Halted, legs spread apart, he stood with nose down, investigating it. Gar rode up to the dog and dismounted.

"It's P.S.'s horse track," Gar confirmed, kneeling. "See that long calk on the shoe. It's anyways three days old. These grass leaves was bruised down long enough ago that they've clean sprung back up again."

Gar stood up, contemplatively. "He's riding off into the piney woods, and that will slow him down some. This is an old cow trail we used to use to bring Mexican cattle up to the Texarkana plantation. We ought to just stay on it. Maybe we can get ahead of him at the old Douglas place."

Blue was hesitant to leave the familiar scent of the palomino horse's tracks, but he followed along reluctantly as they continued on down the trace, through low, red, sandy hills, among the stagnant swamplands of the piney woods. Reaching the cabin Gar had remembered as belonging to early settler John Douglas, Gar said, "Let's hold up here for the night. He's almost bound to come riding out of the woods here. We can set up a watch, and be waiting for him."

Standing watch and watch through the long night produced nothing, but dawn brought an ancient black man riding out of the woods on a spindly jennet marked with the gray hairs of age, the harness marks and healed collar sores of a long life of drawing plantation plows. Gar hailed him down.

They sat astride their contrasting mounts staring at each other until Gar finally ejaculated, "You cain't be Uncle Tater Joe Seeley?"

"Yes, I kin, an' have been since I was borned 'most eighty years ago."

"On Texarkana Plantation?"

"Yes—an' I see it now. You're Gar Rutherford, used to be right there with us during the mean ol' slavery days. I been thinking I seen you awhile back, looking as young as ever."

Gar speculated thoughtfully. "I got a son about the same age I was when you an' me both was at Texarkana. We been waiting here for him."

"Then you ought to be waiting someplace else," the aged man declared gently. "If he come out of the pineys, it musta been early yestidy or the evenin' befo'. I been closing down my sorghum mill up on Hopper's Flat."

Gar said no more, considering that there was no reason to explain the motivation for their search. He changed the subject. "You still working as a hired hand for the plantation?"

"No, no. I rents enough land on shares to raise some peanuts an' truck, and my own cane. Sell the sorghum to the white folks. Plantation don't hardly exist no more. Mistah Bedford done near drank an' diddled hisself to death since the war. When he passed he looked older than me."

"Hmm." Gar gave little thought to the report of his former master's death. "Well, if we missed my boy, I expect we better ride on after him. If you don't mind, Mistah Seeley, ain't no need to say anything about seeing me down around here." So Mistah Bruce was dead; well, I don't feel too lively myself, Gar thought.

Tater Joe Seeley smiled. "See nothin', hear nothin', say nothin'. Times ain't changed that much for black folks in these parts, Rutherford." The old man rode on about his business.

"We'll ride on to Cypress Bayou," Gar told Ross. "P.S. will nearly have to stick to the trace through here. Trammel's Trace they used to call it. I been told Davy Crockett come this way down into Texas."

The early morning's temperature had been cold and raw, but moderated as the day progressed. "It gets cold here," Gar commented, "but we're not likely to see any more ice this far south this early. Them storms kind of skin off along the mountains north of the Red River, go over into Louisiana and bend back up into the Ozarks."

"Your judgment about the weather sure seems better than your guesses about where to catch up with P.S.," Ross said dryly.

Gar let it pass. No need to make an issue here. There would be plenty of time to voice his own mind when, and if, they were able to apprehend the boy.

"The steamboats used to come almost up to here," Gar said, as the trail began to parallel the sluggish stream. "There's a big town not far on down. We used to get goods there, shipped all the way up from New Orleans. There's wharves there, and redbud trees galore. Country sure gets pretty in the springtime of the year. Looky here."

Gar stepped off the copper dun horse where a set of tracks branched off the trace, descending toward the bayou. "That's P.S.'s horse tracks all right. Heah! Blue! Come heah!"

Gar squatted to look closely. "Bank gets so soft a man can't hardly go down to the bayou. He'll bog down. He let the palomino go though. Lucky he got back. See where the horse threshed around there in the muck?"

Gar prowled and studied while the bluetick hound sniffed and put his stamp of approval on the tracks. Then Gar stood up, cogitating. "Way that mud is still oozing in those suck holes where the horse walked, we've been doing some catching up. We ain't that far behind anymore. Let's find a place to get across somewheres here. P.S. ain't going to ride into that town."

They continued on down the bayou, encountering the hulk, wrecked and rotting, of a steamboat that had tried to ascend too far upstream. The wreck thrust out across the mud flats, the prow of its caving hull still jammed firmly aground on the bank.

"Good place to spend the night," Gar offered.

"We ought to keep traveling, right on through the night," Ross admonished.

"Don't want to pass him up somewhere and arrive in Mexico before he does," Gar equivocated. "Lots of water snakes, moccasins, around here. Pilot deck of that stranded riverboat be a lot better than sleeping on the ground. In the morning we can go down off her stern there where it slopes down under the waterline. Swimming water for maybe fifty–sixty feet and we'll come out on that caliche bar."

When, in the early dawn of the succeeding morning, they had gained firm footing on the caliche gravel bar, Gar said, "Sabine River will be our next water. Likely we can cross it walking our horses. Shawnee Town was there. Where the Shawnee Indians lived."

"We surely are seeing the sights," Ross gutturaled. "But not the one sight we need to see the worst way!"

In a less complicated affair Gar would willingly have admitted his desire to see the boy. P.S. was traveling fast and light—and lonesome. Gar's thoughts went sweeping back over his own years of such traveling. He felt a freshet of admiration for his boy's courage and resourcefulness. In his lonely flight, P.S. was traveling over what was, for him, new country. In deep sympathy for the boy, Gar wished he could be with him, helping him.

They would strike the Sabine along in the afternoon if they didn't run up on P.S. somewhere before that. Gar struggled to fill up what might have become a painful silence with talk. "Used to be a courthouse, not far south of here, where they kept their prisoners chained to a big liveoak tree in the yard. Them poor devils was out in every kind of weather. Strung out on that chain for everybody to look at while they was waitin' to be tried, and servin' out their sentences. Sorry warning to anybody who thought to break the law!"

They found the Sabine running knee deep over its stony bed, and P.S. had taken to the river. Blue could not follow his young master into the water and, barking and fretting, ran up and down the bank, each yapping bark yearning with frustration.

Gar worried, "That ain't smart of the boy. Just going to slow him down some more. This river flows near due east, an' he looks to be headed downstream. He surely ain't going to back track himself."

Gar and Ross crossed the Sabine, their horses' strides showering out silvery splashes of the shallow water, and continued along the south bank until Blue, running ahead, found the place where P.S.'s palomino had come up out of the water.

As Gar had surely hoped that he would, P.S. had traveled in the river but briefly. Now his tracks turned southwesterly. The water had dried on the flat riverbed rocks where the horse had climbed up out of the Sabine, but the sharp abrasions of the palomino's hoof marks were still visible. Bits of rock dust along the marks left by the iron shoes' sharp calks still showed signs of having been recently wet.

The drift of the tracks lay southwest toward the Neches. Gar fretted, "He'll be lucky if he don't come down with the fever from drinking that brackish stagnant bayou water yesterday. When he gets to the Neches, there is a big spring comes gushing out of a cleft in the rock where the old cattle trail crosses. He can get all the clear, cold water he needs there."

"You're of two minds about catching him, aren't you?" Ross at last undertook to surmise. "Seemed like there for a while you was feeling better because we were getting farther behind."

I got to make up my mind how it's going to be when we find him, Gar thought. They racked along into the evening. The spring Gar had anticipated at the Neches had ceased to run. The rock cleft from which it once had sprung was filled with caved-in earth, from which good-sized scrub oak trees grew.

"Things sure do change," Gar pondered. He pulled up on the far bank, and sat with his hand on the copper dun's rump, looking back. "I wouldn't have thought that spring would ever dry up. You know, it's near thirty years since I rode down this trail."

They were fully out of the piney woods country now, riding through fertile crop land. Gar once more recommended that they pull up for the night.

"If that dog would mind me," Ross grumbled, "or if I could read the signs, I'd keep on going by myself."

"This is a bad place to be prowling along at night by yourself," Gar countered. "Somebody might ketch you. What used to be slaves are sharecroppin' here for the same mastahs that owned 'em before the war. They say up in the Territory that if you get arrested through here you'll wind up working out your fine on somebody's home place. It's a kind of slavery where you stay in debt to the commissary store just enough ever' week that you don't ever go free."

So, another night, and another day, and Gar pointed out, "That big white house yonder on the ridge belonged to John

Reagan. It's been there since before I can remember. He was a bigwig for the Confederate rebels. Run their post office. A little ways back of that ridge, Fort Houston was strong when I was a boy, after this country first become Texas."

"Seeing that we're not in any rush," Ross said, "I'm going to favor turning into the next town we come to. See if we can't buy a square meal. Living on swamp rabbit and branch water with some kind of an upland bird once in a while is making me gaunt."

"I expect P.S. is tired of riding gaunt, too," Gar said. "Gaunt don't bother me none. I've growed a little roll of fat on my belly to draw on when the vittles get thin. This really ain't no place to patronize no towns, and I hope P.S. don't try it."

As they made a dry and hungry camp that night over a low rise well back off the trail, Gar remarked, "Lots of wild flowers on these prairies in the springtime, Texas flowers, Indian paintbrush, bluebonnets . . ."

Ross seemed finally to resign himself to Gar's pace. "I've been thinking," the dapper but trail-worn marshal reflected. "What you said about near slavery still going on here. We had a minstrel show in a burlesque house in Saint Louis last winter. On my beat down on the riverfront. White actors blacked up with burnt cork. You know them kind. White folks like it. The actors had a tune. Did a dance to it. Called it 'Jumping Jim Crow.'"

"That song been going around," Gar said. "I heard the words to it somewhere. 'My name's Jim Crow. I do just so.'"

"We all going to be doing 'just so' one of these days," Ross predicted. "'Jumping Jim Crow.'"

"When I was a boy at Texarkana," Gar said, "Bedford used to call his field hands 'crows.'"

"We going to be done in by crows," said Ross, "just plain 'Jim Crowed.'"

As they started out again at first light, the land kept changing. The liveoak groves of the bayou and river country gave way to broad, sweeping savannas, well-watered and fertile. The land leveled out, anticipating the spread of the coastal plains beyond.

They encountered a sandy area where normal rainfall had been lacking, leaving a considerable dusty stretch. P.S.'s trail sank into it and disappeared.

"He's brushed it out with broom weeds he picked up back yonder where the liveoaks peter out," Gar said admiringly. "Wonder where he learned to do that?"

Ross scoffed, "You said he was brought up amongst the Creek Indians. Didn't you? They must have taught him a good deal about covering up his tracks. He's been hiding his trail pretty good all the way. I can't hardly ever see it."

"I can," Gar said. "And his scent don't brush out. Ain't no problem for Blue."

"For all the use I am on this peregrination," Ross grumbled, "I might as well be back in Saint Louis." He rode meditatively for a while, then revealed his cogitations. "You got to remember, Gar, your boy is the sum of his father *and* his mother. He's got both of you in him, and is likely to turn up smarter than either one of you."

Above the little south Texas town of Plácido the trail turned directly south. It now impinged on an area of which Gar said, "These Texans had a lot of trouble with the Mexicans years ago. I don't remember about it too good but a bunch of white men signed up together and tried to invade Mexico. Some of them got killed and some was took prisoner. The prisoners had to draw beans from a hat somewhere down in Mexico. If you drew a black bean you got shot—and most of them did."

"Drawing black ain't hardly ever lucky," Ross vouchsafed.

Farther south, in Lavaca County, crossing Cuero Creek, "Rawhides Creek" Gar called it, he yarned, "One time on our way south we found three black men lynched here. They bodies had been riddled with bullets. When we come back through a few weeks later with a herd of Mexican cattle, the birds had picked them lynched men's bones clean. Our trail cook, white man named Soogan, took enough bones to make hisself a set of tuning pegs and a tailboard for his fiddle. It always sounded wonderful after that—had a right weird, haunting tone."

Gar still had to admire the persistent way in which P.S. was traveling. Steady. Taking what little time to rest he had to, to keep from going fuzzy-headed, but no panic running, no giving up, and no lazy stopping and loafing. Empathy for the lonely boy, heading so doggedly across this lonesome country, toward an unknown and foreign place where he knew nobody, plucked at Gar. He almost wished out loud that he could be with P.S., and help him.

Ross must have sensed the pensive depths of Gar's mood. They were riding across the flat, north of Victoria, when Ross said, "It ain't that I don't reckon I know how you feel, but you're not doing what you told the judge you'd do."

The words brought Gar up sharply. He sensed the coming of the hard challenge he had been expecting Ross to throw up to him.

"We are just fooling around," Ross accused bluntly. "Three days ago we was so close you could still see bayou water sucking back into his tracks where his horse had pulled its legs out of that runny mud. Now we're somewhere a far piece behind him again. You been just purposefully dallying. If he makes it into Mexico before we catch up to him, we can't legally follow him down there. Can't nobody else, neither. I know that."

Gar denied it. "I ain't been hurrying much because, to tell the honest truth," he admitted, "I do hate to catch up with him. Ain't no telling what is going to happen then. Seems like the P.S. we been following has got more to him than the selfish boy I thought I'd got to know. This P.S. we're after has got guts. He's climbing uphill all the way. May not give up easy. May not give up at all. What if I have to shoot my own boy? But if he makes it into Mexico before we catch up with him, I'm going to follow him right on in. I'm going to catch up to him sometime, someplace. Maybe it's even up to P.S. when and where."

Abreast of Victoria the trail turned west. They turned, following it, toward the Guadalupe River and the town which lay there. An occasional motte of *encino*, kin to the liveoak, studded these brushy, rolling ranch country prairies. Blue was following the trail. P.S.'s horse was bound to be hot and sweaty in this warm southern climate and leaving a strong scent. The hound ran on so urgently that Gar occasionally had to slow him by whistling him down.

"No use to go running off headlong into something we can't see," Gar cautioned. "It might be dangerous."

The dog hurried them on into town, through quiet streets of gabled, gingerbread-ornamented houses. Streets peacefully lined with box elder, pecan, and locust, streets that led them into the heart of Victoria, Texas, past the town hall, and to the town jail.

Gar and Ross sat, uncertainly, on their horses at the awning-shaded boardwalk curb before the barred windows of the Victoria jailhouse with Blue panting beneath the thin shade of the tie rail, looking up at them, expectant and eager, as though knowing he deserved some kind words and a pat of affection for his achievement.

Gar lifted his hand to check. His U. S. Marshal's badge was firmly pinned to his shirt pocket, and he could clearly see Ross's badge, displayed with equal ostentation. He fumbled in the saddlebag on the copper dun's flank and found his papers. The original, tobacco juice–stained commission, and the warrant for P.S.'s arrest, duly and properly signed by Federal Judge Isaac Parker.

"Better be sure you got your paper, too," he cautioned Ross.

They dismounted.

Entering the jailhouse office, they encountered a fine-looking, handsomely mustachioed Texan, seated at a scarred desk, his feet cocked up on a pulled-out desk drawer. The Texas officer looked up at them, curiously. Further across the long room, another Texan sat at a tall, rolltop desk working patiently on papers spread out before him.

Gar broke the pendent silence. "We looking for a young fellow. Tall, part Indian, part black man. Name of Phenunda Sterling Rutherford."

The near officer, his eyes fixed on the badges of the two black marshals facing him, took his time about answering. His reply, when it came, was laconic.

"I've got a nigger like that. Never did ask him what his name was."

"What charge against him?" Gar asked.

The officer at the back desk looked up curiously.

"Vagrancy." The Texan spoke dryly, reserved and coolly stingy with words.

"He have any money on him?" Gar asked.

The officer nodded. "Not much. Some."

"I expect he rode into town to buy something to eat," Gar said. "I don't think you can hold a man for vagrancy when he comes into town with money to buy something." Gar handed the Texan Judge Parker's warrant.

The officer at the back desk laid aside his pen, covered his ink stand, and gave full attention to the conversation in the front of the office. He, too, had noted the federal marshal's stars worn on Gar's and Ross's shirt fronts. The man at the back desk wore one like it on his vest lapel.

The officer at the front desk removed his boots from the pulled-out drawer and shoved the drawer shut with a bang. He planted his feet firmly on the jailhouse floor, and leaned forward. "We've got enough niggers in Victoria already," he said, "without welcoming any more from outside." But he read the warrant carefully. "Glenn," he said, "why don't you come up here and look at this."

The officer at the back desk got up and came forward, taking the warrant.

"Murder," said the seated officer. "Federal charge."

Scanning the warrant, the standing man introduced himself, "I'm Glenn Osborn, deputy U. S. Marshal for the circuit court. This is the Victoria police chief, Earl Dexter." Neither officer offered to shake hands. "You're law officers? Deputized out of the Western District of Arkansas?"

Gar handed him his commission paper.

The Texas marshal scanned it hurriedly, and asked Ross, "You got one of these?"

Ross Stephens produced his commission and handed it over.

Dexter, still seated at his desk, muttered, "Nigger marshals! What do them damn carpetbagger yankees think they are doing?"

Osborn asked, "What do you aim to do with this prisoner?"

Gar answered, "Deliver him to the District Court at Fort Smith."

Osborn handed the papers to the seated police chief. "I believe I'd honor this warrant, Earl," he said.

The seated Dexter stroked his mustaches thoughtfully. "It would get three niggers out of Texas," he reasoned, but still he sat, stiff-necked and contrary. "You'll have to get him out of town," he told Gar. "We don't allow northern niggers in Victoria after sundown."

Gar, amused at being called "northern," became suddenly and pleasantly talkative. "Fort Smith is south of the Mason-Dixon line. I used to work driving cattle up through Victoria from Mexico. I remember when you had a bad cholera plague here. You had a undertaker, name of Black Peter—did the buryin'. He used to pick up the bodies every morning. Sometimes they was two or three dead in the same house. Sometimes wouldn't nobody answer his call an' he'd go in to find a whole family dead. People dyin' everywhere. Peter got two dollars and a bottle of good whiskey for every corpse he burried. Then the mayor said they wouldn't pay him no more. Peter leaned a stiff corpse up against the mayor's door. Next morning, when his honor opened up the door, the corpse fell in on him. They found the money an' whiskey to start payin' Peter again right away."

The Texas officers listened, wooden-faced. Dexter made no move toward acting on his tentative willingness to turn his black prisoner over to two black marshals. Osborn said, "It is a federal warrant, Earl. You're bound to honor it. Otherwise I'll have to write up some kind of report to answer Fort Smith's questions."

Police Chief Dexter got up abruptly and walked to unlock

the door at the rear of the room. Beyond it, Gar could see the cell block of the jail. He could hear the iron clatter of a cell door being unlocked and opened. Dexter returned herding a handcuffed and downcast P.S. before him.

While the Victoria policeman removed the handcuffs, Gar took the boy's arm. "Come on—" he nearly said, "son," but quickly revised it and said, "boy."

Gar told Marshal Osborn, "He was riding a palomino stud horse."

The handsomely mustached Dexter replied, a little reluctantly, Gar thought, "You'll find it stabled out back. We don't segregate horses." As they left the office, Dexter cautioned, "Be sure you take your own saddle, boy!"

As they quickly saddled P.S.'s palomino, Ross said, "Neither one of them said anything about you and the prisoner having the same name."

"Like they said, the law down here don't pay much attention to niggers' names. If they did, we'd probably still be there."

They rode out of the stable, back through the quiet streets of gabled houses. It was falling dusk. Ross flanked P.S. on the right and Gar on the left as they rode out of town, with Blue slinking along contentedly at the heels of P.S.'s palomino horse. They found a place to camp in a liveoak grove beside a tributary flowing back toward the Guadalupe.

Gar said gently, "We almost caught up with you, son, back at Cypress Bayou. Couldn't have been more than five minutes behind you."

"I was watching you from the tamaracks," P.S. said, his eyes hooded. "Could have shot you. I didn't do it."

Gar said with a morbid grin, "You can't do it now, even if you might like to. What kind of firearms you leave back there at that Victoria jailhouse?"

"My thirty-eight pistol, and a brand new thirty-thirty Winchester rifle."

"How much money?"

"Twenty dollars."

"I didn't want to make a fuss. We'll get Parker's clerk to send a court order down here to forward your property. Your mama buy that thirty-thirty for you, give you that money?"

"Yes, Papa."

He seemed subdued. Gar studied his son pensively. "We'll get on back up to Fort Smith," he said sympathetically, "and straighten out yo' trouble the best way we can."

P.S. said nothing. He sat staring reticently into the fire his father was building. When Ross came walking up from the stream carrying fresh bream he had caught, P.S. got up to help dress them.

Gar said, "A running man lives scared. The longer you run the more scared you git. Pretty soon you got to stop an' make a stand somewhere."

"Git—get," P.S. began, then shut up abruptly, and ducked his head. He seemed tempered, almost meek. Gar thought maybe the long trail behind them had knocked some of the cocky edges off his boy's smarty attitude.

With supper cooked, P.S. fed most of his share to the dog.

"Ain't you hungry?" Gar asked.

"You mean, 'Are you,'" P.S. started out, fell silent, then said, "I'm sorry, Papa. Yes, I'm hungry. I was just rewarding Blue for finding me in that jail. It was terrible, frightful, in there."

"You don't give us any credit for getting you out?" Gar asked bluntly.

"Yes, Papa. I do," the boy said resignedly.

They turned in. P.S. seemed chastened, beaten. Gar thought of the leg-irons in his duffle, then felt ashamed. His commiseration for the boy turned to pity and he was chagrined that he had even thought of so humiliating him. When they awakened in the morning, P.S., his horse, and the shotgun from Gar's saddle boot, were gone.

So was Blue.

CHAPTER 9

The palomino's trail headed south toward Refugio through sand dunes and partially grassed hillocks, a semi-desert fully exposed to the warm rays of the climbing sun.

"I felt so relieved to ketch him without any shooting my good sense gave out on me," Gar declared.

"We're just tired," said Ross. "It was as much my place to think of restraining him as it was yours."

"Anyhow, we're chasing him again. And without no good dog to help us this time."

Ross grinned as he replied, "Without *any* good dog to help us."

Gar gave him a sidelong glare. "You going to git like P.S.?"

Ross grinned wider. "A man ought to be able to take a little correction from his son. Especially if the boy's right."

"You mean I ought to encourage him to start up again? When it looks like he's breaking himself of the habit?"

In firm rebuttal, Ross said, "The more I see of your boy, the more certain I am there is nothing evil in him. Except maybe some bullheaded bad judgment he got from his papa and mama."

Gar slowed, trying to sort out the tracks of the palomino's long-calked shoes from a myriad of others, old and new, that marked the much-used Refugio road, alongside a towering, patchy-grassed rise of hillocks.

When he lifted his eyes and first saw her, sitting high up on the ridge, he thought it was a mirage. She was riding the sidesaddle, straight-backed and erect, her horse standing atop the domelike swell of the savanna, her long skirts swept out like a cape in the coastal breeze. In the hazy distance she looked as young and pretty as when Gar had first seen her, years ago, riding atop that sidesaddle toward Opothleyahola's harness shop with a broken flank cinch for him to mend.

Gar spurred his copper dun horse toward her, disbelieving. The flirty wind was switching her skirts as bewitchingly as she had herself been doing it in that long ago time and place. As he drew near, the fetching image of her summoned up the past even more vividly in Gar's unbelieving awareness. At the foot of the lightly grassed, sandy hill, he pulled up. She came, slowly, riding down to meet him. It was truly Bernice, in her own shapely, though slightly matronly flesh, and her fine-featured attractive face held a superior, condescending look long familiar to Gar.

"It is sure enough you." Gar said it, he knew, dumbly.

She simply stared him down until he finally dropped his gaze.

"How did you do it?" He tried to confront her with his eyes.

From this close, she looked worn and dusty, but still, Gar marveled, fadingly pretty. Drawn and weary but, hell's-fire and damnation, still pretty.

"How did you do it?" he asked again.

"Do what?" Her voice was caustic.

"Get here—"

"A-horseback. Just like you."

"But I left you sick a-bed—"

"A mother whose boy needs her, she can get well enough to go."

"But how did you find us?"

"I'm part Creek and was raised by Indians too, Gar Rutherford!" She said spitefully, "I know how to follow a track better than you do."

Ross Stephens came up alongside them. Bernice ignored his presence. "I saw your camp around daylight. But not my Sonny. Then I found his tracks heading on."

"He got away from us last night," Gar confessed guiltily. "If we don't hurry up after him, he's going to ride on into Mexico."

"Let him," she declared. "I'm going to go and be with him."

"Huh-uh," Gar contested. "I aim to ketch up to him an' take him back to Fort Smith"—his bass voice rumbled as deep as his determination—"even if I have to shoot him."

Bernice cried in horror, "Kill your own son?"

"I didn't say that. I can shoot him without killing him."

"That's fine. Shoot me, too. But kill me!" She resorted to pleading, "Let him alone, Gar. He can have a good life in Mexico. Half the Kickapoos and some of the Cherokees are down there. Mexico treats dark folks better than the U.S.A. White folks squeezed us west with the Indians and I feel their prejudice up there in the Territory, squeezing me tighter all the time."

"Me, too," Gar acceded.

"It's worse on me than it is on you. Black folks don't much like me because I'm part Indian. Indians stay away from me altogether anymore because I'm part black. And you know white folks won't have nothing to do with either a Indian squaw or a nigger woman."

Gar kept still. He could not really dispute any of her argument.

Persuasively, she opened up her offer. "You can come with us, Gar. You got a way of getting along. You can get along down in Mexico, too."

Slowly, he shook his head. "A life on the fly is no good. I lived that way back when the whites was studyin' war and had plenty to do besides chase me. It would be worse now that they ain't no Civil War to keep they attention. They wouldn't think about nothin' but comin' after us. Anyhow, we got to ketch up to P.S. first."

"No, we don't."

"How come? Bernice, do you aim to do that boy's thinking for him from now on? Ain't you ever going to let him have his own say?"

"He's just around the other side of this hill and he can have his say right now."

P.S. came riding the palomino, slowly, around the mound. Blue lagged along behind him, slack-gaited, his tongue lolling.

"Guess all my life, Mama," the young man said, "I've been wondering what I am, Indian or Black? But I sure ain't Mexican. It's been on my mind ever since Papa talked last night. I hadn't ought to have run off the first time. It's just made trouble for everybody. I'll go back."

Bernice despaired. "I married a fool and he has sired another one."

They debated, halfheartedly. Bernice was insistent that she would never agree to surrender. So Gar led off north, knowing the long return could only begin by starting. Ross and P.S. fell in alongside him. Bernice came following along grudgingly, under protest.

When they reached the Victoria turnoff Gar baited her with a question. He was overwhelmingly curious, but trying, as much as anything, to improve her sullen, angry humor.

"How come you passed up Ross an' me?" he asked.

"When I got close to Victoria," she said, "I heard there was a town named Refugio south of here. That sounded like a place somebody would run to, so I didn't pay any 'tention to you all. I just picked up Sonny's trail where you all camped last night."

"How did you hear about Refugio?" Gar found it hard to credit that, while there was no doubt that she was here, she could have accomplished all that journey alone.

"I talked to the Indians," she said. "There's still a few Karakawas and Copanoes living around here. They said the Spaniards built Our Lady of Refuge church a hundred years ago. The whites started coming in and the Spaniards told them not to, but they kept on coming anyway. They had a big fight. The Spaniards, the Texans call them Mexicans, didn't keep no prisoners. They shot them. There was a lot of bloody killing then. Still is. But it's mostly Mexicans getting killed now."

"But how did you persuade P.S. to wait for you?" Gar persisted.

"Wasn't nothing to that," she said mildly. "When Sonny saw me coming along behind him this morning he pulled up and stopped. He might run from you, but Sonny would always come to his mama," she finished smugly.

On that triumphant note Bernice shut up, retreated within herself, and refused to say any more about her traveling until they approached the Neches crossing almost two days later. Here she volunteered another of her adventures while she had been on the way south.

"Right out yonder by the river crossing I got caught by a Anderson County law. He gave me my choice of going to work for him on his pig farm or going to jail, which wasn't no choice at all. I took the farm. When we got there, he offered me another choice—being his 'house woman,' or slopping pigs. That wasn't no choice either, an' when that cracker gave me an invitational look that was so lewd I knew what he was thinking, I stole the ice pick from where he had stuck it in the screen door frame.

"He offered me a bathtub full of hot water, which I was glad to take, but then when he come to join me in it, I fetched that ice pick up from under the soapy water and stuck it through his bare leg. He fell down. I pulled it out an' pinned his big arm muscle to the pine floor. He wasn't doing much but a lot of wiggling an' hollering when I grabbed my clothes and headed for the barn. Believe me, I was careful not to leave no tracks at all for about fifteen miles south of there."

Her narrative was satisfyingly convincing. Gar knew how willful, and how resourceful, she had always been. It still seemed incredible to Gar that a woman, even his own woman, could have made such a trek alone, but it deepened his pride in her. At Cypress Bayou, she had spent a night on the way in the pilothouse of the same wrecked and abandoned steamboat they had.

Nearing Texarkana, she said to Gar, "These piney woods sure is a sorry country. I don't see how you stayed around here, growing up, as long as you did."

She had avoided the snowstorm in the Kiamichis by being two days behind it. "I got out of my sickbed as soon as I could after you left me there, and started following you. It was hard going for a while. But the way you was fooling along I was able

to keep from getting any farther behind. Then I started gaining
up on you and kept coming closer all the way."

Gar wanted to bend west around through Rentiesville. "We
ought to tell ol' man Butler to go after his mules."

"I already done that," said Bernice. "I stopped and told him
Sonny had shot that thief Nash and if he would go on up to
Yahola he could probably round up his mules before they scat-
tered too far. Let's don't take any detours. If we got to take
Sonny to Fort Smith let's get on over there."

The weather had grown steadily colder during their coming
north. It was a chill winter sun that cast its pale and sickly light
on the Fort Smith courthouse the late December afternoon they
arrived there. Ross Stephens rode away immediately, leaving
Gar and Bernice alone to face the grim chore of putting their
boy in the Fort Smith jail. For Bernice it was an unrelieved
agony; for Gar, who knew what to expect, it was almost impossible.

They took P.S. into the courthouse for the process of booking
him. Coming back out, they paused on the courthouse stone
porch. The jail was a cellar dungeon beneath the courthouse, its
entry down through the stairwell beneath the high stone porch.
As they took P.S. down into the stairwell the stench that rose toward them was so foul and stinking it drove them back.

Filled with sickness and dread Gar led them on down into the
jail vestibule. The musty basement was divided into two com-
partments separated by a heavy stone wall, with the ceiling a
scant eight feet above the wet, rough stone floor. As they entered the vestibule they could see the evil-smelling, crowded
prisoners squatted on wooden benches among a scattering of
slop buckets. In the small vestibule, fenced off with rough lumber, sat the jailer. He handed P.S. a single blanket, unlocked
the gate, and motioned him on inside.

Bernice turned away retching, stifling a sob, and said, "My
God, Gar, we can't leave him here."

He took her arm, leading her back into the stairwell. Ross came down the steps to meet them. "I thought maybe Dan Wells could help us find someplace else to confine your boy. This jail was built for fifty prisoners. They've got nearly a hundred in it."

"Dan can't help us?" Gar asked.

Ross shook his head. "There isn't any hope." He reached in and picked up scraps of bread and meat from the vestibule floor. They were crawling with maggots. "Maybe the best thing we can do is hang around the courthouse, Gar. Sleep here at night until you can get some kind of hearing. That way, your boy will anyway know that there's somebody close by."

"Unless Parker sends us out after somebody else."

"We'll have to figure it out so that just one of us goes. The other one has to stay here," Ross said.

They took Bernice to the same boardinghouse where they had left Winged Trudy to wait for her sons to get out of jail. The hunchbacked, aged woman was still there. She tried to comfort Bernice.

"My boys is there, serving out they sentence. They are still alive," she declared. "I got me a night job in the cotton mill so's I could stay here to keep track of them. I didn't figure I'd ever hear of your man putting his own boy in there. I reckon we all do what we have to do. We'll work on a hex medicine to confound their jailers and hoodoo to strengthen those boys, honey."

Gar and Ross returned to the courthouse. George Maledon was busy at his gallows, preparing for an execution. The two black marshals watched the skeletal Maledon prepare the gallows traps with weighted bags of sand and trip them, letting the heavy bags fall through, testing the strength of the ropes that left the bags suspended and swinging, six feet above the ground.

Ross took their horses and the bluetick hound to the courthouse stable. He returned carrying their blanket rolls, and suggested supper. Gar said he didn't want anything, so they waited until they were summoned by Judge Parker.

The weary, ailing judge sat alone in his chamber. He chided plaintively, "You served your earlier warrants with dispatch and promptitude, Rutherford. This one took a great deal more time."

"When you're chasing your own son, your honor," Gar said, "it's a good deal different."

"Hmmm."

"Fact is, my boy was better at giving us the slip and staying ahead of us than I expected. He can take care of himself, when he's of a mind to."

"You have him lodged in jail now?"

"Yes, sir. His mother is wanting to know, is there some way we can get him out of that pest house?"

"I've been giving a deal of study to these charges against him. One, the deceased man, was a known criminal seemingly engaged in the commission of another crime. Horse, or mule, stealing. But the girl—"

"My boy didn't know she was anywhere around, your honor," Gar said.

"Then you must plead accidental homicide," said Parker.

"I don't know how to go at that," Gar admitted, more humbly, he realized, than he had ever spoken.

"I'll see that an attorney is assigned to the case," Parker said. "Since the charge is murder, your son cannot be admitted to bail."

"Yes, sir."

"We are preparing to carry out the Fowler executions in the morning," Parker said. "I am asking that off-duty marshals be present here at the courthouse. It will be a simultaneous, quintuple hanging. There will be a great crowd of the morbid and curious. Should any of the Fowler gang have criminal friends in the crowd, there may be trouble."

The judge dismissed them.

Gar rolled out his blankets that night by one of the jail's small, half-underground windows. Ross lay down by another. Through the barred, tight-shut window, the stench crept out. There was no way to contact P.S. When a patrolling town constable questioned their presence, they showed their badges and said they were there on orders of Judge Parker.

The long night dragged sleeplessly past, and the grim activities of a hanging day commenced. During the cold, cloudy morning, rumors told of postponement, waiting for relatives of the condemned men to arrive. The crowd swelled, a strangely morose, suppressed, yet avid gathering of Arkansawyers and ragged frontiersmen from the Indian Territory, many of them accompanied by women. Several brought children. They were all miserable in the raw cold of the day, gathering in bunches to gossip, cowering in the shelter of building corners for protection from the damp, chilling wind that blew up from the river, but determined not to miss the sensations of this banner execution.

Gar watched hawkers work among the crowd, crying their wares of hot drinks and food gone cold, congealed in the bleakness of the wintry day. He listened to ribald jests about hanging and death, and coarse laughter. By midafternoon the delays had made the waiting horde impatient and they began clustering about Maledon's gallows, shoving in for the closest possible view of the spectacle that must surely come soon.

When it appeared that the fierce crowding might topple the scaffold, workers came from the courthouse and set fire to the dry brown grass beneath the gallows platform. Beating the flames back with wet gunnysacks from the wooden stanchions which supported the platform, the fire also burned on outward, driving back and scattering the crowd. The grisly machine of death with its crossbar of suspended nooses was left standing more stark than before, in the center of the blackened yard of burned grass.

The crowd did not long remain dispersed. Sanguinary rumors increased, passing harshly from mouth to vicious mouth, that the macabre event was at hand, and the five outlaws appeared together outside the courthouse door. Gar could see the dull-witted Bennie Gault, callous-jowled Sim Davis, black Hector March, predominantly Indian Lucky Sampson, and dark Rufus Fowler himself, standing bunched and heavily guarded on the courthouse portico. He was momentarily glad that, however distasteful the duty of marshaling this ragtag mob of spectators, he had been spared the grim chore of escorting the outlaws to the gallows.

He thought, *I helped catch 'em, and God knows they've earned what's coming, but all of a sudden I've got no stomach to watch 'em die.* He knew that his son's presence in the dungeon jail beneath the courthouse, charged with one of the same crimes for which these felons were about to swing, had everything to do with his sudden horror of the spectacle.

The guard of escorting marshals made passage through the crowd and the procession of prisoners to the gallows began. The crowd clogged the passage before and behind them and surged up toward Maledon's gibbet. Now not only the courthouse yard was jammed with turbulent humanity, the wall around it was lined with spectators. The roofs of nearby buildings were covered with people, perching, stretching, peering, watching, avid to drink in every horrifying detail.

The outlaws ascended to the scaffold platform. The hangropes were adjusted around their necks. Black hoods were brought out to lower over their faces. But, remarkably, only four men finally stood hooded. By some odd omission, it seemed that only four black hoods had been prepared for the execution. The hoods were snatched off and there was some discussion among the authorities around the hang-noosed men. Then it was apparently decided that since only four hoods were available, no one would be masked.

The noisy crowd hushed as the five men were asked for their last words. Progressively, down the line, Gault, then Davis, shook their heads to indicate they had nothing to say. Belatedly then, Bennie Gault shouted excitedly, "Hell's-fare, look at the people! Whut's gonna happen?" Sim Davis grumbled loudly, "I come here to die. Not to talk." His sullen words flowed out turgidly, like a viscous substance, over the utter silence that followed Bennie Gault's shout.

Hector March said, "If there's a preacher here, I would like for him to pray for me."

Somewhere beyond where Gar stood, a pious voice lifted promptly, addressing itself to the Almighty. The crowd stood patiently quiet through the long, sanctimonious prayer. Lucky Sampson uttered no refusal to speak; he just stared out at the spectators with phlegmatic Indian face.

Rufus Fowler began to recite a poem probably composed by himself during his time in jail:

> I dreamt I saw an angel bright
> with two wings white clear through.
> It was my mother, saintly and light—

The gallows trap sprung.

The five outlaws dropped through the opened floor and jerked up short. George Maledon had done his expert work. None of them, except Fowler himself, moved again. Rufus Fowler jerked convulsively, then hung as inert as his confederates. The jail doctor began to pass along the line, pronouncing them dead.

Gar turned away. He was deeply thankful above all, that Bernice had not been there. The crowd noise had become a dull, insensate animal sound; a subdued, primitive ululation of inchoate beasts primally aroused. Gar was surprised to note that it was growing dark. During his fixation on the deadly events, afternoon had passed into evening without notice.

The spectators were in no hurry to disperse. Glancing upward, Gar saw Judge Isaac Parker standing alone in the window of his courtroom. The fat old jurist was standing like a specter, his window wide open in spite of the cold of the darkening evening. His shoulders were shaking, perhaps from the chill, but as Parker turned away from the window his back was slumped and bent. It appeared to Gar that the aging man was crying.

Someone near Gar said grimly, "They got a plenty more down there in that jail that ought to swing the same way."

A companion beside the man who had spoken added, "Murderers, robbers, rapers, scum the lot of 'em."

A conversation was springing up around these men, within hearing of where Gar stood beside the stairwell down into the jail dungeon.

Someone contributed, "I saw 'em bring another young nigger in here yesterday afternoon."

"Yeah. That was the one that killed that Indian girl over by Yahola."

"No, no," a man contradicted loudly. "I heard it was a white woman he raped."

Ross moved up beside Gar. "I smell a stink, and it isn't coming up out of the jail," he said. "Is something making up around here?"

One of the men suggested conspiratorially, "We ought to git together while there's a bunch of us here. We ought to bust down that jail door. Git that nigger kid an' a flock of his buddies. Hoist them up where them carrion baits are swinging out there now!"

He started a movement toward the gallows. "Come on. Let's cut them down—"

But strong leadership was forming. The man who had declared that he had heard it was a white woman who had been raped lifted his arms. They were the thick arms of a man of hard physical work. His clothing was soiled and caked with muddy dirt. He had a cowpen smell and looked like a river bottom farmer. "Hold back a minute, boys," he cautioned. "I'm Asa Goss. I come into town for all these neck rope parties. They'll take those carcasses down. Let 'em. No use getting in a hurry and messing something up. Let's fall back and get organized."

A lieutenant promptly appointed himself. This one reminded Gar of Trudy Cabot's son Squint, but he was white, or part Indian, instead of black. A burly, town-dressed youth with prominent outthrust rump.

"I hear what you're saying," he told Goss, then hushed his voice to a conniving whisper. "Pass the word around. Round up everbody who takes an interest. Tell 'em to take the time to get their guns. Once it gets full dark we can poleaxe them jail doors."

Thrusting his rump out, he reached to scratch his crotch. With an anticipatory grin of pleasure, he moved out through the crowd, proceeding off in the opposite direction from Goss, each of them pausing frequently, gathering adherents as they went.

In the gloomy dusk beside the jail stairs, Ross said to Gar, "We had better go and talk to Judge Parker."

Gar led off toward the courthouse back entrance. Reaching its narrow stone stairs they climbed up single file. Gar tried the door. It was locked. He rattled it, then doubled up his fist and banged on its thick oaken portal. After a while, a voice from inside answered, "Who's there? What do you want?" It was Dan Wells.

"It's me, Dan. Gar Rutherford with Ross Stephens. We need to talk to the judge."

The door cracked open. "He's gone home, boys." It started to shut again then Dan said, "Oh, I wanted to tell you fellows. I went down to Bokoshe and tried to find some cached money for Trudy Cabot. Didn't find a dime. But she's got a job. Seems to be getting along—"

Gar broke in urgently. "We just listened to some jaybirds planning to bust into the jail and have them a lynching bee."

Dan Wells heard their information soberly, but he said, "I wouldn't worry about it. A couple blowhards wanting to attract attention. The likes of them turn up here every once in a while. They make some wind, but it dies down."

"I expect I wouldn't worry about it," Gar admitted, "if my boy wasn't down there in that jail."

Wells understood. He granted, "I'd feel the same. Go on over and talk to his honor. I'm not as young as I used to be, but I can keep things in hand here."

They set out afoot through darkened Fort Smith, crossing dimly lighted Garrison Street, then covered two more blocks to arrive on Isaac Parker's front porch. The house was dark.

"He's gone somewhere," Ross concluded.

Gar demurred. "Hang five men in the afternoon, then go out socializing in the evening? It don't sound right. Maybe he ain't got home yet." He lifted his fist and knocked.

No reply.

Gar knocked again.

Still silence.

They turned together to leave the porch.

Ross asked, "Where now?"

"Back to the courthouse," Gar said grimly. "We git our artillery together and ready to start shooting."

They heard the faint sound of a door opening somewhere in the house. Light filtered into the parlor, illuminating the curtained, frosted front door glass. Behind it a shadowy form appeared and a woman's voice called softly, "This is Mrs. Parker. What do you want?"

"Ma'am," Gar tried to modulate the fearful excitement in his deep voice. "This is Marshals Gar Rutherford and Ross Stephens. We need to talk to the judge."

"He has retired for the night," she replied.

Didn't take him long, Gar thought. "It's important, ma'am," he insisted.

"I fixed him a hot lemonade and made him go to bed," came her uneasy reply. "He came home with a chill. I think he's coming down with the grippe."

Ross spoke up, supporting Gar. "We won't keep him up, Mrs. Parker. But I think he'd blame us if we don't tell him the information we're bringing. Could we see him for just a minute?"

Unwillingly, she opened the door. "Well," she fretted, "all right. For just a minute. Wait here, I'll get the lamp." She moved off, apologizing, "I'm sorry it took me so long to answer the door. I was in the upper part of the house."

Bringing the lamp, she escorted them upstairs to the sickroom. "He is running a fever," she said as she softly opened the door. Isaac Parker turned heavily in the bed, its cornshuck ticking crackling.

He was dull-eyed, blinking as he stared at them in the

lamplight, clearly not well. He sat up to hear Gar out, and declared doggedly, "I'll not have my jail delivered. Who's down there?"

"We talked to Dan Wells," Gar said.

"Good. Go back. Tell him my orders are to call in the available marshals. I'll be there as soon as I can get up and dressed."

Trying to ignore Mrs. Parker's evident upset, Gar and Ross descended the stairs listening to her protest, pleading with her husband to let his marshals handle this matter and stay in bed through the night. When they arrived at the courthouse, Dan Wells told them, "You men might be right. Look over there. You can see a half dozen bonfires burning on the river bluffs behind the old garrison. I've sent for the four marshals who were here this afternoon to take the prisoners to the gallows. If they're still around town they ought to be here before long. Is the judge going to come in?"

"It's hard to say," Ross averred. "His wife was working at persuading him not to. He looks mighty sick."

"He spends too many hours here," Dan said. "I've alerted the jailers. There's two of them and three of us. We've got ninety-seven prisoners. Maybe this will just blow over."

They waited. Gar's impatience was contagious and seemed gradually to communicate itself to the others. The four marshals, Ives, Oates, Toller, and Jones, trickled in with complaints that it was impossible even to enjoy a short beer, a pinochle game, your wife's company, or a decent night's sleep while riding for Isaac Parker.

Nearly an hour passed before the judge arrived. He was visibly flushed with fever, manifestly fatigued, but as dogged and determined as when Gar and Ross had left him in his bedroom. "I'll stay here until midnight," he said. "Surely by then we'll know if anything is developing. I'll be in my chambers."

Gar knew there was a leather couch in the chambers. At least the ailing jurist could lie down in there. Gar returned to the window. The more distant fires on the bluffs had faded and were flickering out. They had been replaced by a single, high-blazing fire near the former garrison's flagstaff, a hundred yards from the courthouse.

Fort Smith had been abandoned as a military post soon after the Civil War, but the former garrison buildings still stood along the river bluffs, interspaced across the intervening quadrangle of the parade ground. Remarkably, Gar could see no human in the reaching circle of firelight at the base of the tall iron flagpole.

He stood castigating himself because he had not helped his son escape into Mexico, had not gone on there with the boy, when he had the chance. Flames were reflecting on the fort's old saluting cannon. The smoothbore fieldpiece, a cast-iron Civil War relic, had been left for the use of the G.A.R. on the Fourth of July and at other patriotic celebrations. Beside it stood a symbolic rack of cannonballs.

Ross came to stand beside Gar.

"Maybe they decided to give it up," he said.

Gar chafed, "Looks like we ought to be able to see them."

"Or be hearing from them. Maybe a note—a threatening, made under a flag of truce—some kind of move."

Behind them, Dan Wells said, "Ives, you, Oates, and Toller unlimber your guns and take the hall windows. If it comes to trouble we'll have to defend all sides."

There was a rush of men out of the darkness.

Gar counted five in the group that gathered around the cannon. Some of them began to light pine torches. The torches flickered like fireflies as they were passed back through the mob. The bulk of the mob became dimly visible, hanging back in the edge of darkness beyond the reach of the firelight. The horde was growing. Faint figures were seen, running in from the far side of the parade ground to join the milling throng barely discernible beyond the flagstaff.

Of the five who had run in toward the firelit cannon, one had carried a long pole with a wad of rags bundled around its end. Another had lugged a heavy box. Two more struggled with an

even weightier box, and set it down with a jolting thump beside
the cannon. The one with the lighter box opened it now and
began pouring its contents, black powder, down the mouth of
the cannon.

Ross turned. "Mr. Wells," he said, "you had better call Judge
Parker."

The carrier of the pole ram with its bundled end of rag wad-
ding ran it down into the cannon and shoved hard, packing the
powder. Gar recognized him—the burly dirt farmer who had
urged the forming of the mob. The shorter youth, who had appointed himself lieutenant, leaned to open the heavier box and
dump its contents, lug bolts, nuts, and lengths of chain, in a
heap beside the cannon. He stepped back then to scratch his
wide rump, and Gar got an abrupt shock.

A remaining man who ran back now to seize a flickering
torch from one of the mobsters was strikingly familiar. He
looked seedy but pompous, and as he came hurrying back to
stand like a Prussian beside the touchhole of the cannon, Gar recognized him. It was Jake Hesse.

The judge came to look out the adjoining window. The men
around the cannon began throwing into it the lengths of chain,
lug bolts, and nuts. The load of rusty junk was rammed home
and all five took hold to train the gun, shoving its barrel down
for a low trajectory.

"They are not aiming at us," Parker decided. "They intend to
try to blow a hole in the wall of the jail."

"That junk is more dangerous than a load of grape," Dan
Wells said. "There won't be enough left of some prisoners to
lynch." He stepped back to the wall gunrack and took down a
.50 caliber Sharps buffalo rifle. Gar, Ross, and Jones drew their
.45s. Dan Wells knelt, silently lifted a window a few inches,
rested the Sharps on the sill, and aimed.

Judge Parker touched him on the shoulder. "No, Marshal
Wells. Let them shoot."

One of the gunners primed the touchhole with a dribble of

powder, and Hesse laid his torch on the primer. There was a hiss of upward flame and the cannon fired. Its massive detonation tore the ancient gun apart in a roaring explosion.

The cannon's total disintegration left the area around the flagpole swept clean. The bonfire, blown away by the explosion, had scattered its coals and embers across the dry yard and grass fires sprung up. The flames revealed shards of iron from the shattered cannon beneath floating clouds of clearing smoke a considerable distance from the broken remains of the gun carriage on which the cannon had been mounted. The downed gunners lay scattered among the wreckage.

"That cannon has been sitting there rusting since the Civil War," Parker said. "Safe enough for firing a small saluting charge of powder alone. But a charge sufficient to propel the scrap iron with which they had loaded it—I assumed would be too much." He paused. "Yet if we had fired first and killed one of those men . . . I hesitate to contemplate the seriousness of the charges that would have been laid against us."

Torches flared at the inert and prostrate men were carried from the field.

His voice rumbling deep in his chest, Gar said, "Jake Hesse was out there."

Parker nodded. "That Hesse was among them is proof that you were right, Marshal Rutherford. His principal purpose was to obtain your son."

The mob was scattering out, away from the parade ground, disappearing into the dark.

"Our lynch gang has lost its fervor," said Parker. "I think they are done for the night. Perhaps it would be wise to hold your son's hearing early in the morning, and remove him from this area. Marshal Wells, would you assist me home?"

The ailing judge indeed appeared exhausted, even feeble, though seeking to maintain his independence. While trying to seem self-sufficient, he clung to Dan Wells's arm as they left the courthouse. Gar, looking at his flushed face and trembling hand, wondered how high a fever the old man was running.

CHAPTER 10

The morning Fort Smith newspaper published a scare-headline account of the lynching attempt. Ross read portions of it to Gar and Bernice as they sat at breakfast in her boardinghouse:

> . . . *the post's field piece was too decrepit to withstand a shot fired in anger. Among the dead, victims of their own ill-advised attempt to invade the federal jail, are three men identified as Asa Goss, Jake Hesse, and "Shorty" Rule, said to have been ring leaders in the plot. It has been learned that Hesse concocted and spread unfounded rumors that a young negro in the jail, Phenunda Rutherford, son of one of Parker's deputy marshals, had raped and killed a white woman . . .*

Ross, in disgust, tossed the newspaper on the table. "We had better get over to the court. It's near time for the 'Oyez, oyez,' and I feel pretty sure your son P.S. is going to be the first up on the docket."

When they entered the courtroom it was nearly empty. Only preliminary hearings were to be held during the morning. No cases were docketed to go before a jury, and none had been impaneled. The jury box was empty. Gar, Ross, and Bernice found seats easily. P.S. was brought up from the jail.

As the bailiff seated her son at the counsel table Bernice wrinkled her nose. "He has picked up the smell of that jail. I can smell it from here."

They stood as Parker made his entry and took his place behind the bench. *He looks sicker than he did last night,* Gar thought, with a feeling of admiration for the man's determination to do his duty regardless of what plagued him. The judge's voice was weak, mumbling, and sometimes unclear as he appointed Fort Smith attorney Malcolm Rice to represent P.S.

Ross whispered, "That man"—he was looking with awe at the judge—"is right on the edge of fever delirium."

The widely feared arbiter of justice for the Indian Territory was having perceptible trouble in keeping his mind from wandering. Elegantly waistcoated Lawyer Rice rose to ask for a postponement to become acquainted with the case of his client.

"Denied," ruled the judge. "Have the accused take the stand and sworn." He was plainly aware that he still had the first and final authority over the lives of the defendants who faced him.

Bernice stood up. "Your honor, I would like to take my son over to the boardinghouse. He needs a chance to clean up. He wants a shave, and his clothes in bad shape. Already, before he starts, he looks, and smells, guilty. And I know he ain't."

Shocked, Gar reached up to grab her arm. "Bernice, set down," he gasped.

She jerked loose. "I know enough to know it ain't right for a boy to be tried dirty and *looking* guilty, when he innocent."

"Madam," Parker said wearily. "Your son is not being tried. This is only a preliminary hearing."

"Whatever," Bernice spat out, "he deserves a chance to look his best. And why ain't that lawyer you appointed saying so?"

"Bernice," Gar again whispered cautiously. "Set down and shut up. The judge knows how to run his courtroom."

"Maybe he knows how to put my boy in prison, too. I want to hear something about this lawyer. Does he know how to keep him out?"

Gar stood up, grasping both her arms, forcing her to face him. "The judge knows how to throw you out of this courtroom. If he do, don't *no* lawyer know how to get you back in."

She struggled to free herself.

"Mrs. Rutherford," Parker said weakly, "you must be patient and let us proceed."

Something in Parker's tired voice, with its tone of defeat and helplessness, seemed to mollify her. She stopped struggling and, tentatively, sat down.

P.S. moved into the witness chair. Parker motioned Malcolm Rice away. "I would like to hear, in this young man's own words, an account of the events that led to his presence here."

With straightforward sincerity, young P.S. related how he had happened to see Dick Nash driving the herd through Pleasant Hill. Sure the mules were stolen, he had gone home to arm himself, and followed. By the time he had reached Yahola, Nash had penned the animals in the sagging, broken corrals there and taken refuge in the deserted, former cookhouse.

"I yelled at him, your honor," P.S. testified. "He came out shooting and was trying to kill me."

The judge cleared his throat, saying hoarsely, "My attitude toward mule and horse thieves in this frontier environment is well known. A citizen has every right to pursue such a felon, and to make a citizen's arrest. If he was shooting at you, you had the right to defend yourself."

Bernice was up again. "What you mean 'if he was shooting at you?' My son don't lie. We can get the Reverend Haworth and plenty other Pleasant Hill folks to come over here and testify that Phenunda don't lie."

Gar pulled her bodily down. "Woman, if you don't set an' keep your mouth shut I'm going to carry you out of here myself, screaming and hollering if you want to be. I'll dump you in the street!"

Ross Stephens stared at Gar and Bernice, appalled. Attorney Rice eyed them in wonder, with dropped jaw. The few spectators in the courtroom were grinning, laughing, buzzing with gossip.

Judge Parker seemed to ignore them, so debilitated with fever and sickness as to find it necessary to concentrate all his remaining strength on examining the witness. "What about the girl?" he asked.

"I didn't know she was there; never saw her," P.S. admitted hesitantly. "I sure didn't mean to—" his voice broke, "we was going to get married—" He choked off a sob of anguish and leaned against the witness box railing.

"Counselor Rice, would you approach the bench?" said the judge.

Bernice, as if trying to do so surreptitiously, rose to a half crouch and followed the bewildered lawyer. Gar came at her heels. As they neared the judge's bench, Gar could hear Parker murmur weakly, "I am going to advise you, Mr. Rice, to have the accused plead guilty to a charge of accidental homicide."

Malcolm Rice, who had spoken not a word, simply looked at P.S. questioningly.

The boy moaned. "Yes sir, your honor," he choked. "I think I would want to do that."

Parker's gavel rose and fell. Not forcefully, as in the past, but in relief at P.S.'s agreement, as he went on resignedly. "Then I sentence you to three years in the federal prison at Leavenworth, Kansas." He addressed himself to Gar and Bernice. "He will be safe from the rumor mongers there," Parker said. "With good behavior, he can be released when he has served a third of his sentence." In frailty, but with sternness, the redoubtable hanging judge told Gar and Bernice, "Marshal Rutherford, madam, in one year your son can be free to have another chance. But the conspicuously discordant atmosphere of your lives, which must be carried over into your home, cannot be helpful to him. A young man who must live in an inharmonious household cannot be expected to develop good judgment. Thus he chose as his future wife a young woman who quickly fell short of his expectations. I would urge that you mend your ways. He will need your help in the future. The spirit of bickering you have displayed in this courtroom is a sorry encouragement to a young man trying to prepare himself for a useful life."

The judge lowered his forehead to rest on his folded arms on the desk. Gar thought he was only resting for a moment, but Parker's body went slack. He hung precariously balanced between desk and chair, then slid to the floor. Ross ran around the railing to kneel over him, and Gar was beside him instantly.

"Let's move his chair. Lay him out," Gar said.

The bailiff came running, and as Chief Marshal Dan Wells came from the clerk's office, Bernice was leaning over the judge's bench. Gar could hear her whisper, "Come on, Phenunda. Come with me. The judge has fainted."

Gar left Ross, the bailiff, and Wells to look after Isaac Parker and strode back around the courtroom railing. There he stood staring at Bernice, and at P.S. Dan Wells called for a doctor, and a stretcher.

P.S. said, "Mama, you go on back to that place where you're staying. Dad, will you walk back down to the jail with me?"

Wells and Ross were lifting the unconscious Parker on the stretcher as Gar and P.S. walked out the hall door of the courtroom. In the stairwell leading down to the jail, they paused to talk.

"I'm going to have to find something else to call you, son," Gar said thoughtfully. "Seems like I always called you P.S., mocking you, in a scornful kind of way. I don't feel like that no more."

"You go right on calling me P.S., Papa," his son ordered. "I have sure enough been a P.S. on your life."

"No, you ain't. It's a fact I didn't know about you till you was plumb growed up, but you, and your momma and me, we got to realize we are all important to one another."

"I wish Etta could have been—" P.S. began, brokenly.

Gar tried to cross the barrier of restraint that lay between him and his son by laying a hand on the boy's shoulder. "Son, I had strong doubts about that girl, and they proved out."

"It's a good thing the court didn't question me too hard about why I went after Dick Nash, Papa. I wasn't chasing him so much because of Mr. Butler's mules. I went after him because I knew he was trying to make time with Etta. I meant to kill him, Papa. The fact that Etta was already there—I didn't know—I wouldn't have shot—"

"You've got to put it out of your mind, son. Everybody hates horse thieves and what's past can't be changed. There is still time ahead. Plenty of time, maybe. Let's try to use it good."

P.S. stood with his head bowed.

Gar asked, "Can you put in a year and maybe more in that jail up there?"

His son nodded. "You put in near thirty years as a slave, didn't you?"

"We can't understand all these things, I guess," Gar admitted. "We just got to try to take 'em as they come."

P.S. turned to go on down into the dungeon. "I'll be coming back," he assured his father.

Gar held on to him. "And your mother and I will be here. Don't forget that. We'll be waiting." Gar let him go.

P.S. went on into the stinking basement. Gar heard the jailer's key unlock the jail door, and the door clang shut. He climbed up out of the stairwell and was halfway up the courthouse steps when Dan Wells met him.

"Where is the prisoner? Your boy?" the chief marshal asked.

Gar gestured toward the basement. "In jail," he said.

A look of relief crossed Wells's elderly face. "Good. I'm arranging for Ross Stephens to transport him to Leavenworth."

"How is Judge Parker?" Gar asked.

"Dying."

Gar's face went blank.

"We're taking him home," Wells said. "The doctor says he may not last long."

"He came out last night sick, and again this morning—for my son," Gar faltered.

"There is another matter," Wells said. "Frank Eads' appeal has been granted. The Supreme Court apparently feels that Isaac Parker is too severe on such scoundrels."

"When did the judge find out?"

"The decision came this morning. There will be more appeals granted now. We suspect that Judge Parker's court will be split up. Parts of its jurisdiction will go to Paris, Texas, to Wichita, and Fort Scott in Kansas, then to courts established in the Indian Territory. This court and his work here was Isaac Parker's life. I agree with the doctor that he is not likely to live long without it."

"Judge Parker, out of a job," Gar found the thought incredible.

"You're going to be out, too," Wells observed.

"Yes," Gar pondered. "I wouldn't expect none of those other courts to commission a black man deputy marshal."

"I'm going up to Tulsa and apply for their job as police chief," Wells said. "It's open. If I'm hired, Gar, would you come up there as an officer for me?"

"To police white folks?"

"A law enforcement officer of your caliber will always be needed, Gar," Uncle Dan equivocated.

"But not to arrest white folks," Gar said. "It'll be back to patrolling a beat in black town for such as Ross an' me. Jim Crow is getting strong, and mighty close."

Dan Wells stood with lowered gaze, studying his boots.

Gar looked toward the courthouse stable. "I expect I better saddle up, go get Bernice, and take her home."

EPILOGUE

When Gar Rutherford died of old age many years later, after
the turn of the century, the following newspaper article appeared:

*Tulsa, Oklahoma (Interstate News Service). Gar Rutherford
is gone. He is dead after an illness of some months' duration,
having passed away at his home yesterday.*

*The news was flashed to various law enforcement agencies in
the state immediately after his passing and numerous expres-
sions of regret are being received. Former Marshal Rutherford
was widely respected.*

*He served for years as a deputy for the Isaac Parker court,
headquartered in Fort Smith. When that famous court was
divided he became an officer of this city under Police Chief Dan
Wells, serving in that capacity until his recent illness.*

*His exact age is not known, for he was born in slavery, but
his recollections and his long years of service indicate that he
was well past eighty. Only a few days before his passing, this re-
porter was able to interview him at his home. The account of
that interview is published here for the first time:*

*"We understand, Mr. Rutherford, that in your long career of
law enforcement, you were forced to kill many men!"*

"No. Only one."

"How did that happen?"

*"It got down to where it was him, or me. When you get there
another law takes over besides the laws the fugitive broke."*

"What law is that?"

"The law of survival."

"I believe you once had some trouble with the law yourself,

didn't you? Something about a fight with a man you'd hired to transport your prisoners."

"He poured hot grease on my dog. I poured some on him."

"What was the outcome of that?"

"He filed some charges against me, kept on trying to get revenge 'til he got killed himself trying."

"And you once hunted down your own son, did you not? Sent him to prison, I believe."

"Yes. He served his time, got out, and has never been in trouble since."

"How did his mother, your wife, react to your arresting your own son?"

"Not good. We had our troubles over that, and other things, but we're still together."

"We understand, also, that you are opposed to separate but equal facilities for the races."

"They're separate. But not equal."

"What do you foresee, regarding segregation?"

"It will end."

"Why?"

"Because it's wrong. Bad things, like most good ones too, do end. We got rid of being slaves. We'll get rid of Jim Crow."

"How about prejudice?"

"There are all kinds of prejudice. Young folks against old ones. Prejudice against Indians, Jews, Mexicans—even church folks fighting each other. I expect we'll be trying to do better that way from now on."

ABOUT THE AUTHOR

Mr. Burchardt is a native Oklahoman and the author of numerous Western novels. He is a past president of the Western Writers of America, is a retired Naval Reserve officer, and was for twenty-three years the editor-in-chief of *Oklahoma Today* magazine. He has received the Western Heritage Award presented by the National Cowboy Hall of Fame, as well as the University of Oklahoma Professional Writing Award, and has twice won the Tepee Award of the Oklahoma Writers' Federation for the Best Novel of the Year by an Oklahoman.